Sarah Orne Jewett

The king of Folly Island and other People

Sarah Orne Jewett

The king of Folly Island and other People

ISBN/EAN: 9783743314184

Manufactured in Europe, USA, Canada, Australia, Japa

Cover: Foto ©Andreas Hilbeck / pixelio.de

Manufactured and distributed by brebook publishing software
(www.brebook.com)

Sarah Orne Jewett

The king of Folly Island and other People

THE KING OF FOLLY ISLAND

AND OTHER PEOPLE

BY

SARAH ORNE JEWETT

BOSTON AND NEW YORK
HOUGHTON, MIFFLIN AND COMPANY
The Riverside Press, Cambridge
1888

NOTE.

Two of these stories, "Mère Pochette" and "The King of Folly Island," are reprinted from *Harper's Magazine*; "Law Lane" and "Miss Peck's Promotion" from *Scribner's*; and "The Landscape Chamber," "Miss Tempy's Watchers," and "The Courting of Sister Wisby" from *The Atlantic*. "A Village Shop" is now printed for the first time.

CONTENTS.

	PAGE
THE KING OF FOLLY ISLAND	1
THE COURTING OF SISTER WISBY	50
THE LANDSCAPE CHAMBER	81
LAW LANE	115
MISS PECK'S PROMOTION	167
MISS TEMPY'S WATCHERS	208
A VILLAGE SHOP	229
MÈRE POCHETTE	291

THE KING OF FOLLY ISLAND.

I.

THE September afternoon was nearly spent, and the sun was already veiled in a thin cloud of haze that hinted at coming drought and dustiness rather than rain. Nobody could help feeling sure of just such another golden day on the morrow; this was as good weather as heart could wish. There on the Maine coast, where it was hard to distinguish the islands from the irregular outline of the main-land, where the summer greenness was just beginning to change into all manner of yellow and russet and scarlet tints, the year seemed to have done its work and begun its holidays.

Along one of the broad highways of the bay, in the John's Island postmaster's boat, came a stranger — a man of forty-two or forty-three years, not unprosperous but hardly satisfied, and ever on the quest for entertainment, though he called his pleasure by the hard name of work, and liked himself the better for such a wrong translation. Fate had made him a business man of good success and reputation; inclination, at least so he thought, would have led him another way, but his business ventures pleased him more than the best of his holidays. Somehow life was more interesting if one took it by contraries; he persuaded himself that he had been looking forward to this solitary ramble for many months, but the truth remained that he had found it provokingly hard to break away from his city office, his clerks, and his accounts. He had grown much richer in this last twelve-month, and as he leaned back in the stern of the boat with his arm over the rudder, he was pondering with great perplexity the troublesome question what he ought to do with so much money, and why he should have had it put into his careless hands at all. The bulk of it must be only a sort of reservoir for the sake of a later need and ownership. He thought with scorn of some liberal gifts for which he had been aggravatingly thanked and praised, and made such an impatient gesture with his shoulder that the boat gave a surprised flounce out of its straight course, and the old skipper, who was carefully inspecting the meagre contents of the mail-bag, nearly lost his big silver spectacles overboard. It would have been a strange and awesome calamity. There were no new ones to be bought within seven miles.

"Did a flaw strike her?" asked Jabez Pennell, who looked curiously at the sky and sea and then at his passenger. "I've known of a porpus h'isting a boat, or mought be you kind o' shifted the rudder?"

Whereupon they both laughed; the passenger with a brilliant smile and indescribably merry sound, and the old postmaster with a mechanical grimace of the face and a rusty chuckle; then he turned to his letters again, and adjusted the rescued spectacles to his weather-beaten nose. He thought the stranger, though a silent young man, was a friendly sort of chap, boiling over with fun, as it were; whereas he was really a little morose — so much for Jabez's knowledge of human nature. "Feels kind o' strange, 't is likely; that's better than one o' your forrard kind," mused Jabez, who took the visitor for one of the rare specimens of commercial travelers who sometimes visited

John's Island — to little purpose it must be confessed. The postmaster cunningly concealed the fact that he kept the only store on John's Island; he might as well get his pay for setting the stranger across the bay, and it was nobody's business to pry into what he wanted when he got there. So Jabez gave another chuckle, and could not help looking again at the canvas-covered gun case with its neat straps, and the well-packed portmanteau that lay alongside it in the bows.

"I suppose I can find some place to stay in overnight?" asked the stranger, presently.

"Do' know 's you can, I 'm sure," replied Mr. Pennell. "There ain't no reg'lar boarding places onto John's Island. Folks keep to theirselves pretty much."

"I suppose money is of some object?" gently inquired the passenger.

"Waal, yes," answered Jabez, without much apparent certainty. "Yes, John's Island folks ain't above nippin' an' squeezin' to get the best of a bargain. They 're pretty much like the rest o' the human race, an' want money, whether they 've got any use for it or not. Take it in cold weather, when you 've got pork enough and potatoes and them things in your sullar, an' it blows an' freezes so 't ain't wuth while to go out, 'most all that money 's good for is to set an' look at. Now I need to have more means than most on 'em," continued the speaker, plaintively, as if to excuse himself for any rumor of his grasping ways which might have reached his companion. " Keeping store as I do, I have to handle " — But here he stopped short, conscious of having taken a wrong step. However, they were more than half across now, and the mail was overdue; he would not be forced into going back when it was ascertained that he refused to even look at any samples.

But the passenger took no notice of the news that he was sailing with the chief and only merchant of John's Island, and even turned slowly to look back at the shore they had left, far away now, and fast growing dim on the horizon. John's Island was, on the contrary, growing more distinct, and there were some smaller fragments of land near it; on one he could already distinguish a flock of sheep that moved slowly down a barren slope. It was amazing that they found food enough all summer in that narrow pasture. The suggestion of winter in

this remote corner of the world gave Frankfort a feeling of deep pity for the sheep, as
well as for all the other inhabitants. Yet
it was worth a cheerless year to come occasionally to such weather as this; and he
filled his lungs again and again with the
delicious air blown to him from the inland
country of bayberry and fir balsams across
the sparkling salt-water. The fresh northwest wind carried them straight on their
course, and the postmaster's passenger could
not have told himself why he was going to
John's Island, except that when he had apparently come to the end of everything on
an outreaching point of the main-land, he
had found that there was still a settlement
beyond — John's Island, twelve miles distant, and communication would be that day
afforded. " Sheep farmers and fishermen —
a real old-fashioned crowd," he had been
told. It was odd to go with the postmaster:
perhaps he was addressed by fate to some
human being who expected him. Yes, he
would find out what could be done for the
John's-Islanders; then a wave of defeat
seemed to chill his desire. It was better to
let them work toward what they needed and
wanted ; besides, " the gift without the giver

were dumb." Though after all it would be a kind of satisfaction to take a poor little neighborhood under one's wing, and make it presents of books and various enlightenments. It would n't be a bad thing to send it a Punch and Judy show, or a panorama.

"May I ask your business?" interrupted Jabez Pennell, to whom the long silence was a little oppressive.

"I am a sportsman," responded John Frankfort, the partner in a flourishing private bank, and the merchant-postmaster's face drooped with disappointment. No bargains, then, but perhaps a lucrative boarder for a week or two; and Jabez instantly resolved that for not a cent less than a dollar a day should this man share the privileges and advantages of his own food and lodging. Two dollars a week being the current rate among John's-Islanders, it will be easily seen that Mr. Pennell was a man of far-seeing business enterprise.

II.

On shore, public attention was beginning to centre upon the small white sail that was crossing the bay. At the landing there was at first no human being to be seen, unless one had sharp eyes enough to detect the sallow, unhappy countenance of the postmaster's wife. She sat at the front kitchen window of the low-storied farm-house that was perched nearly at the top of a long green slope. The store, of which the post-office department was a small fraction, stood nearer the water, at the head of the little harbor. It was a high, narrow, smartly painted little building, and looked as if it had strayed from some pretentious inland village, but the tumble-down shed near by had evidently been standing for many years, and was well acquainted with the fish business. The landing-place looked still more weather-beaten; its few timbers were barnacled and overgrown with sea-weeds below high-water mark, and the stone-work was rudely put together. There was a litter of drift-wood, of dilapidated boats and empty barrels and broken lobster pots, and a little higher on the shore stood a tar kettle, and, more prominent still, a melancholy pair of high chaise wheels, with their thorough-braces drawn uncomfortably tight by exposure to many seasonings of relentless weather.

The tide was high, and on this sheltered side of the island the low waves broke with a quick, fresh sound, and moved the pebbles gently on the narrow beach. The sun looked more and more golden red, and all the shore was glowing with color. The faint reddening tinge of some small oaks among the hemlocks farther up the island shore, the pale green and primrose of a group of birches, were all glorified with the brilliant contrast of the sea and the shining of the autumn sky. Even the green pastures and browner fields looked as if their covering had been changed to some richer material, like velvet, so soft and splendid they looked. High on a barren pasture ridge that sheltered the landing on its seaward side the huckleberry bushes had been brightened with a touch of carmine. Coming toward John's Island one might be reminded of some dull old picture that had been cleansed and wet, all its colors were suddenly grown so clear and gay.

Almost at the same moment two men appeared from different quarters of the shore, and without apparently taking any notice of each other, even by way of greeting, they seated themselves side by side on a worm-

eaten piece of ship timber near the tar pot.
In a few minutes a third resident of the
island joined them, coming over the high
pasture slope, and looking for one moment
giant-like against the sky.

"Jabez need n't grumble to-day on account
o' no head-wind," said one of the first com-
ers. "I was mendin' a piece o' wall that
was overset, an' I see him all of a sudden,
most inshore. My woman has been expecting a letter from her brother's folks in Castine. I s'pose ye 've heard? They was all
down with the throat distemper last we knew
about 'em, an' she was dreadful put about
because she got no word by the last mail.
Lor', now wa'n't it just like Jabe's con-
trairiness to go over in that fussin' old dory
o' his with no sail to speak of?"

"Would n't have took him half the time
in his cat-boat," grumbled the elder man of
the three. "Thinks he can do as he 's a
mind to, an' we 've got to make the best
on 't. Ef I was postmaster I should look
out, fust thing, for an abler boat nor any
he 's got. He 's gittin nearer every year,
Jabe is."

"'T ain't fa'r to the citizens," said the
first speaker. "Don't git no mail but twice

a week anyhow, an' then he l'iters round long 's he 's a mind to, dickerin' an' spoutin' politics over to the Foreside. Folks may be layin' dyin', an' there 's all kinds o' urgent letters that ought to be in owners' hands direct. Jabe need n't think we mean to put up with him f'rever;" and the irate islander, who never had any letters at all from one year's end to another's looked at both his companions for their assent.

"Don't ye git riled so, Dan'el," softly responded the last-comer, a grizzled little fisherman-farmer, who looked like a pirate, and was really the most amiable man on John's Island — "don't ye git riled. I don' know as, come to the scratch, ary one of us would want to make two trips back an' forrard every week the year round for a hunderd an' twenty dollars. Take it in them high December seas, now, an' 'long in Jenoary an' March. Course he accommodates himself, an' it comes in the way o' his business, an' he gits a passenger now an' then. Well, it all counts up, I s'pose."

"There 's somebody or 'nother aboard now," said the opponent. "They may have sent over for our folks from Castine. They was headin' on to be dangerous, three

o' the child'n and Wash'n'ton himself. I
may have to go up to-night. Dare say
they 've sent a letter we ain't got. Darn
that Jabe! I 've heard before now of his
looking over everything in the bag comin'
over — sortin' he calls it, to save time — but
't would n't be no wonder ef a letter blowed
out o' his fingers now an' again."

"There 's King George a-layin' off, ain't
he?" asked the peace-maker, who was whit-
tling a piece of dry kelp stalk that he had
picked up from the pebbles, and all three
men took a long look at the gray sail beyond
the moorings.

"What a curi's critter that is!" exclaimed one of the group. "I suppose, now,
nothin 's goin' to tempt him to set foot on
John's Island long 's he lives — do you?"
but nobody answered.

"Don' know who he 's spitin' but himself,"
said the peace-maker." I was underrunning
my trawl last week, an' he come by with
his fare o' fish, an' hove to to see what I
was gittin'. Me and King George 's al'a's
kind o' fellowshiped a little by spells. I
was off to the Banks, you know, that time
he had the gran' flare up an' took himself
off, an' so he ain't counted me one o' his
enemies."

"I always give my vote that he wa'n't in his right mind; 't wa'n't all ugliness, now. I went to school with him, an' he was a clever boy as there was," said the elder man, who had hardly spoken before. "I never more 'n half blamed him, however 't was, an' it kind o' rankled me that he should ha' been drove off an' outlawed hisself this way. 'T was Jabe Pennell; he thought George was stan'in' in his light 'bout the postmastership, an' he worked folks up, an' set 'em agin him. George's mother's folks did have a kind of a punky spot somewhere in their heads, but he never give no sign o' anything till Jabe Pennell begun to hunt him an' dare him."

"Well, he 's done a good thing sence he bought Folly Island. I hear say King George is gittin' rich," said the peaceful pirate. "'T was a hard thing for his folks, his wife an' the girl. I think he 's been more scattery sence his wife died, anyway. Darn! how lonesome they must be in winter! I should think they 'd be afeared a sea would break right over 'em. Pol'tics be hanged, I say, that 'll drive a man to do such things as them — never step foot on any land but his own agin! I tell ye we 've each on us got rights."

This was unusual eloquence and excitement on the speaker's part, and his neighbors stole a furtive look at him and then at each other. He was an own cousin to King George Quint, the recluse owner of Folly Island — an isolated bit of land several miles farther seaward — and one of the listeners reflected that this relationship must be the cause of his bravery.

The post-boat was nearly in now, and the three men rose and went down to the water's edge. The sail was furled, and the old dory slipped about uneasily on the low waves. The postmaster was greeted by friendly shouts from his late maligners, but he was unnecessarily busy with his sail and with his packages amidships, and took his time, as at least one spectator grumbled, about coming in. King George had also lowered his sail and taken to his oars, but just as he would have been alongside, the postmaster caught up his own oars, and pulled smartly toward the landing. This proceeding stimulated his pursuer to a stern-chase, and presently the boats were together, but Pennell pushed straight on through the low waves to the strand, and his pursuer lingered just outside, took in his oars, and dropped his killock over the bow. He knew perfectly well that the representative of the government would go ashore and take all the time he could to sort the contents of the mail-bag in his place of business. It would even be good luck if he did not go home to supper first, and keep everybody waiting all the while. Sometimes his constituents had hailed him from their fishing-boats on the high seas, and taken their weekly newspaper over the boat's side, but it was only in moments of great amiability or forgetfulness that the King of Folly Island was so kindly served. This was tyranny pure and simple. But what could be done? So was winter cold, and so did the dog-fish spoil the trawls. Even the John's-Islanders needed a fearless patriot to lead them to liberty.

The three men on the strand and King George from the harbor were all watching with curious eyes the stranger who had crossed in Jabez Pennell's boat. He was deeply interested in them also; but at that moment such a dazzling glow of sunlight broke from the cloud in the west that Frankfort turned away to look at the strange, remote landscape that surrounded him. He felt as if he had taken a step backward into an earlier age — these men had the look of pioneers or of colonists — yet the little country-side showed marks of long occupancy. He had really got to the outer boundary of civilization.

" Now it 's too bad o' you, Jabez, to keep George Quint a-waitin'," deprecated the peace-maker. " He 's got a good ways to go 'way over to Folly Island, an' like 's not he means to underrun his trawl too. We all expected ye sooner with this fair wind." At which the postmaster gave an unintelligible growl.

" This 'ere passenger was comin' over, calc'latin' to stop a spell, an' wants to be accommodated," he announced presently.

But one of the group on the strand interrupted him. He was considered the wag of that neighborhood. " Ever b'en to Folly Island, stranger?" he asked, with great civility. " There's the King of it, layin' off in his boat. George!" he called lustily, " I want to know ef you can't put up a trav'ler that wants to view these parts o' the airth?"

Frankfort somehow caught the spirit of the occasion, and understood that there was a joke underlying this request. Folly Island had an enticing sound, and he listened eagerly for the answer. It was well known by everybody except himself that Jabez Pennell monopolized the entertainment of the traveling public, and King George roared back, delightedly, that he would do the best he could on short notice, and pulled his boat farther in. Frankfort made ready to transfer his luggage, and laughed again with the men on the shore. He was not sorry to have a longer voyage in that lovely sunset light, and the hospitality of John's Island, already represented by these specimens of householders, was not especially alluring. Jabez Pennell was grumbling to himself, and turned to go to the store. King George reminded him innocently of some groceries which he had promised to have ready, and always fearful of losing one of his few customers, he nodded and went his way. It seemed to be a strange combination of dependence and animosity between the men. The King followed his purveyor with a blasting glance of hatred, and turned his boat, and held it so that Frankfort could step in and reach back afterward for his possessions.

In a few minutes Mr. Pennell returned

with some packages and a handful of news-
papers.

"Have ye put in the cough drops?" asked
the fisherman, gruffly, and was answered by
a nod of the merchant's head.

"Bring them haddick before Thu'sday,"
he commanded the island potentate, who
was already setting his small sail.

The wind had freshened. They slid out
of the bay, and presently the figures on the
shore grew indistinct, and Frankfort found
himself outward bound on a new tack toward
a low island several miles away. It seemed
to be at considerable distance from any
other land; the light of the sun was full
upon it. Now he certainly was as far away
as he could get from city life and the busy
haunts of men. He wondered at the curious
chain of circumstances that he had followed
that day. This man looked like a hermit,
and really lived in the outermost island of
all.

Frankfort grew more and more amused
with the novel experiences of the day. He
had wished for a long time to see these
Maine islands for himself. A week at
Mount Desert had served to make him very
impatient of the imported society of that re-

nowned watering-place, so incongruous with the native simplicity and quiet. There was a serious look to the dark forests and bleak rocks that seemed to have been broken into fragments by some convulsion of nature, and scattered in islands and reefs along the coast. A strange population clung to these isolated bits of the world, and it was rewarding to Frankfort's sincere interest in such individualized existence that he should now be brought face to face with it.

The boat sailed steadily. A colder air, like the very breath of the great sea, met the voyagers presently. Two or three lighthouse lamps flashed out their first pale rays like stars, and evening had begun. Yet there was still a soft glow of color over the low seaboard. The western sky was slow to fade, and the islands looked soft and mirage-like in the growing gloom. Frankfort found himself drifting away into dreams as if he were listening to music; there was something lulling in the motion of the boat. As for the King, he took no notice of his passenger, but steered with an oar and tended the sheet and hummed a few notes occasionally of some quaint minor tune, which must have been singing itself more plainly to his own consciousness. The stranger waked from his reverie before very long, and observed with delight that the man before him had a most interesting face, a nobly moulded forehead, and brave, commanding eyes. There was truly an air of distinction and dignity about this King of Folly Island, an uncommon directness and independence. He was the son and heir of the old Vikings who had sailed that stormy coast and discovered its harborage and its vines five hundred years before Columbus was born in Italy, or was beggar to the surly lords and gentlemen of Spain.

The silence was growing strange, and provoking curiosity between the new-made host and guest, and Frankfort asked civilly some question about the distance. The King turned to look at him with surprise, as if he had forgotten his companionship. The discovery seemed to give him pleasure, and he answered, in a good clear voice, with a true fisherman's twang and brogue: "We 're more 'n half there. Be you cold?" And Frankfort confessed to a stray shiver now and then, which seemed to inspire a more friendly relationship in the boat's crew. Quick as thought, the King pulled off his own rough coat and wrapped it about the shoulders of the paler city man. Then he stepped forward along the boat, after handing the oar to his companion, and busied himself ostentatiously with a rope, with the packages that he had bought from Pennell. One would have thought he had freed himself from his coat merely as a matter of convenience; and Frankfort, who was not a little touched by the kindness, paid his new sovereign complete deference. George Quint was evidently a man whom one must be very careful about thanking, however, and there was another time of silence.

"I hope my coming will not make any trouble in your family," ventured the stranger, after a little while.

"Bless ye, no!" replied the host. "There 's only Phebe, my daughter, and nothing would please her better than somebody extra to do for. She 's dreadful folksy for a girl that 's hed to live alone on a far island, Phebe is. 'T ain't every one I 'd pick to carry home, though," said the King, magnificently. "'T has been my plan to keep clear o' humans much as could be. I had my fill o' the John's-Islanders a good while ago."

"Hard to get on with?" asked the listener, humoring the new tone which his ears had caught.

"I could get on with 'em ef 't was anyways wuth while," responded the island chieftain. "I did n't see why there was any need o' being badgered and nagged all my days by a pack o' curs like them John's-Islanders. They 'd hunt ye to death if ye was anyways their master; and I got me a piece o' land as far off from 'em as I could buy, and here I be. I ain't stepped foot on any man's land but my own these twenty-six years. Ef anybody wants to deal with me, he must come to the water's edge."

The speaker's voice trembled with excitement, and Frankfort was conscious of a strange sympathy and exhilaration.

"But why did n't you go ashore and live on the main-land, out of the way of such neighbors altogether?" he asked, and was met by a wondering look.

"I did n't belong there," replied the King, as if the idea had never occurred to him before. "I had my living to get. It took me more than twelve years to finish paying for my island, besides what hard money I laid down. Some years the fish is mighty shy.

I always had an eye to the island sence I was a boy; and we 've been better off here, as I view it. I was some sorry my woman should be so fur from her folks when she was down with her last sickness."

The sail was lowered suddenly, and the boat rose and fell on the long waves near the floats of a trawl, which Quint pulled over the bows, slipping the long line by with its empty hooks until he came to a small haddock, which he threw behind him to flop and beat itself about at Frankfort's feet as if imploring him not to eat it for his supper. Then the sprit-sail was hoisted again, and they voyaged toward Folly Island slowly with a failing breeze. The King stamped his feet, and even struck his arms together as if they were chilled, but took no notice of the coat which his guest had taken off again a few minutes before. To Frankfort the evening was growing mild, and his blood rushed through his veins with a delicious thrill. The island loomed high and black, as if it were covered with thick woods; but there was a light ashore in the window of a small house, and presently the pilgrim found himself safe on land, quite stiff in his legs, but very serene in temper. A brisk little dog leaped about him with clamorous barks, a large gray cat also appeared belligerent and curious; then a voice came from the doorway: " Late, ain't you, father?"

Without a word of reply, the King of that isle led the way to his castle, haddock in hand. Frankfort and the dog and cat followed after. Before they reached the open door, the light shone out upon a little wilderness of bright flowers, yellow and red and white. The King stepped carefully up the narrow pathway, and waited on the step for his already loyal subject to enter.

" Phebe," he said, jokingly, " I 've brought ye some company — a gentleman from Lord knows where, who could n't seem to content himself without seeing Folly Island."

Phebe stepped forward with great shyness, but perfect appreciation of the right thing to be done. " I give you welcome," she said, quietly, and offered a thin affectionate hand. She was very plain in her looks, with a hard-worked, New England plainness, but as Frankfort stood in the little kitchen he was immediately conscious of a peculiar delicacy and refinement in his surroundings. There was an atmosphere in this out-of-the-way corner of civilization that he missed in

all but a few of the best houses he had ever
known.

The ways of the Folly Island housekeeping were too well established to be thrown
out of their course by even so uncommon
an event as the coming of a stranger. The
simple supper was eaten, and Frankfort was
ready for his share of it. He was touched
at the eagerness of his hostess to serve him,
at her wistful questioning of her father to
learn whom he had seen and what he had
heard that day. There was no actual exile
in the fisherman's lot after all; he met his
old acquaintances almost daily on the fishing grounds, and it was upon the women of
the household that an unmistakable burden
of isolation had fallen. Sometimes a man
lived with them for a time to help cultivate
the small farm, but Phebe was skilled in
out-door handicrafts. She could use tools
better than her father, the guest was told
proudly, and that day she had been digging
potatoes — a great pleasure evidently, as
anything would have been that kept one out-
of-doors in the sunshiny field.

When the supper was over, the father
helped his daughter to clear away the table
as simply and fondly as could be, and as if

it were as much his duty as hers. It was very evident that the cough drops were for actual need; the poor girl coughed now and then with a sad insistence and hollowness. She looked ill already, so narrow-chested and bent-shouldered, while a bright spot of color flickered in her thin cheeks. She had seemed even elderly to Frankfort when he first saw her, but he discovered from something that was said that her age was much less than his own. What a dreary lifetime! he thought, and then reproached himself, for he had never seen a happier smile than poor Phebe gave her father at that moment. The father was evidently very anxious about the cough; he started uneasily at every repetition of it, with a glance at his guest's face to see if he also were alarmed by the foreboding. The wind had risen again, and whined in the chimney. The pine-trees near the house and the wind and sea united in a solemn, deep sound which affected the new-comer strangely. Above this undertone was the lesser, sharper noise of waves striking the pebbly beach and retreating. There was a loneliness, a remoteness, a feeling of being an infinitesimal point in such a great expanse of sea and stormy sky, that was almost too heavy to be borne. Phebe knitted steadily, with an occasional smile at her own thoughts. The tea-kettle sang and whistled away; its cover clicked now and then as if with hardly suppressed cheerfulness, and the King of Folly Island read his newspaper diligently, and doled out bits of information to his companions. Frankfort was surprised at the tenor of these. The reader was evidently a man of uncommon depth of thought and unusual common-sense. It was both less and more surprising that he should have chosen to live alone; one would imagine that his instinct would have led him among people of his own sort. It was no wonder that he had grown impatient of such society as the postmaster's; but at this point of his meditation the traveler's eyes began to feel strangely heavy, and he fell asleep in his high-backed rocking-chair. What peacefulness had circled him in! the rush and clamor of his business life had fallen away as if he had begun another existence, without the fretful troubles of this present world.

"He's a pretty man," whispered Phebe to her father, and the old fisherman nodded a grave assent, and folded his hands upon the county newspaper while he took a

long honest look at the stranger within his
gates.

The next morning Frankfort made his
appearance in the kitchen at a nobly early
hour, to find that the master of the house
had been out in his boat since four o'clock,
and would not be in for some time yet.
Phebe was waiting to give him his breakfast, and soon after he saw her going to the
potato field, and joined her. The sun was
bright, and the island was gay with color;
the asters were in their best pale lavender
and royal purple tints ; the bay was flecked
with sails of fishing-boats, because the mackerel had again struck in; and outside the isl-
and, at no great distance, was the highway
of the coasting vessels to and from the eastern part of the state and the more distant
provinces. There were near two hundred
craft in sight, great and small, and John
Frankfort dug his potatoes with intermittent
industry as he looked off east and west at
such a lovely scene. They might have been
an *abbé galant* and a dignified *marquise,*
he and Phebe — it did not matter what
work they toyed with. They were each
filled with a charming devotion to the other,

a grave reverence and humoring of the mutual desire for quiet and meditation. Toward noon the fishing-boat which Phebe had known constantly and watched with affectionate interest was seen returning deep laden, and she hastened to the little landing. Frankfort had already expressed his disdain of 'a noonday meal, and throwing down his hoe, betook himself to the highest point of the island. Here was a small company of hemlocks, twisted and bent by the northeast winds, and on the soft brown carpet of their short pins, our pilgrim to the outer boundaries spent the middle of the day. A strange drowsiness, such as he had often felt before in such bracing air, seemed to take possession of him, and to a man who had been perplexing himself with hard business problems and erratic ventures in financiering, potato-digging on a warm September day was not exciting.

The hemlocks stood alone on the summit of the island, and must have been a landmark for the King to steer home by. Before Frankfort stretched a half-cleared pasture, where now and then, as he lazily opened his eyes, he could see a moving sheep's back among the small birches and fern and juniper. Behind him were the cleared fields and the house, and a fringe of forest trees stood all round the rocky shore of the domain. From the water one could not see that there was such a well-arranged farm on Folly Island behind this barrier of cedars, but the inhabitants of that region thriftily counted upon the natural stockade to keep the winter winds away.

The sun had changed its direction altogether when he finally waked, and shone broadly down upon him from a point much nearer the western horizon. At that moment the owner of the island made his appearance, looking somewhat solicitous.

"We did n't know what had become of ye, young man," he said, in a fatherly way. "'T ain't nateral for ye to go without your dinner, as I view it. We 'll soon hearten ye up, Phebe an' me; though she don't eat no more than a chippin'-sparrer, Phebe don't," and his face returned to its sadder lines.

"No," said Frankfort; "she looks very delicate. Don't you think it might be better to take her inland, or to some more sheltered place, this winter?"

The question was asked with hesitation,

but the speaker's kind-heartedness was in all his words. The father turned away and snapped a dry hemlock twig with impatient fingers.

"She would n't go withouten me," he answered, in a choked voice, "an' my vow is my vow. I shall never set foot on another man's land while I 'm alive."

The day had been so uneventful, and Folly Island had appeared to be such a calm, not to say prosaic place, that its visitor was already forgetting the thrill of interest with which he had first heard its name. Here again, however, was the unmistakable tragic element in the life of the inhabitants ; this man, who should be armed and defended by his common-sense, was yet made weak by some prejudice or superstition. What could have warped him in this strange way ? for, indeed, the people of most unenlightened communities were prone to herd together, to follow each other's lead, to need a dictator, no matter how much they might rebel at his example or demands. This city gentleman was moved by a deep curiosity to know for himself the laws and charts of his new-found acquaintance's existence ; he had never felt a keener interest in a first day's acquaintance with any human being.

"Society would be at a stand-still," he said, with apparent lightness, "if each of us who found his neighbors unsatisfactory should strike out for himself as you have done."

The King of Folly Island gave a long shrewd look at his companion, who was still watching the mackerel fleet; then he blushed like a girl through all the sea-changed color of his cheeks.

"Look out for number one, or else number two's got to look out for you," he said, with some uncertainty in the tone of his voice.

"Yes," answered Frankfort, smiling. "I have repeated that to myself a great many times. The truth is, I don't belong to my neighbors any more than you do."

"I expect that you have got a better chance nor me; ef I had only been started amon'st Christians, now!" exclaimed Quint, with gathering fury at the thought of his John's-Islanders.

"Human nature is the same the world over," said the guest, quietly, as if more to himself than his listener. "I dare say that the fault is apt to be our own;" but there was no response to this audacious opinion.

Frankfort had risen from the couch of hemlock pins, and the two men walked toward the house together. The cares of modern life could not weigh too heavily on such a day. The shining sea, the white sails, gleaming or gray-shadowed, and the dark green of the nearer islands made a brilliant picture, and the younger man was impatient with himself for thinking the armada of small craft a parallel to the financial ventures which were made day after day in city life. What a question of chance it was, after all, for either herring or dollars — some of these boats were sure to go home disappointed, or worse, at night; but at this point he shrugged his shoulders angrily because he could not forget some still undecided ventures of his own. How degraded a man became who chose to be only a money-maker! The zest of the chase for wealth and the power of it suddenly seemed a very trivial and foolish thing to Frankfort, who confessed anew that he had no purpose in making his gains.

"You ain't a married man; live a bachelor life, don't ye?" asked the King, as if in recognition of these thoughts, and Frankfort, a little startled, nodded assent.

" Makes it a sight easier," was the unexpected response. " You don't feel as if you might be wronging other folks when you do what suits you best. Now my woman was wuth her weight in gold, an' she lays there in the little yard over in the corner of the field — she never fought me, nor argued the p'int again after she found I was sot, but it aged her, fetchin' of her away from all her folks, an' out of where she was wonted. I did n't foresee it at the time."

There was something martyr-like and heroic in the exile's appearance as he spoke, and his listener had almost an admiration for such heroism, until he reminded himself that this withdrawal from society had been willful, and, so far as he knew, quite selfish. It could not be said that Quint had stood in his lot and place as a brave man should, unless he had left John's Island as the Pilgrim Fathers left England, for conscientious scruples and a necessary freedom. How many pilgrims since those have falsely made the same plea for undeserved liberty !

" What was your object in coming here ? " the stranger asked, quietly, as if he had heard no reason yet that satisfied him.

" I wanted to be by myself ; " and the

King rallied his powers of eloquence to make excuses. "I wa'n't one that could stand them folks that overlooked an' harried me, an' was too mean to live. They could go their way, an' I mine; I would n't harm 'em, but I wanted none of 'em. Here, you see, I get my own livin'. I raise my own hog, an' the women-folks have more hens than they want, an' I keep a few sheep a-runnin' over the other side o' the place. The fish o' the sea is had for the catchin', an' I owe no man anything. I should ha' b'en beholden if I'd stopped where we come from;" and he turned with an air of triumph to look at Frankfort, who glanced at him in return with an air of interest.

"I see that you depend upon the larger islands for some supplies — cough drops, for instance?" said the stranger, with needless clearness. "I cannot help feeling that you would have done better to choose a less exposed island — one nearer the main-land, you know, in a place better sheltered from the winds."

"They do cut us 'most in two," said the King, meekly, and his face fell. Frankfort felt quite ashamed of himself, but he was conscious already of an antagonistic feeling.

Indeed, this was an island of folly; this man, who felt himself to be better than his neighbors, was the sacrificer of his family's comfort; he was heaping up riches, and who would gather them? Not the poor pale daughter, that was certain. In this moment they passed the corner of the house, and discovered Phebe herself standing on the doorstep, watching some distant point of the sea or sky with a heavy, much battered spy-glass.

She looked pleased as she lowered the glass for a moment, and greeted Frankfort with a silent welcome.

"Oh, so 't is; now I forgot 't was this afternoon," said Quint. "She's a-watchin' the funeral; ain't you, daughter? Old Mis' Danforth, over onto Wall Island, that has been layin' sick all summer — a cousin o' my mother's," he confessed, in a lower tone, and turned away with feigned unconcern as Frankfort took the spy-glass which Phebe offered. He was sure that his hostess had been wishing that she could share in the family gathering. Was it possible that Quint was a tyrant, and had never let this grown woman leave his chosen isle? Freedom, indeed!

He forgot the affairs of Folly Island the

next moment, as he caught sight of the strange procession. He could see the coffin with its black pall in a boat rowed by four men, who had pushed out a little way from shore, and other boats near it. From the low gray house near the water came a little group of women stepping down across the rough beach and getting into their boats; then all fell into a rude sort of orderliness, the hearse-boat going first, and the procession went away across the wide bay toward the main-land. He lowered the glass for an instant, and Phebe reached for it eagerly.

"They were just bringing out the coffin before you came," she said, with a little sigh; and Frankfort, who had seen many pageants and ceremonials, rebuked himself for having stolen so much of this rare pleasure from his hostess. He could still see the floating funeral. Though it was only a far-away line of boats, there was a strange awe and fascination in watching them follow their single, steady course.

"Danforth's folks bury over to the Foreside," explained the King of Folly Island; but his guest had taken a little book from his pocket, and seated himself on a rock that made one boundary of the gay, disorderly garden. It was very shady and pleasant at this side of the house, and he was too warm after his walk across the unshaded pastures. It was very hot sunshine for that time of the year, and his holiday began to grow dull. Was he, after all, good for nothing but money-making? The thought fairly haunted him; he had lost his power of enjoyment, and there might be no remedy.

The fisherman had disappeared; the funeral was a dim speck off there where the sun glittered on the water, yet he saw it still, and his book closed over his listless fingers. . Phebe sat on the door-step knitting now, with the old glass laid by her side ready for use. Frankfort looked at her presently with a smile.

"Will you let me see your book?" she asked, with a child's eagerness; and he gave it to her.

"It is an old copy of Wordsworth's shorter poems," he said. "It belonged to my mother. Her name was the same as yours."

"She spelled it with the *o*," said Phebe, radiant with interest in this discovery, and closely examining the flyleaf. "What a pretty hand she wrote! Is it a book you like?"

"I like it best because it was hers, I am afraid," replied Frankfort, honestly. "Yes, it does one good to read such poems; but I find it hard to read anything in these days; my business fills my mind. You know so little, here on your island, of the way the great world beyond pushes and fights and wrangles."

"I suppose there are some pleasant folks," said Phebe, simply. "I used to like to read, but I found it made me lonesome. I used to wish I could go ashore and do all the things that folks in books did. But I don't care now; I would n't go away from the island for anything."

"No," said Frankfort, kindly; "I would n't if I were you. Go on dreaming about the world; that is better. And it does people good to come here and see you so comfortable and contented," he added, with a tenderness in his voice that was quite foreign to it of late years. But Phebe gave one quick look at the far horizon, her thin cheeks grew very rosy, and she looked down again at her knitting.

Presently she went into the house. At tea-time that evening the guest was surprised to find the little table decked out for a festival, with some flowered china, and a straight-backed old mahogany chair from the best room in his own place of honor. Phebe looked gay and excited, and Frankfort wondered at the feast, as well as the master of the house, when they came to take their places.

"You see, you found me unawares last night, coming so unexpected," said the poor pale mistress. "I did n't want you to think that we had forgotten how to treat folks."

And somehow the man whose face was usually so cold and unchanging could hardly keep back his tears while, after the supper was cleared away, he was shown a little model of a meeting-house, steeple and all, which Phebe had made from card-board and covered with small shells a winter or two before. She brought it to him with a splendid sense of its art, and Frankfort said everything that could be said except that it was beautiful. He even begged to be told exactly how it was done, and they sat by the light together and discussed the poor toy, while the King of Folly Island dozed and waked again with renewed pleasure as he contemplated his daughter's enjoyment. But she coughed very often, poor Phebe, and the guest wondered if the postmaster's supply of drugs were equal to this pitiful illness. Poor Phebe! and winter would be here soon!

Day after day, in the bright weather, Frankfort lingered with his new friends, spending a morning now and then in fishing with his host, and coming into closer contact with the inhabitants of that part of the world.

Before the short visit was over, the guest was aware that he had been very tired and out of sorts when he had yielded to the desire to hide away from civilization, and had drifted, under some pilotage that was beyond himself, into this quiet haven. He felt stronger and in much better spirits, and remembered afterward that he had been as merry as a boy on Folly Island in the long evenings when Phebe was busy with her knitting-work, and her father told long and spirited stories of his early experiences along the coast and among the fisherman. But business cares began to fret this holiday-maker, and as suddenly as he had come he went away again on a misty morning that promised rain. He was very sorry when he said good-by to Phebe; she was crying as he left the house, and a great wave of compassion poured itself over Frankfort's heart. He never should see her again, that was certain; he wished that he could spirit her away to some gentler climate, and half spoke his thought as he stood hesitating that last minute on the little beach. The next moment he was fairly in the boat and pushing out from shore. George Quint looked as hardy and ruddy and weather-beaten as his daughter was pale and faded, like some frost-bitten flower that tries to lift itself when morning comes and it feels the warmth of the sun. The tough fisherman, with his pet doctrines and angry aversions, could have no idea of the loneliness of his wife and daughter all these unvarying years on his Folly Island. And yet how much they had been saved of useless rivalries and jealousies, of petty tyranny from narrow souls! Frankfort had a bitter sense of all that, as he leaned back against the side of the boat, and sailed slowly out into the bay, while Folly Island seemed to retreat into the gathering fog and slowly disappear. His thoughts flew before him to his office, to his clerks and accounts; he thought of his wealth which was buying him nothing, of his friends who were no friends at all, for

he had pushed away some who might have
been near, strangely impatient of famil-
iarity, and on the defense against either
mockery or rivalry. He was the true King
of Folly Island, not this work-worn fisherman; he had been a lonelier and a more
selfish man these many years.

George Quint was watching Frankfort
eagerly, as if he had been waiting for this
chance to speak to him alone.

"You seem to be a kind of solitary creatur'," he suggested, with his customary
frankness. " I expect it never crossed your
thought that 't would be nateral to git married?"

"Yes, I thought about it once, some
years ago," answered Frankfort, seriously.

"Disapp'inted, was you? Well, 't was
better soon nor late, if it had to be," said
the sage. "My mind has been dwellin' on
Phebe's case. She was a master pooty gal
'arlier on, an' I was dreadful set against
lettin' of her go, though I call to mind there
was a likely chap as found her out, an' made
bold to land an' try to court her. I drove
him, I tell you, an' ducked him under when
I caught him afterward out a-fishin', an' he
took the hint. Phebe did n't know what

was to pay, though I dare say she liked to have him follerin' about."

Frankfort made no answer, — he was very apt to be silent when you expected him to speak, — and presently the King resumed his suggestions.

"I 've been thinking that Phebe ought to have some sort o' brightenin' up. She pines for her mother: they was a sight o' company for each other. Now I s'pose you could n't take no sort o' fancy for her in course o' time? I 've got more hard cash stowed away than folks expects, an' you should have everything your own way. I could git a cousin o' mine, a widow woman, to keep the house winters, an' you an' the gal need n't only summer here. I take it you 've got some means?"

Frankfort found himself smiling at this pathetic appeal, and was ashamed of himself directly, and turned to look seaward. "I 'm afraid I could n't think of it," he answered. "You don't suppose" —

"Lor' no," said George Quint, sadly, shifting his sail. "*She* ain't give no sign, except that I never see her take to no stranger as she has to you. I thought you might kind of have a feelin' for her, an' I knowed you thought the island was a sightly place; 't would do no harm to speak, leastways."

They were on their way to John's Island, where Frankfort was to take the postmaster's boat to the main-land. Quint found his fog-bound way by some mysterious instinct, and at their journey's ends the friends parted with little show of sentiment or emotion. Yet there was much expression in Quint's grasp of his hand, Frankfort thought, and both men turned more than once as the boats separated, to give a kindly glance backward. People are not brought together in this world for nothing, and poor Quint had no idea of the confusion that his theories and his manner of life had brought into the well-regulated affairs of John Frankfort. Jabez Pennell was brimful of curiosity about the visit, but he received little satisfaction. " Phebe Quint was the pootiest gal on these islands some ten years ago," he proclaimed, " an' a born lady. Her mother's folks was ministers over to Castine."

The winter was nearly gone when Frankfort received a letter in a yellow envelope, unbusiness-like in its appearance. The King of Folly Island wrote to say that Phebe had been hoping to get strength enough to thank him for the generous Christmas-box which Frankfort had sent. He had taxed both his imagination and memory to supply the minor wants and fancies of the islanders.

But Phebe was steadily failing in health, and the elderly cousin had already been summoned to take care of her and to manage the house-keeping. The King wrote a crabbed hand, as if he had used a fish-hook instead of a pen, and he told the truth about his sad affairs with simple, unlamenting bravery. Phebe only sent a message of thanks, and an assurance that she liked to think of Frankfort's being there in the fall. She would soon send him a small keepsake.

One morning Frankfort opened a much-crushed bundle which lay upon his desk, and found this keepsake, the shell meeting-house, which looked sadly trivial and astray. He was entirely confused by its unexpected appearance; he did not dare to meet the eyes of an office-boy who stood near; there was an uncomfortable feeling in his throat, but he bravely unfastened a letter from the battered steeple, and read it slowly, without a very clear understanding of the words : —

"Dear Friend" (said poor Phebe), —
"I was very thankful for all that you sent
in the box — I take such pleasure in the
things. I find it hard to write, but I think
about you every day. Father sends his best
respects. We have had rough weather, and
he stays right here with me. You must
keep your promise, and come back to the isl-
and ; he will be lonesome, and you are one
that takes father just right. It seems as if
I had n't been any use in the world, but it
rests me, laying here, to think what a sight
of use you must be. And so good-by."

A sudden vision of the poor girl came
before his eyes as he saw her stand on the
door-step the day they watched the boat
funeral. She had worn a dress with a quaint
pattern, like gray and yellowish willow
leaves as one sees them fallen by the country roadsides. A vision of her thin, stoop-
ing shoulders and her simple, pleasant look
touched him with real sorrow. "Much use
in the world!" Alas! alas! how had her
affection made her fancy such a thing!

The day was stormy, and Frankfort
turned anxiously to look out of the window
beside him, as he thought how the wind

must blow across the distant bay. He felt a strange desire to sweep away everything that might vex poor Phebe or make her less comfortable. Yet she must die, at any rate, before the summer came. The King of Folly Island would reign only over his sheep pastures and the hemlock-trees and pines. Much use in the world! The words stung him more and more.

The office-boy still stood waiting, and now Frankfort became unhappily conscious of his presence. "I used to see one o' them shell-works where I come from, up in the country," the boy said, with unexpected forbearance and sympathy; but Frankfort dismissed him with a needless question about the price of certain railroad bonds, and dropped the embarrassing gift, the poor little meeting-house, into a deep lower drawer of his desk. He had hardly thought of the lad before except as a willing, half mechanical errand-runner; now he was suddenly conscious of the hopeful, bright young face. At that moment a whole new future of human interests spread out before his eyes, from which a veil had suddenly been withdrawn, and Frankfort felt like another man, or as if there had been a revivifying of his old, uninterested, self-occupied nature. Was there really such a thing as taking part in the heavenly warfare against ignorance and selfishness? Had Phebe given him in some mysterious way a legacy of all her unsatisfied hopes and dreams?

THE COURTING OF SISTER WISBY.

ALL the morning there had been an increasing temptation to take an out - door holiday, and early in the afternoon the temptation outgrew my power of resistance. A far-away pasture on the long southwestern slope of a high hill was persistently present to my mind, yet there seemed to be no particular reason why I should think of it. I was not sure that I wanted anything from the pasture, and there was no sign, except the temptation, that the pasture wanted anything of me. But I was on the farther side of as many as three fences before I stopped to think again where I was going, and why.

There is no use in trying to tell another person about that afternoon unless he distinctly remembers weather exactly like it. No number of details concerning an Arctic ice-blockade will give a single shiver to a child of the tropics. This was one of those perfect New England days in late summer, when the spirit of autumn takes a first stealthy flight, like a spy, through the ripening country - side, and, with feigned sympathy for those who droop with August heat, puts her cool cloak of bracing air about leaf and flower and human shoulders. Every living thing grows suddenly cheerful and strong ; it is only when you catch sight of a horror-stricken little maple in swampy soil, — a little maple that has second sight and foreknowledge of coming disaster to her race, — only then does a distrust of autumn's friendliness dim your joyful satisfaction.

In midwinter there is always a day when one has the first foretaste of spring ; in late August there is a morning when the air is for the first time autumn like. Perhaps it is a hint to the squirrels to get in their first supplies for the winter hoards, or a reminder that summer will soon end, and everybody had better make the most of it. We are always looking forward to the passing and ending of winter, but when summer is here it seems as if summer must always last. As I went across the fields that day, I found myself half lamenting that the world must fade again, even that the best of her budding and bloom was only a preparation for another spring-time, for an awakening beyond the coming winter's sleep.

The sun was slightly veiled; there was a chattering group of birds, which had gathered for a conference about their early migration. Yet, oddly enough, I heard the voice of a belated bobolink, and presently saw him rise from the grass and hover leisurely, while he sang a brief tune. He was much behind time if he were still a housekeeper; but as for the other birds, who listened, they cared only for their own notes. An old crow went sagging by, and gave a croak at his despised neighbor, just as a black reviewer croaked at Keats: so hard it is to be just to one's contemporaries. The bobolink was indeed singing out of season, and it was impossible to say whether he really belonged most to this summer or to the next. He might have been delayed on his northward journey; at any rate, he had a light heart now, to judge from his song, and I wished that I could ask him a few questions, — how he liked being the last man among the bobolinks, and where he had taken singing lessons in the South.

Presently I left the lower fields, and took a path that led higher, where I could look beyond the village to the northern country mountainward. Here the sweet fern grew, thick and fragrant, and I also found myself heedlessly treading on pennyroyal. Near by, in a field corner, I long ago made a most comfortable seat by putting a stray piece of board and bit of rail across the angle of the fences. I have spent many a delightful hour there, in the shade and shelter of a young pitch-pine and a wild-cherry tree, with a lovely outlook toward the village, just far enough away beyond the green slopes and tall elms of the lower meadows. . But that day I still had the feeling of being outward bound, and did not turn aside nor linger. The high pasture land grew more and more enticing.

I stopped to pick some blackberries that twinkled at me like beads among their dry vines, and two or three yellow-birds fluttered up from the leaves of a thistle, and then came back again, as if they had complacently discovered that I was only an overgrown yellow-bird, in strange disguise but perfectly harmless. They made me feel as if I were an intruder, though they did not offer to peck at me, and we parted company very soon. It was good to stand at last on the great shoulder of the hill. The wind was coming in from the sea, there was a fine fragrance from the pines, and the air grew sweeter every moment. I took new pleasure in the thought that in a piece of wild pasture land like this one may get closest to Nature, and subsist upon what she gives of her own free will. There have been no drudging, heavy-shod ploughmen to overturn the soil, and vex it into yielding artificial crops. Here one has to take just what Nature is pleased to give, whether one is a yellow-bird or a human being. It is very good entertainment for a summer wayfarer, and I am asking my reader now to share the winter provision which I harvested that day. Let us hope that the small birds are also faring well after their fashion, but I give them an anxious thought while the snow goes hurrying in long waves across the buried fields, this windy winter night.

I next went farther down the hill, and got a drink of fresh cool water from the brook, and pulled a tender sheaf of sweet flag beside it. The mossy old fence just beyond was the last barrier between me and the pasture which had sent an invisible messenger earlier in the day, but I saw that somebody else had come first to the rendezvous: there was a brown gingham cape-bonnet and a sprigged shoulder-shawl bobbing up and down, a little way off among the junipers. I had taken such uncommon pleasure in being alone that I instantly felt a sense of disappointment; then a warm glow of pleasant satisfaction rebuked-my selfishness. This could be no one but dear old Mrs. Goodsoe, the friend of my childhood and fond dependence of my maturer years. I had not seen her for many weeks, but here she was, out on one of her famous campaigns for herbs, or perhaps just returning from a blueberrying expedition. I approached with care, so as not to startle the gingham bonnet; but she heard the rustle of the bushes against my dress, and looked up quickly, as she knelt, bending over the turf. In that position she was hardly taller than the luxuriant junipers themselves.

"I 'm a-gittin' in my mulleins," she said briskly, "an' I 've been thinking o' you these twenty times since I come out o' the house. I begun to believe you must ha' forgot me at last."

"I have been away from home," I explained. "Why don't you get in your pennyroyal too? There's a great plantation of it beyond the next fence but one."

"Pennyr'yal!" repeated the dear little old woman, with an air of compassion for inferior knowledge; "'t ain't the right time, darlin'. Pennyr'yal's too rank now. But for mulleins this day is prime. I've got a dreadful graspin' fit for 'em this year; seems if I must be goin' to need 'em extry. I feel like the squirrels must when they know a hard winter's comin'." And Mrs. Goodsoe bent over her work again, while I stood by and watched her carefully cut the best full-grown leaves with a clumsy pair of scissors, which might have served through at least half a century of herb-gathering. They were fastened to her apron-strings by a long piece of list.

"I'm going to take my jack-knife and help you," I suggested, with some fear of refusal. "I just passed a flourishing family of six or seven heads that must have been growing on purpose for you."

"Now be keerful, dear heart," was the anxious response; "choose 'em well. There's odds in mulleins same's there is in angels. Take a plant that 's all run up to stalk, and there ain't but little goodness in the leaves. This one I 'm at now must ha' been stepped on by some creatur' and blighted of its bloom, and the leaves is han'- some! When I was small I used to have a notion that Adam an' Eve must a took mul- leins fer their winter wear. Ain't they just like flannel, for all the world? · I 've had ex- perience, and I know there 's plenty of sick- ness might be saved to folks if they 'd quit horse-radish and such fiery, exasperating things, and use mullein drarves in proper season. Now I shall spread these an' dry 'em nice on my spare floor in the garrit, an' come to steam 'em for use along in the winter there 'll be the vally of the whole summer's goodness in 'em, sartin." And she snipped away with the dull scissors, while I listened respectfully, and took great pains to have my part of the harvest present a good appearance.

"This is most too dry a head," she added presently, a little out of breath. "There! I can tell you there 's win'rows o' young doctors, bilin' over with book-larnin', that is truly ignorant of what to do for the sick, or how to p'int out those paths that well

people foller toward sickness. Book-fools I
call 'em, them young men, an' some on 'em
never 'll live to know much better, if they
git to be Methuselahs. In my time every
middle-aged woman, who had brought up a
family, had some proper ideas o' dealin' with
complaints. I won't say but there was some
fools amongst *them*, but I 'd rather take my
chances, unless they 'd forsook herbs and
gone to dealin' with patent stuff. Now my
mother really did sense the use of herbs and
roots. I never see anybody that come up
to her. She was a meek-looking woman,
but very understandin', mother was."

" Then that 's where you learned so much
yourself, Mrs. Goodsoe," I ventured to say.

" Bless your heart, I don't hold a candle
to her; 't is but little I can recall of what
she used to say. No, her l'arnin' died with
her," said my friend, in a self-depreciating
tone. " Why, there was as many as twenty
kinds of roots alone that she used to keep
by her, that I forget the use of; an' I 'm
sure I should n't know where to find the
most of 'em, any. There was an herb " —
airb, she called it — " an herb called masterwort, that she used to get way from Pennsylvany; and she used to think everything

of noble-liverwort, but I never could seem
to get the right effects from it as she could.
Though I don't know as she ever really did
use masterwort where somethin' else would n't
a served. She had a cousin married out in
Pennsylvany that used to take pains to get
it to her every year or two, and so she felt
't was important to have it. Some set more
by such things as come from a distance, but
I rec'lect mother always used to maintain
that folks was meant to be doctored with
the stuff that grew right about 'em ; 't was
sufficient, an' so ordered. That was before
the whole population took to livin' on wheels,
the way they do now. 'T was never my
idee that we was meant to know what's
goin' on all over the world to once. There's
goin' to be some sort of a set-back one o'
these days, with these telegraphs an' things,
an' letters comin' every hand's turn, and
folks leavin' their proper work to answer
'em. I may not live to see it. 'T was allowed to be difficult for folks to git about
in old times, or to git word across the country, and they stood in their lot an' place,
and were n't all just alike, either, same as
pine-spills."

We were kneeling side by side now, as if

in penitence for the march of progress, but
we laughed as we turned to look at each
other.

"Do you think it did much good when
everybody brewed a cracked quart mug of
herb-tea?" I asked, walking away on my
knees to a new mullein.

"I've always lifted my voice against the
practice, far 's I could," declared Mrs. Goodsoe; "an' I won't deal out none o' the herbs
I save for no such nonsense.   There was
three houses along our road, — I call no
names, — where you could n't go into the
livin' room without findin' a mess o' herb-
tea drorin' on the stove or side o' the fireplace, winter or summer, sick or well.   One
was thoroughwut, one would be camomile,
and the other, like as not, yellow dock; but
they all used to put in a little new rum to
git out the goodness, or keep it from spilin'."
(Mrs. Goodsoe favored me with a knowing
smile.)   "Land, how mother used to laugh!
But, poor creaturs, they had to work hard,
and I guess it never done 'em a mite o'
harm; they was all good herbs.   I wish you
could hear the quawkin' there used to be
when they was indulged with a real case o'
sickness.   Everybody would collect from

far an' near; you 'd see 'em coming along the road and across the pastures then; everybody clamorin' that nothin' would n't do no kind o' good but her choice o' teas or drarves to the feet. I wonder there was a babe lived to grow up in the whole lower part o' the town; an' if nothin' else 'peared to ail 'em, word was passed about that 't was likely Mis' So-and-So's last young one was goin' to be foolish. Land, how they 'd gather! I know one day the doctor come to Widder Peck's and the house was crammed so 't he could scercely git inside the door; and he says, just as polite, ' Do send for some of the neighbors ! ' as if there wa'n't a soul to turn to, right or left. You 'd ought to seen 'em begin to scatter."

" But don't you think the cars and telegraphs have given people more to interest them, Mrs. Goodsoe ? Don't you believe people's lives were narrower then, and more taken up with little things ? " I asked, unwisely, being a product of modern times.

" Not one mite, dear," said my companion stoutly. " There was as big thoughts then as there is now; these times was born o' them. The difference is in folks themselves; but now, instead o' doin' their own house-keepin' and watchin' their own neighbors, — though that was carried to excess, — they git word that a niece's child is ailin' the other side o' Massachusetts, and they drop everything and git on their best clothes, and off they jiggit in the cars. 'T is a bad sign when folks wears out their best clothes faster 'n they do their every-day ones. The other side o' Massachusetts has got to look after itself by rights. An' besides that, Sunday-keepin' 's all gone out o' fashion. Some lays it to one thing an' some another, but some o' them old ministers that folks are all a-sighin' for did preach a lot o' stuff that wa'n't nothin' but chaff; 't wa'n't the word o' God out o' either Old Testament or New. But everybody went to meetin' and heard it, and come home, and was set to fightin' with their next door neighbor over it. Now I 'm a believer, and I try to live a Christian life, but I 'd as soon hear a surveyor's book read out, figgers an' all, as try to get any simple truth out o' most sermons. It 's them as is most to blame."

"What was the matter that day at Widow Peck's?" I hastened to ask, for I knew by experience that the good, clear-minded soul beside me was apt to grow unduly vexed and distressed when she contemplated the state of religious teaching.

"Why, there wa'n't nothin' the matter, only a gal o' Miss Peck's had met with a dis'pintment and had gone into screechin' fits. 'T was a rovin' creatur' that had come along hayin' time, and he'd gone off an' forsook her betwixt two days; nobody ever knew what become of him. Them Pecks was 'Good Lord, anybody!' kind o' gals, and took up with whoever they could get. One of 'em married Heron, the Irishman; they lived in that little house that was burnt this summer, over on the edge o' the plains. He was a good-hearted creatur', with a laughin' eye and a clever word for everybody. He was the first Irishman that ever came this way, and we was all for gettin' a look at him, when he first used to go by. Mother's folks was what they call Scotch-Irish, though; there was an old race of 'em settled about here. They could foretell events, some on 'em, and had the second sight. I know folks used to say mother's grandmother had them gifts, but mother was never free to speak about it to us. She remembered her well, too."

"I suppose that you mean old Jim Heron, who was such a famous fiddler?" I asked

with great interest, for I am always delighted
to know more about that rustic hero, parochial Orpheus that he must have been !

"Now, dear heart, I suppose you don't remember him, do you?" replied Mrs. Goodsoe,
earnestly.   "Fiddle!   He'd about break
your heart with them tunes of his, or else set
your heels flying up the floor in a jig, though
you was minister o' the First Parish and all
wound up for a funeral prayer. I tell ye
there ain't no tunes sounds like them used
to. It used to seem to me summer nights
when I was comin' along the plains road,
and he set by the window playin', as if there
was a bewitched human creatur' in that old
red fiddle o' his. He could make it sound
just like a woman's voice tellin' somethin'
over and over, as if folks could help her out
o' her sorrows if she could only make 'em
understand. I've set by the stone-wall and·
cried as if my heart was broke, and dear
knows it wa'n't in them days. How he would
twirl off them jigs and dance tunes! He
used to make somethin' han'some out of 'em
in fall an' winter, playin' at huskins and
dancin' parties; but he was unstiddy by
spells, as he got along in years, and never
knew what it was to be forehanded. Every-

body felt bad when he died; you could n't help likin' the creatur'. He 'd got the gift — that 's all you could say about it.

"There was a Mis' Jerry Foss, that lived over by the brook bridge, on the plains road, that had lost her husband early, and was left with three child'n. She set the world by 'em, and was a real pleasant, ambitious little woman, and was workin' on as best she could with that little farm, when there come a rage o' scarlet fever, and her boy and two girls was swept off and laid dead within the same week. Every one o' the neighbors did what they could, but she 'd had no sleep since they was taken sick, and after the funeral she set there just like a piece o' marble, and would only shake her head when you spoke to her. They all thought her reason would go; and 't would certain, if she could n't have shed tears. An' one o' the neighbors — 't was like mother's sense, but it might have been somebody else — spoke o' Jim Heron. Mother an' one or two o' the women that knew her best was in the house with her. 'T was right in the edge o' the woods and some of us younger ones was over by the wall on the other side of the road where there was a couple of old willows, — I remember just how the brook damp felt; and we kept quiet 's we could, and some other folks come along down the road, and stood waitin' on the little bridge, hopin' somebody 'd come out, I suppose, and they 'd git news. Everybody was wrought up, and felt a good deal for her, you know. By an' by Jim Heron come stealin' right out o' the shadows an' set down on the doorstep, an' 't was a good while before we heard a sound; then, oh, dear me! 't was what the whole neighborhood felt for that mother all spoke in the notes, an' they told me afterwards that Mis' Foss's face changed in a minute, and she come right over an' got into my mother's lap, — she was a little woman, — an' laid her head down, and there she cried herself into a blessed sleep. After awhile one o' the other women stole out an' told the folks, and we all went home. He only played that one tune.

"But there!" resumed Mrs. Goodsoe, after a silence, during which my eyes were filled with tears. "His wife always complained that the fiddle made her nervous. She never 'peared to think nothin' o' poor Heron after she 'd once got him."

"That 's often the way," said I, with harsh cynicism, though I had no guilty person in

my mind at the moment; and we went straying off, not very far apart, up through the
pasture. Mrs. Goodsoe cautioned me that
we must not get so far off that we could not
get back the same day. The sunshine began
to feel very hot on our backs, and we both
turned toward the shade. We had already
collected a large bundle of mullein leaves,
which were carefully laid into a clean, calico
apron, held together by the four corners, and
proudly carried by me, though my companion regarded them with anxious eyes. We
sat down together at the edge of the pine
woods, and Mrs. Goodsoe proceeded to fan
herself with her limp cape-bonnet.

"I declare, how hot it is! The east wind's
all gone again," she said. "It felt so cool
this forenoon that I overburdened myself
with as thick a petticoat as any I 've got. I 'm
despri't afeared of having a chill, now that I
ain't so young as once. I hate to be housed
up."

"It 's only August, after all," I assured
her unnecessarily, confirming my statement
by taking two peaches out of my pocket, and
laying them side by side on the brown pine
needles between us.

"Dear sakes alive!" exclaimed the old

lady, with evident pleasure. "Where did you get them, now? Does n't anything taste twice better out-o'-doors? I ain't had such a peach for years. Do le's keep the stones, an' I 'll plant 'em; it only takes four year for a peach pit to come to bearing, an' I guess I 'm good for four year, 'thout I meet with some accident."

I could not help agreeing, or taking a fond look at the thin little figure, and her wrinkled brown face and kind, twinkling eyes. She looked as if she had properly dried herself, by mistake, with some of her mullein leaves, and was likely to keep her goodness, and to last the longer in consequence. There never was a truer, simple-hearted soul made out of the old-fashioned country dust than Mrs. Goodsoe. I thought, as I looked away from her across the wide country, that nobody was left in any of the farm-houses so original, so full of rural wisdom and reminiscence, so really able and dependable, as she. And nobody had made better use of her time in a world foolish enough to sometimes under-value medicinal herbs.

When we had eaten our peaches we still sat under the pines, and I was not without pride when I had poked about in the ground

with a little twig, and displayed to my
crony a long fine root, bright yellow to the
eye, and a wholesome bitter to the taste.

"Yis, dear, goldthread," she assented in-
dulgently. "Seems to me there's more of
it than anything except grass an' hardhack.
Good for canker, but no better than two or
three other things I can call to mind; but I
always lay in a good wisp of it, for old
times' sake. Now, I want to know why you
should a bit it, and took away all the taste
o' your nice peach? I was just thinkin'
what a han'some entertainment we 've had.
I 've got so I 'sociate certain things with
certain folks, and goldthread was somethin'
Lizy Wisby could n't keep house without,
no ways whatever. I believe she took so
much it kind o' puckered her disposition."

"Lizy Wisby?" I repeated inquiringly.

"You knew her, if ever, by the name of
Mis' Deacon Brimblecom," answered my
friend, as if this were only a brief preface
to further information, so I waited with
respectful expectation. Mrs. Goodsoe had
grown tired out in the sun, and a good story
would be an excuse for sufficient rest. It
was a most lovely place where we sat, half-
way up the long hillside; for my part, I was

perfectly contented and happy. "You've
often heard of Deacon Brimblecom?" she
asked, as if a great deal depended upon his
being properly introduced.

"I remember him," said I. "They
called him Deacon Brimfull, you know, and
he used to go about with a witch-hazel
branch to show people where to dig wells."

"That's the one," said Mrs. Goodsoe,
laughing. "I did n't know 's you could go
so far back. I 'm always divided between
whether you can remember everything I
can, or are only a babe in arms."

"I have a dim recollection of there being
something strange about their marriage," I
suggested, after a pause, which began to appear dangerous. I was so much afraid the
subject would be changed.

"I can tell you all about it," I was
quickly answered. "Deacon Brimblecom
was very pious accordin' to his lights in his
early years. He lived way back in the
country then, and there come a rovin'
preacher along, and set everybody up that
way all by the ears. I 've heard the old
folks talk it over, but I forget most of his
doctrine, except some of his followers was
persuaded they could dwell among the an-

gels while yet on airth, and this Deacon
Brimfull, as you call him, felt sure he was
called by the voice of a spirit bride. So
he left a good, deservin' wife he had, an'
four children, and built him a new house
over to the other side of the land he 'd had
from his father. They did n't take much
pains with the buildin', because they expected to be translated before long, and
then the spirit brides and them folks was
goin' to appear and divide up the airth
amongst 'em, and the world's folks and on-
believers was goin' to serve 'em or be sent
to torments. They had meetins about in
the school-houses, an' all sorts o' goins on ;
some on 'em went crazy, but the deacon held
on to what wits he had, an' by an' by the
spirit bride did n't turn out to be much of
a housekeeper, an' he had always been used
to good livin', so he sneaked home ag'in.
One o' mother's sisters married up to Ash
Hill, where it all took place ; that 's how I
come to have the particulars."

" Then how did he come to find his Eliza
Wisby ? " I inquired. " Do tell me the
whole story ; you 've got mullein leaves
enough."

" There 's all yisterday's at home, if I

have n't," replied Mrs. Goodsoe. "The way he come a-courtin' o' Sister Wisby was this: she went a-courtin' o' him.

"There was a spell he lived to home, and then his poor wife died, and he had a spirit bride in good earnest, an' the child'n was placed about with his folks and hers, for they was both out o' good families; and I don't know what come over him, but he had another pious fit that looked for all the world like the real thing. He had n't no family cares, and he lived with his brother's folks, and turned his land in with theirs. He used to travel to every meetin' an' conference that was within reach of his old sorrel hoss's feeble legs; he j'ined the Christian Baptists that was just in their early prime, and he was a great exhorter, and got to be called deacon, though I guess he wa'n't deacon, 'less it was for a spare hand when deacon timber was scercer 'n usual. An' one time there was a four days' protracted meetin' to the church in the lower part of the town. 'T was a real solemn time; something more 'n usual was goin' forward, an' they collected from the whole country round. Women folks liked it, an' the men too; it give 'em a change, an' they was quartered

round free, same as conference folks now.
Some on 'em, for a joke, sent Silas Brimblecom up to Lizy Wisby's, though she'd
give out she could n't accommodate nobody,
because of expectin' her cousin's folks.
Everybody knew 't was a lie; she was
amazin' close considerin' she had plenty to
do with. There was a streak that wa'n't
just right somewheres in Lizy's wits, I always thought. She was very kind in case o'
sickness, I 'll say that for her.

"You know where the house is, over there
on what they call Windy Hill? There the
deacon went, all unsuspectin', and 'stead o'
Lizy 's resentin' of him she put in her own
hoss, and they come back together to evenin'
meetin'. She was prominent among the
sect herself, an' he bawled and talked, and
she bawled and talked, an' took up more 'n
the time allotted in the exercises, just as if
they was showin' off to each other what they
was able to do at expoundin'. Everybody
was laughin' at 'em after the meetin' broke
up, and that next day an' the next, an' all
through, they was constant, and seemed to
be havin' a beautiful occasion. Lizy had
always give out she scorned the men, but
when she got a chance at a particular one

't was altogether different, and the deacon seemed to please her somehow or 'nother, and — There! you don't want to listen to this old stuff that 's past an' gone?"

"Oh yes, I do," said I.

"I run on like a clock that 's onset her striking hand," said Mrs. Goodsoe mildly. "Sometimes my kitchen timepiece goes on half the forenoon, and I says to myself the day before yisterday I would let it be a warnin', and keep it in mind for a check on my own speech. The next news that was heard was that the deacon an' Lizy — well, opinions differed which of 'em had spoke first, but them fools settled it before the protracted meetin' was over, and give away their hearts before he started for home. They considered 't would be wise, though, considerin' their short acquaintance, to take one another on trial a spell; 't was Lizy's notion, and she asked him why he would n't come over and stop with her till spring, and then, if they both continued to like, they could git married any time 't was convenient. Lizy, she come and talked it over with mother, and mother disliked to offend her, but she spoke pretty plain; and Lizy felt hurt, an' thought they was showin' excellent judgment, so much harm come from hasty unions and folks comin' to a realizin' sense of each other's failin's when 't was too late.

" So one day our folks saw Deacon Brim- full a-ridin' by with a gre't coopful of hens in the back o' his wagon, and bundles o' stuff tied on top and hitched to the exes underneath ; and he riz a hymn just as he passed the house, and was speedin' the old sorrel with a willer switch. 'T was most Thanksgivin' time, an' sooner 'n she ex- pected him. New Year's was the time she set ; but he thought he 'd better come while the roads was fit for wheels. They was out to meetin' together Thanksgivin' Day, an' that used to be a gre't season for marryin' ; so the young folks nudged each other, and some on' 'em ventured to speak to the couple as they come down the aisle. Lizy carried it off real well ; she wa'n't afraid o' what nobody said or thought, and so home they went. They 'd got out her yaller sleigh and her hoss ; she never would ride after the deacon's poor old creatur', and I believe it died long o' the winter from stiffenin' up.

" Yes," said Mrs. Goodsoe emphatically, after we had silently considered the situa- tion for a short space of time, — " yes, there

was consider'ble talk, now I tell you! The
raskil boys pestered 'em just about to death
for a while. They used to collect up there
an' rap on the winders, and they'd turn out
all the deacon's hens 'long at nine o'clock
'o night, and chase 'em all over the dingle;
an' one night they even lugged the pig right
out o' the sty, and shoved it into the back
entry, an' run for their lives. They'd stuffed
its mouth full o' somethin', so it could n't
squeal till it got there. There wa'n't a
sign o' nobody to be seen when Lizy hasted
out with the light, and she an' the deacon
had to persuade the creatur' back as best
they could; 't was a cold night, and they
said it took 'em till towards mornin'. You
see the deacon was just the kind of a man
that a hog would n't budge for; it takes a
masterful man to deal with a hog. Well,
there was no end to the works nor the talk,
but Lizy left 'em pretty much alone. She
did 'pear kind of dignified about it, I must
say!"

"And then, were they married in the
spring?"

"I was tryin' to remember whether it was
just before Fast Day or just after," responded my friend, with a careful look at

the sun, which was nearer the west than either of us had noticed. "I think likely 't was along in the last o' April, any way some of us looked out o' the window one Monday mornin' early, and says, 'For goodness' sake! Lizy 's sent the deacon home again!' His old sorrel havin' passed away, he was ridin' in Ezry Welsh's hoss-cart, with his hen-coop and more bundles than he had when he come, and he looked as meechin' as ever you see. Ezry was drivin', and he let a glance fly swiftly round to see if any of us was lookin' out; an' then I declare if he did n't have the malice to turn right in towards the barn, where he see my oldest brother, Joshuay, an' says he real natural, 'Joshuay, just step out with your wrench. I believe I hear my kingbolt rattlin' kind o' loose.' Brother, he went out an' took in the sitooation, an' the deacon bowed kind of stiff. Joshuay was so full o' laugh, and Ezry Welsh, that they could n't look one another in the face. There wa'n't nothing ailed the kingbolt, you know, an' when Josh riz up he says, 'Goin' up country for a spell, Mr. Brimblecom ?'

" 'I be,' says the deacon, lookin' dreadful mortified and cast down.

" ' Ain't things turned out well with you an' Sister Wisby ?' says Joshuay. ' You had ought to remember that the woman is the weaker vessel.'

" ' Hang her, let her carry less sail, then !' the deacon bu'st out, and he stood right up an' shook his fist there by the hen-coop, he was so mad; an' Ezry's hoss was a young creatur', an' started up an set the deacon right over backwards into the chips. We did n't know but he 'd broke his neck ; but when he see the women folks runnin' out, he jumped up quick as a cat, an' clim' into the cart, an' off they went. Ezry said he told him that he could n't git along with Lizy, she was so fractious in thundery weather ; if there was a rumble in the day-time she must go right to bed an' screech, and if 't was night she must git right up an' go an' call him out of a sound sleep. But everybody knew he 'd never a gone home unless she 'd sent him.

" Somehow they made it up agin right away, him an' Lizy, and she had him back. She 'd been countin' all along on not havin' to hire nobody to work about the gardin an' so on, an' she said she wa'n't goin' to let him have a whole winter's board for nothin'. So the old hens was moved back, and they was married right off fair an' square, an' I don't know but they got along well as most folks. He brought his youngest girl down to live with 'em after a while, an' she was a real treasure to Lizy; everybody spoke well o' Phebe Brimblecom. The deacon got over his pious fit, and there was consider'ble work in him if you kept right after him. He was an amazin' cider-drinker, and he airnt the name you know him by in his latter days. Lizy never trusted him with nothin', but she kep' him well. She left everything she owned to Phebe, when she died, 'cept somethin' to satisfy the law. There, they're all gone now: seems to me sometimes, when I get thinkin,' as if I 'd lived a thousand years ! "

I laughed, but I found that Mrs. Goodsoe's thoughts had taken a serious turn.

" There, I come by some old graves down here in the lower edge of the pasture," she said as we rose to go. " I could n't help thinking how I should like to be laid right out in the pasture ground, when my time comes; it looked sort o' comfortable, and I have ranged these slopes so many summers. Seems as if I could see right up through the turf and tell when the weather was pleasant, and get the goodness o' the sweet fern. Now, dear, just hand me my apernful o' mulleins out o' the shade. I hope you won't come to need none this winter, but I 'll dry some special for you."

" I 'm going home by the road," said I, " or else by the path across the meadows, so I will walk as far as the house with you. Are n't you pleased with my company?" for she demurred at my going the least bit out of the way.

So we strolled toward the little gray house, with our plunder of mullein leaves slung on a stick which we carried between us. Of course I went in to make a call, as if I had not seen my hostess before; she is the last maker of muster-gingerbread, and before I came away I was kindly measured for a pair of mittens.

" You 'll be sure to come an' see them two peach-trees after I get 'em well growin'?" Mrs. Goodsoe called after me when I had said good-by, and was almost out of hearing down the road.

THE LANDSCAPE CHAMBER.

I.

I was tired of ordinary journeys, which
involved either the loneliness and discomfort
of fashionable hotels, or the responsibilities
of a guest in busy houses. One is always
doing the same things over and over ; I now
promised myself that I would go in search
of new people and new scenes, until I was
again ready to turn with delight to my familiar occupations. So I mounted my horse
one morning, without any definite plan of
my journey, and rode eastward, with a
business-like haversack strapped behind the
saddle. I only wished that the first day's
well-known length of road had been already
put behind me. One drawback to a woman's
enjoyment of an excursion of this sort is the
fact that when she is out of the saddle she
is uncomfortably dressed. But I compro-
mised matters as nearly as possible by wear-

ing a short corduroy habit, light both in color and weight, and putting a linen blouse and belt into my pack, to replace the stiff habit-waist. The wallet on the saddle held a flat drinking-cup, a bit of chocolate, and a few hard biscuit, for provision against improbable famine. Autumn would be the best time for such a journey, if the evenings need not be so often spent in stuffy rooms, with kerosene lamps for company. This was early summer, and I had long days in which to amuse myself. For a book I took a much-beloved small copy of "The Sentimental Journey."

After I left my own neighborhood I was looked at with curious eyes. I was now and then recognized with surprise, but oftener viewed with suspicion, as if I were a criminal escaping from justice. The keepers of the two country taverns at which I rested questioned me outright, until I gave a re-assuring account of myself. Through the middle of the day I let the horse stand un-saddled in the shade, by the roadside, while I sat near, leaning against the broad trunk of a tree, and ate a bit of luncheon, or slept, or read my book, or strolled away up the shore of a brook or to the top of a hill. On the third or fourth day I left my faithful companion so long that he grew restless, and at last fearful, as petted horses will. The silence and strangeness of the place and my disappearance frightened him. When I returned, I found that the poor creature had twisted a forward shoe so badly that I could neither pull it off altogether, nor mount again. There was nothing to do but to lead him slowly to some farm-house, where I could get assistance; so on went the saddle, and away we plodded together sadly along the dusty road. The horse looked at me with anxious eyes, and was made fretful by the difficulty of the projecting shoe. I should have provided myself with some pincers, he seemed to tell me; the foot was aching from the blows I had given it with a rough-edged stone in trying to draw the tenacious nails. It was all my fault, having left him in such a desolate place, fastened to a tree that grew against a creviced ledge of rock. We were both a little sulky at this mischance so early in the careless expedition.

The sea was near, and the salt-marshes penetrated deep into the country, like abandoned beds of rivers winding inland among the pine woods and upland pastures. The higher land separated these marshes, like a succession of low promontories trending seaward, and the road climbed and crossed over from one low valley to another. There had been no houses for some distance behind us. I knew that there was a village with a good tavern a few miles ahead; so far, indeed, that I had planned to reach it at sundown. I began to feel very tired, and the horse tossed his head more and more impatiently, resenting my anxious, dragging hold upon the rein close at his mouth. There was nobody to be seen; the hills became steeper, the unshaded strips of marshland seemed hotter, and I determined at last to wait until some traveler appeared who could give us assistance. Perhaps the blacksmith himself might be out adventuring that afternoon.

We halted by some pasture bars in the shade of an old cider-apple tree, and I threw the bridle over a leaning post in the unsteady fence; and there the horse and I waited, and looked at each other reproachfully. It was some time before I discovered a large rusty nail lying in the short grass, within reach of my hand. My pocket-knife was already broken, because I had tried to use it for a lever, and this was just what I needed. I quickly caught up the disabled hoof again, and with careful prying the tough nails loosed their hold at last, and the bent shoe dropped with a clink. The horse gave a whinny of evident relief, and seemed to respect me again, and I was ready to mount at once; in an instant life lost its depressing aspect. "Keep your feet out of clefts now!" I said joyfully, with a friendly stroke of the good creature's neck and tangled mane, and a moment afterward we were back in the stony road. Alas, the foot had been strained, and our long halt had only stiffened it. I was mounted on three feet, not four. Nothing was to be done but to go forward, step by step, to the far-away village, or to any friendly shelter this side of it.

The afternoon was waning: sometimes I rode, sometimes I walked; those three miles of marsh and hill seemed interminable. At last I saw the chimneys of a house; the horse raised his head high, and whinnied loud and long.

These chimneys were most reassuring; being high and square, they evidently belonged to a comfortable house of the last century, and my spirits rose again. The country was still abandoned by human beings. I had seen no one since noon, but the road was little used, and was undoubtedly no longer the main highway of that region. I wondered what impression I should make in such a migratory guise. The saddle and its well-stuffed haversack and my own dustiness amused me unexpectedly, and I understood for the first time that the rest and change of this solitary excursion had done me much good. I was no longer listless and uninterested, but ready for adventure of any sort. It had been a most sensible thing to go wandering alone through the country. But now the horse's ankle was swollen. I grew anxious again, and looked at the chimneys with relief. Presently I came in sight of the house.

It was disappointing, for the first view gave an impression of dreariness and neglect. The barn and straggling row of out-buildings were leaning this way and that, mossy and warped; the blinds of the once handsome house were broken; and everything gave evidence of unhindered decline from thrift and competence to poverty and ruin. A good colonial mansion, I thought, abandoned by its former owners, and tenanted now by some shiftless outcasts of society, who ask but meagre comfort, and are indifferent to the decencies of life. Full of uncertainty, I went along the approach to the barn, noticing, however, with surprise that the front yard had been carefully tended; there were some dark crimson roses in bloom, and broken lines of box which had been carefully clipped at no remote period. Nobody was in sight. I went to the side door, and gave a knock with my whip at arm's length, for the horse was eager to reach the uninviting, hungry-looking stable. Some time elapsed before my repeated summons were answered; then the door slowly opened, and a woman just this side of middle age stood before me, waiting to hear my errand. She had a pathetic look, as if she were forced by circumstances to deny all requests, however her own impulses might lead her toward generosity. I was instantly drawn toward her, in warm sympathy: the blooming garden was hers; she was very poor. I would plead my real fatigue, and ask for a night's lodging, and perhaps my holiday might also give her pleasure. But a curious hardness drew her face into forbidding angles, even as her sweet and womanly eyes watched me with surprised curiosity.

"I should be very sorry to take the horse any farther to-day," said I, after stating my appealing case. "I will give you as little trouble as possible." At this moment the haggard face of an elderly man peered at me over her shoulder.

"We don't keep tavern, young lady," he announced, in an unexpectedly musical, low voice, "but since your horse is" —

"I am ready to pay any price you ask," I interrupted, impatiently; and he gave me an eager look and then came to the outer step, ignoring both his daughter and me, as he touched the horse with real kindliness. "'T is a pretty creature!" he said, admiringly, and at once stooped stiffly down to examine the lifted foot. I explained the accident in detail, grateful for such intelligent sympathy, while he stroked the lamed ankle.

"There's no damage done," he assured me presently, looking up with transient self-forgetfulness. "A common liniment will do; there's a bottle in the house, but 't will cost you something," and his face clouded again.

I turned to the daughter, who gave me a

strange, appealing look. Her eyes begged me entreatingly, " Give him his own way; " her firm-set mouth signified her assent to the idea that I had no right to demand favors.

"Do what you think best," I said, "at your own price. I shall be very grateful to you;" and having come to this understanding, the father and I unbuckled the saddle-girths, while the daughter stood watching us. The old man led the limping horse across the green dooryard to a weather-beaten stable, talking to him in a low tone. The creature responded by unusual docility. I even saw him, though usually so suspicious and fretful with strangers, put his head close to his leader's shoulder with most affectionate impulse. I gathered up my belongings,—my needments, as somebody had called them, after Spenser's fashion, in the morning,— and entered the door.

II.

Along the by-ways and in the elder villages of New England stand many houses like this, from which life and vigor have long been ebbing, until all instincts of self-preservation seem to have departed. The commonplace, thrifty fears of increasing damage from cracks, or leaks, or falling plaster no longer give alarm; as age creeps through the human frame, pilfering the pleasures of enthusiasm and activity one by one, so it is with a decaying house. The old man's shrewd eyes alone seemed unrelated to his surroundings. What sorrow or misfortune had made him accept them? I wondered, as I stared about the once elegant room. Nothing new had been brought to it for years; the leather-bound books in the carved secretary might have belonged to his grandfather. The floor was carpetless and deeply worn; the faded paper on the walls and the very paint looked as old as he. The pinch of poverty could nowhere be much sharper than here, but the exquisite cleanness and order of the place made one ignore the thought of poverty in its common aspect, for all its offensive and repulsive qualities were absent. I sat down in a straight-backed mahogany chair, feeling much relieved, and not without gratitude for this unexpected episode. The hostess left me alone. I was glad enough to have the long day shortened a little, and to find myself in this lonely, mysterious house. I was pleased by the thought that the price of my food and lodging would be very welcome, and I grew more and more eager to know the history of my new friends. I have never been conscious of a more intense desire to make myself harmonious, or to win some degree of confidence. And when the silence of the old sitting-room grew tiresome I went out to the stable, whence my host had not returned, and was quite reconciled at finding that I was looked upon by him, at least, merely as an appendage to my four-footed companion.

The old man regarded me with indifference, and went on patiently rubbing the horse's foot. I was silent after having offered to take his place and being contemptuously refused. His clothes were curiously old and worn, patched bravely, and an embroidery of careful darns. The color of them was not unlike the dusty gray of long-neglected cobwebs. There was unusual delicacy and refinement in his hands and feet, and I was sure, from the first glance at my new friends and the first sound of their voices, that they had inherited gentle blood, though such an inheritance had evidently come through more than one generation to whom had been sternly denied any approach to luxury or social advantage. I have often noticed in country villages the descendants of those clergymen who once ruled New England sternly and well, and while they may be men and women of undeveloped minds, without authority and even of humble circumstances, they yet bear the mark of authority and dignified behavior, like silver and copper coins with a guinea stamp.

I was more and more oppressed by the haunting sense of poverty, for I saw proofs everywhere that the inhabitants of the old house made no practical protest against its slow decay. The woman's share of work was performed best, as one might see by their mended clothes; but the master's domain was hopelessly untended, not only as to the rickety buildings, but in the land itself, which was growing wild bushes at its own sweet will, except for a rough patch near the house, which had been dug and planted that year. Was this brooding, sad old man discouraged by life? Did he say to himself, "Let things be; they will last my time"? I found myself watching his face with intense interest, but I did not dare to ask questions, and only stood and watched him. The sad mouth of the man might have been a den from which stinging wild words could assail a curious stranger. I was afraid of what he might say to me, yet I longed to hear him speak.

The summer day was at its close. I moved a step forward to get away from the level sunbeams which dazzled my eyes, and ventured to give some news about myself and the lonely journey that had hitherto brought me such pleasure. The listener looked up with sincere attention, which made me grow enthusiastic at once, and I described my various experiences, and especially the amusing comments which I had heard upon my mode of traveling about the country. It amazed me to think that I was within sixty miles of home and yet a foreigner. At last I asked a trivial question about some portion of the scenery, which was pleasantly answered. The old man's voice was singularly sweet and varied in tone, the exact reverse of a New Englander's voice of the usual rural quality. I was half startled at seeing my horse quickly turn his head to look at the speaker, as if with human curiosity equal to my own. I felt a thrill of vague apprehension. I was unwise enough for a moment to dread taking up my residence in this dilapidated mansion;

a creeping horror, such as one feels at hearing footsteps behind one in a dark, strange place, made me foolishly uneasy, and I stood looking off across the level country through the golden light of closing day, beyond the marshes and beyond the sand dunes to the sea. What had happened to this uncanny father and daughter, that they were contented to let the chances of life slip by untouched, while their ancestral dwelling gradually made itself ready to tumble about their ears?

I could see that the horse's foot was much better already, and I watched with great sympathy the way that the compassionate, patient fingers touched and soothed the bruised joint. But I saw no sign of any other horse in the stable, save a few stiffened, dusty bits of harness hung on a high peg in the wall; and as I looked at these, and renewed my wonder that such a person should have no horse of his own, especially at such a distance from any town, the old man spoke again.

"Look up at that bit of dry skin over the harnesses," said he. "That was the pretty ear of the best mare that ever trod these roads. She leaped the stable-yard gate one day, caught her foot in a rope, and broke her neck. She was like those swallows one minute, and the next she was a heap of worthless flesh, a heavy thing to be dragged away and hidden in the earth." His voice failed him suddenly, poor old fellow; it told me that he had suffered cruel sorrows that made this loss of a pleasure almost unbearable. So far life had often brought me successes, and I had gained a habit of expecting my own enterprises to be lucky. I stood appalled before this glimpse of a defeated life and its long procession of griefs.

Presently the master of the place went into the house, and returned with a worn wooden trencher of bits of hard bread and some meal. The hungry creature in the stall whinnied eagerly, and nestled about, while our host ascended the broken stairway to the stable loft; and after waiting for some time, I heard the rustle of an armful of hay which came down into the crib. I looked that way, and was not surprised, when I noticed the faded, dusty dryness of it, to see my dainty beast sniff at it with disappointment, and look round at me inquiringly. The old man joined me, and I protested hastily against such treatment of my favorite.

"Cannot we get somebody to bring some better hay, and oats enough for a day or two, if you are unprovided?" I asked.

"The creature must not be overfed," he said, grudgingly, with a new harsh tone. "You will heat the foot, and we must keep the beast quiet. Anything will serve to-night; to-morrow he can graze all day, and keep the foot moving gently; next day, he can be shod."

"But there is danger in giving him green grass," I suggested. "This is too rich pasturage about the house; surely you know enough of horses to have learned that. He will not be fit to ride, either. If I meant to give him a month of pasture, it would be another thing. No; send somebody for at least an armful of decent hay. I will go myself. Are there houses near?"

The old man had gone into the stall, and was feeding the hungry horse from the trencher. I was startled to see him snatch back two or three bits of the bread and put them into his pocket, as if, with all his fondness for the horse and a sincere desire to make him comfortable, he nevertheless grudged the food. I became convinced that the poor soul was a miser. He certainly played the character exactly, and yet there was an appealing look in his eyes, which, joined with the tones of his voice, made me sure that he fought against his tyrannous inclinations. I wondered irreverently if I should be killed that night, after the fashion of traditional tavern robberies, for the sake of what might be found in my pocket, and sauntered toward the house. It remained to be proved whether the daughter was the victim or the upholder of her father's traits.

I had the satisfaction of finding that the daughter was just arranging a table for supper. As I passed the wide-open door of a closet, I was tempted to look in by the faint ancient odor of plum cakes and Madeira wine which escaped; but I never saw a barer closet than that, or one that looked hungrier in spite of the lingering fragrance of hospitality. It gave me a strange feeling as if there were a still subtler link with the past, and some invisible presence would have me contrast the house's former opulence with its present meagreness. When we sat at table I was not surprised to find, on a cloth that was half covered with darns and patches, some pieces of superb old English silver and delicate china. The fare was less than frugal, but was nobly eked out with a dish of field strawberries, as if kind Nature had come to the rescue. Cream there was none, nor sugar, nor even tea or butter. I had an aching sense of the poverty of the family, and curiously questioned in my own mind how far they found it possible to live without money. There was some thin, crisp corn bread, which had been baked in the morning, or whenever there had last been a fire. It was very good. Perhaps my entertainers even gathered their own salt from the tide-pools to flavor the native corn. Look where I would, I could see nothing for which money had been lately spent; here was a thing to be wondered at in this lavish America, and 'I pushed back my chair at last, while I was still half hungry, from a dread that there would be nothing for breakfast unless I saved it then.

The father and daughter were very agreeable, I must confess; they talked with me about my journey now, and my plans, as if they were my personal friends, and the strange meal was full of pleasure, after all. What had brought a lady and gentleman to such a pass?

After supper the daughter disappeared for

a time, busy with her household cares; a little later the father went out of the stable and across the fields, before I could call to him or offer my company. He walked with a light, quick step, like an Indian, as if he were used to taking journeys on foot. I found myself uncommonly tired; the half illness which had fettered me seemed to have returned, after the unusual anxiety and weariness of the afternoon, and I longed to go to bed and to sleep. I had been interested in much that my entertainers had said of the early history of that part of the country, and while we sat at the table I had begun to look forward to a later evening talk, but almost before daylight faded I was forced to go to bed.

My hostess led me through a handsome empty hall, of the wide and stately colonial type, to a comfortable upper room, furnished with a gloomy-looking curtained bedstead and heavy mahogany furniture of the best old fashion. It seemed as if the room had been long unused, and also as if the lower part of the house were in a much worse state of disrepair and threadbareness than this. But the two large windows stood open to the fading sky and sweet country air, and I bade my hostess good-night cheerfully. She lingered to see if I were comfortable; it was the first time I had been alone with her. "You can see that we are not used to entertaining company," she whispered, reddening with sensitiveness, and smiling apologetically. "Father has kept everybody away for so many years that I rarely have any one to speak to, or anything to do but to keep the poor old house clean. Father means to be kind, but he " — and she turned away, much embarrassed by my questioning look — "he has a monomania; he inherits it from my grandfather. He fears want, yet seems to have no power to provide against it. We are poor, God knows, yet we have resources; or had them once," she added, sorrowfully. "It was the horse that made him willing to let you in. He loves horses, yet he has long denied himself even that useful pleasure."

"But surely he ought to be controlled," I urged. "You must have suffered."

"I know all that you are eager to say," she replied; "but I promised my dear mother to be patient with him. It will not be long. now; he is very feeble. I have a horror that this habit of parsimony has rooted itself too deeply in my own life to be shaken off. You will hear mockery enough of us among the farmers."

"You surely have friends?"

"Only at a distance," said she, sadly. "I fear that they are no longer friends. I have *you*," she added, turning to me quickly, in a pathetic way that made me wish to put my arms about her. "I have been longing for a friendly face. Yes, it is very hard," and she drearily went out of the door, and left me alone with the dim light of the sky outside, the gloomy shadows of the room within. I tried to fancy some clew to the weird misery of this poverty-stricken household, as I lay down; but I fell asleep very soon, and slept all night, without even a dream.

III.

Daylight brought a new eagerness and a less anxious curiosity about my strange entertainers. I opened my eyes in broad sunlight. I was puzzled by the unfamiliar India-cotton hangings of the great bedstead; then I caught sight of my dusty habit and my riding-cap and whip, near by. I instantly resolved that even if I found my horse in the restored condition there was every reason to expect, I would make this house my headquarters for as long time as its owners would keep me, or I could content myself. I would try to show some sisterly affection to the fast-aging woman who was so enslaved by her father's delusions. I had come out in search of adventure; it would be a difficult task to match my present surroundings.

I listened for the sound of footsteps or voices from below, but it was still very early, and I looked about the long-untenanted room with deliberate interest and scrutiny. As I changed my position a little, I caught sight of a curious old painting on the large oval panel above the empty fireplace. The colors were dull, the drawing was quaintly conventional, and I recognized the subject, though not immediately. The artist had pleased himself by making a study of the old house itself, and later, as I dressed, I examined it in detail.

From the costume of the figures I saw that it must have been painted more than a hundred years before. In astonishing contrast to the present condition, it appeared like a satirical show of the house's possibilities. Servants held capering steeds for gay gentlemen to mount, and ladies walked together in fine attire down the garden alleys of the picture. Once a hospitable family had kept open house behind the row of elms, and once the follies of the world and the fashions of brilliant, luxurious life had belonged to this decayed and withering household. I wondered if the miserly old man, to whose strangely sweet and compelling voice I had listened the evening before, could bear to look at this picture, and acknowledge his unlikeness to his prosperous ancestors.

It was well for me that the keeping of hens is comparatively inexpensive, for I breakfasted comfortably, and was never so heartily rejoiced at the vicinity of a chicken-coop. My proposal to stay with my new friends for a few days met with no opposition from either host or hostess; and again, as I looked in their pinched and hopeless faces, I planned some secret excuses for making a feast of my own, or a happy holiday. The fields and hills of the old picture were still unchanged, but what ebb and flow of purpose, of comfort, of social condition, had enriched and impoverished the household!

"Where did she sleep?" asked the master of the house, suddenly, with a strange, suspicious glance at his daughter.

"In the landscape chamber," the pale

woman said, without lifting her eyes to his, though she grew whiter and thinner as she spoke.

I looked at him instinctively to see his eyes blaze with anger, and expected a torrent of abuse, because he was manifestly so much displeased.   Nothing was said, but with a feeling of uneasiness we left the table, and I went out to the kitchen with my new friend.

"There is no reason why I should not have put you into the landscape chamber," she told me instantly. "It is a fancy of my father's. I had aired that room thoroughly in the morning, but the front guest-chambers have been closed for some time."

"Who painted the strange old picture?" I asked. "Some member of the family?" But I was answered that it was the work of a Frenchman, who was captured in war-time, and paroled under the charge of her great-grandfather.

"He must have had a gay visit," I suggested, "if he has left a faithful picture of the house as he saw it."

"The house used to be like that always," was the faint response, and the speaker hesitated, as if she considered whether we did right in discussing her family history; then she turned quickly away. "I believe we are under some miserable doom. Father will be sure to tell you so, at any rate," she added, with an effort at gayety. "He believes that he fights against it, but I always say that he was cowardly, and accepted it," and she sighed wearily.

I looked at her with fresh surprise and conjecture. I forgot for the time this great, busy, prosaic world of which we were both a part, and I felt as if I had lost a score of years for each day's journey, and had gone backward into the past. New England holds many strange households within its borders, but there could not be another which approached this. The very air of the house oppressed me, and I strayed out into the beautiful wide fields, and found my spirits rising again at once. I turned at last to look back at the group of gray buildings in the great level landscape. They were such a small excrescence upon the fruitful earth, those roofs which covered awful stagnation and hindrance of the processes of spiritual life and growth. What power could burst the bonds, and liberate the man and woman I had left, from a mysterious tyranny?

I was bareheaded and the morning grew

very hot. I went toward a group of oaks,
to shelter myself in the shade, and found the
ancient burying-place of the family. There
were numerous graves, but none were marked
except the oldest. There was a group of
rude but stately stones, with fine inscriptions,
yet curiously enough the latest of them bore
a date soon after the beginning of the century; all the more recent graves were low
and unmarked in any way. The family fortunes had waned long ago, perhaps; I might
be wronging the present master of the house,
though I remembered what had been said to
me of some mysterious doom. I could not
help thinking of my new acquaintances most
intently, and was startled at the sound of
footsteps. I saw the old man, muttering
and bending his head until he could see nothing but the ground at his feet. He only
picked up some dead branches that had fallen
from the oaks, and went away toward the
house again; always looking at the ground,
as if he expected to find something. It came
to my mind with greater distinctness that he
was a miser, poor only by his own choice;
and I indignantly resolved to urge the daughter to break her allegiance to him for a time,
to claim her own and set herself free. But

the miser had no cheerful sense of his hoards, no certainty of a munificence which was more to him than any use of it; there was a look upon his face as of a preying conscience within, a gnawing reptile of shame and guilt and evil memory. Had he sacrificed all sweet family life and natural ties to his craving for wealth? I watched the bent and hungry figure out of sight.

When I reached the house again, I went through the open door of the wide hall, and gained my landscape chamber without being seen by any one. I was tired and dizzy with the unusual heat, and, quickly drawing the close shutters, I threw myself on the bed to rest. All the light in the room came from the shaded hall; there was absolute silence, except some far-off country sounds of birds high in the air or lowing cattle. The house itself was still as a tomb.

I went to sleep, but it was not sound sleep. I grew heavy and tired with my own weight. I heard soft footsteps coming up the stairs; some one stopped as if to listen outside the wide-open door; then the gray, shadowy figure of the old man stood just within, and his eyes peered about the room. I was behind the curtains; one had been unfastened, and hid me from his sight at first, but as he took one step forward he saw me, lying asleep. He bent over me, until I felt my hair stir with his breath, but I did not move. His presence was not frightful, strange to say; I felt as if I were only dreaming. I opened my eyes a little as he went away, apparently satisfied, to the closet door, and unlocked it, starting and looking at me anxiously as the key turned in the lock. Then he disappeared. I had a childish desire to shut him in and keep him prisoner, for reasons that were not clear to myself. Whether he only wished to satisfy himself that a concealed treasure was untouched I do not know, but presently he came out, and carefully locked the door again, and went away on tiptoe. I fancied that he lingered before the picture above the chimney-place, and wondered if his conscience pricked him as he acknowledged the contrast between past and present. Then he groaned softly, and went out. My heart began to beat very fast. I sprang up and tried to lock the door into the hall. My enthusiasm about spending a few days in this dismal place suddenly faded out, for I could not bear the thought that the weird old man was free to prowl about at his own sad will. But as I stood undecided in my doorway, a song sparrow perched on the sill of the wide hall window, and sang his heart away in a most cheerful strain. There was something so touching and appealing in the contrast that I felt a wistful clutch at my throat while I smiled, as one does when tears are coming like April showers to one's eyes. Without thinking what I did, I went back into the room, threw open the shutters again, and stood before the dingy landscape. How the horses pranced up to the door, and how fine the ladies were in their hoop-petticoats and high feathers! I imagined that the picture had been a constant rebuke to the dwellers in the house through their wasting lives and failing fortunes. In every human heart, said I, there is such a picture of the ideal life, — the high possibilities and successes, the semblance of duties done and of spiritual achievements. It forever measures our incompleteness by its exact likeness to that completeness which we would not fight hard enough to win. But as I looked up at the panel, the old landscape became dim, and I knew that it was only because a cloud was hiding the sun ; yet I was glad to leave the shadows of the room, and to hurry down the wide stairway.

I saw nothing of the daughter, though I searched for her, and even called her, through the house.   When I reached the side door I found her father crossing the yard, and wondered if he would show any consciousness of our having so lately met. He stood still and waited for me, and my first impulse made me ask, " What did you want just now ? I was not asleep when you .were in my room ; you frightened me."

" Do not be afraid," he answered with unexpected patience.   " You must take us as you find us.   It is a sad old house, but you need not be afraid; we are much more afraid of you ! " and we both smiled ami- ably.

" But your daughter," said I ; " I have been asking her to come away for a time, to visit me or take a journey.   It would be much better for you both ; and she needs a change and a little pleasuring.   God does not mean that we shall make our lives ut- terly dismal."   I was afraid, and did not dare to meet the old man's eyes after I had spoken so plainly.

He laughed coldly, and glanced at his mended coat-sleeve.

"What do you know about happiness? You are too young," said he. "At your age I thought I knew the world. What difference would it make if the old place here were like the gay ghost of it in our landscape chamber? The farmers would be jealous of our luxury; reverence and respect would be turned into idle curiosity. This quiet countryside would be disgraced by such a flaunting folly. No, we are very comfortable, my child and I; you must not try to disturb us," and he looked at me with a kind of piteous suspicion.

There was a large block of stone under one of the old elms, which had been placed there long ago for a mounting-block, and here we seated ourselves. As I looked at my companion, he seemed like a man unused to the broad light of day. I fancied that a prisoner, who had just ended many years of dungeon life, would wear exactly such a face. And yet it was such a lovely summer day of a joyful world, if he would only take or make it so. Alas, he matched the winter weather better. I could not bear to think of the old house in winter!

"Who is to blame?" said the old man suddenly, in a strange eager tone which startled me, and made me shrink away from him. "We are in bondage. I am a generous-hearted man, yet I can never follow my own impulses. I longed to give what I had with a lavish hand, when I was younger, but some power restrained me. I have grown old while I tried to fight it down. We are all in prison while we are left in this world, — that is the truth; in prison for another man's sin." For the first time I understood that he was not altogether sane. "If there were an ancestor of mine, as I have been taught, who sold his soul for wealth, the awful price was this, and he lost the power of using it. He was greedy for gain, and now we cannot part with what we have, even for common comfort. His children and his children's children have suffered for his fault. He has lived in the hell of watching us from generation to generation; seeing our happiness spoiled, our power of usefulness wither away. Wherever he is, he knows that we are all misers because he was miserly, and stamped us with the mark of his own base spirit. He has watched his descendants shrivel up and disappear one by one, poor and ungenerous in God's world. We fight against the doom of it, but it wins at last. Thank God, there are only two of us left."

I had sprung to my feet, frightened by the old man's vehemence. I could not help saying that God meant us to be free and unconquered by any evil power; the gray, strange face looked blindly at me, and I could not speak again. This was the secret of the doom, then. I left the old man crying, while I hurried away to find the mistress of the desolate house, and appeal to her to let me send a companion for her father, who could properly care for him here, or persuade him to go away to some place where he would forget his misery among new interests and scenes. She herself must not be worn out by his malady of unreason.

But I only dashed my sympathy against the rock of her hopelessness. " I think we shall all disappear some night in a winter storm, and the world will be rid of us, — father and the house and I, all three," she said, with bitter dreariness, and turned to her work again.

Early that evening, I said good-by to my new friends, for the horse was sound, and not to be satisfied by such meagre stabling. Our host seemed sorry to let the creature go, and stood stroking him affectionately after I had mounted. "How the famous old breed holds its own!" he said wistfully. "I should like to have seen the ancestor who has stamped his likeness so unmistakably on all his descendants."

"But among human beings," I could not resist saying, "there is freedom, thank God! We can climb to our best possibilities, and outgrow our worst inheritance."

"No, no!" cried the old man bitterly "You are young and fortunate. Forget us, if you can; we are of those who have no hope in a world of fate."

I looked back again and again, as I rode away. It was a house of shadows and strange moods, and I was glad when I had fairly left it behind me; yet I looked forward to seeing it again. I well remember the old man's clutch at the money I offered him, and the kiss and the bunch of roses that the daughter gave to me. But late that evening I was not sorry to shut myself into my prosaic room at a village hotel, rather than try to sleep again behind the faded figured curtains of the landscape chamber.

LAW LANE.

I.

THE thump of a flat-iron signified to an educated passer-by that this was Tuesday morning; yesterday having been fair and the weekly washing-day unhindered by the weather. It was undoubtedly what Mrs. Powder pleased herself by calling a good orthodox week; not one of the disjointed and imperfect sections of time which a rainy Monday forced upon methodical housekeepers. Mrs. Powder was not a woman who could live altogether in the present, and whatever she did was done with a view to having it cleared out of the way of the next enterprise on her list. " I can't bear to see folks do their work as if every piece on 't was a tread-mill," she used to say, briskly. "Life means progriss to me, and I can't dwell by the way no more 'n sparks can fly downwards. 'T ain't the way I 'm built, nor none of the Fisher tribe."

The hard white bundles in the shallow splint-basket were disappearing, one by one, and taking their places on the decrepit clothes-horse, well ironed and precisely folded. The July sunshine came in at one side of Mrs. Powder's kitchen, and the cool northwest breeze blew the heat out again from the other side. Mrs. Powder grew uneasy and impatient as she neared the end of her task, and the flat-iron moved more and more vigorously. She kept glancing out through the doorway and along the country road as if she were watching for somebody.

"I shall just have to git ready an' go an' rout her out myself, an' take my chances," she said at last with a resentful look at the clock, as if it were partly to blame for the delay and had ears with which to listen to proper rebuke. The round moon-face had long ago ceased its waxing and waning across the upper part of the old dial, as if it had forgotten its responsibility about the movements of a heavenly body in its pleased concern about housekeeping.

"See here!" said Mrs. Powder, taking a last hot iron from the fire. "You ain't a-keepin' time like you used to; you're gettin' lazy, I must say. Look at this 'ere sun-mark on the floor, that calls it full 'leven o'clock, and you want six minutes to ten. I 've got to send word to the clock-man and have your in'ards all took apart; you got me to meetin' more 'n half an hour too late, Sabbath last."

To which the moon-face did not change its beaming expression; very likely, being a moon, it was not willing to mind the ways of the sun.

"Lord, what an old thing you be!" said Mrs. Powder, turning away with a chuckle. "I don't wonder your sense kind of fails you!" And the clock clucked at her by way of answer, though presently it was going to strike ten at any rate.

The hot iron was now put down hurriedly, and the half-ironed night-cap was left in a queer position on the ironing-board. A small figure had appeared in the road and was coming toward the house with a fleet, barefooted run which required speedy action. "Here you, Joel Smith!" shouted the old woman. "Jo—el!" But the saucy lad only doubled his pace and pretended not to see or hear her. Mrs. Powder could play at that game, too, and did not call again, but quietly went back to her ironing

and tried as hard as she could to be provoked. Presently the boy came panting up
the slope of green turf which led from the
road to the kitchen doorstep.

"I did n't know but you spoke as I ran
by," he remarked, in an amiable tone. Mrs.
Powder took no heed of him whatever.

"I ain't in no hurry; I kind o' got running," he explained, a moment later; and
then, as his hostess stepped toward the
stove, he caught up the frilled night-cap and
tied it on in a twinkling. When Mrs. Powder turned again, the sight of him was too
much for her gravity.

"Them frills is real becoming to ye," she
announced, shaking with laughter. "I declare for 't if you don't favor your gran'ma
Dodge's looks. I should like to have yer
folks see ye. There, take it off now; I 'm
most through my ironin' and I want to clear
it out o' the way."

Joel was perfectly docile and laid the
night-cap within reach. He had a temptation to twitch it back by the end of one
string, but he refrained. "Want me to go
drive your old brown hen-turkey out o' the
wet grass, Mis' Powder? She 's tolling her
chicks off down to'a'ds the swamp," he offered.

"She's raised up families enough to know how by this time," said Mrs. Powder, "an' the swamp's dry as a bone."

"I'll split ye up a mess o' kindlin'-wood whilst I'm here, jest as soon's not," said Joel, in a still more pleasant tone, after a long and anxious pause.

"There, I'll get ye your doughnuts, pretty quick. They ain't so fresh as they was Saturday. I s'pose that's what you're driving at." The good soul shook with laughter. Joel answered as well for her amusement as the most famous of comic actors; there was something in his appealing eyes, his thin cheeks and monstrous freckles, and his long locks of sandy hair, which was very funny to Mrs. Powder. She was always interested, too, in fruitless attempts to satisfy his appetite. He listened now, for the twentieth time, to her opinion that the bottomless pit alone could be compared to the recesses of his being. "I should like to be able to say that I had filled ye up jest once!" she ended her remarks, as she brought a tin pan full of doughnuts from her pantry.

"Heard the news?" asked small Joel, as he viewed the provisions with glistening eyes. He bore likeness to a little hungry woodchuck, or muskrat, as he went to work before the tin pan.

"What news?" Mrs. Powder asked, suspiciously. "I ain't seen nobody this day."

"Barnet's folks has got their case in court."

"They ain't!" and while a solemn silence fell upon the kitchen, the belated old clock whirred and rumbled and struck ten with persistent effort. Mrs. Powder looked round at it impatiently; the moon-face confronted her with the same placid smile.

"Twelve o'clock's the time you git your dinner, ain't it, Mis' Powder?" the boy inquired, as if he had repeated his news like a parrot and had no further interest in its meaning.

"I don't plot for to get me no reg'lar dinner this day," was the unexpected reply. "You can eat a couple or three o' them nuts and step along, for all I care. An' I want you to go up Lyddy Bangs's lane and carry her word that I'm goin' out to pick me some blueberries. They'll be ripened up elegant, and I've got a longin' for 'em. Tell her I say 't is our day — she'll know; we've be'n after 'arly blueberries together this forty years, and Lyddy knows where to meet with me; there by them split rocks."

The ironing was finished a few minutes afterward, and the board was taken to its place in the shed. When Mrs. Powder returned, Joel had stealthily departed; the tin pan was turned upside down on the seat of the kitchen chair. "Good land!" said the astonished woman, "I believe he'll bu'st himself to everlastin' bliss one o' these days. Them doughnuts would have lasted me till Thursday, certain."

"Gimme suthin' to eat, Mis' Powder?" whined Joel at the window, with his plaintive countenance lifted just above the sill. But he set forth immediately down the road, with bulging pockets and the speed of a light-horseman.

II.

Half an hour later the little gray farm-house was shut and locked, and its mistress was crossing the next pasture with a surprisingly quick step for a person of her age and weight. An old cat was trotting after her, with tail high in the air, but it was plain to see that she still looked for danger, having

just come down from the woodpile, where
she had retreated on Joel's first approach.
She kept as close to Mrs. Powder as was
consistent with short excursions after crick-
ets or young, unwary sparrows, and opened
her wide green eyes fearfully on the lookout
for that evil monster, the boy.

There were two pastures to cross, and
Mrs. Powder was very much heated by the
noonday sun and entirely out of breath
when she approached the familiar rendezvous and caught sight of her friend's cape-
bonnet.

"Ain't there no justice left?" was her
indignant salutation. "I s'pose you 've
heard that Crosby's folks have lost their
case? Poor Mis' Crosby! 't will kill her,
I 'm sure. I 've be'n calculatin' to go berryin' all the forenoon, but I could n't git
word to you till Joel came tootin' by. I
thought likely you 'd expect notice when
you see what a good day 't was."

" I did," replied Lyddy Bangs, in a tone
much more serious than her companion's.
She was a thin, despairing little body, with
an anxious face and a general look of disappointment and poverty, though really the
more prosperous person of the two. "Joel

told me you said 't was our day," she added.
" I 'm wore out tryin' to satisfy that boy;
he 's always beggin' for somethin' to eat
every time he comes nigh the house. I
should think they 'd see to him to home;
not let him batten on the neighbors so."

" You ain't been feedin' of him, too ? "
laughed Mrs. Powder. " Well, I declare, I
don't see whar he puts it ! " and she fanned
herself with her apron. " I always forget
what a sightly spot this is."

" Here 's your pussy - cat, ain't she ? "
asked Lyddy Bangs, needlessly, as they sat
looking off over the valley. Behind them
the hills rose one above another, with their
bare upland clearings and great stretches of
pine and beech forest. Beyond the wide
valley was another range of hills, green and
pleasant in the clear mid-day light. Some
higher mountains loomed, sterile and stony,
to northward. They were on the women's
right as they sat looking westward.

" It does seem as if folks might keep the
peace when the Lord's give 'em so pooty a
a spot to live in," said Lyddy Bangs, re-
gretfully. " There ain't no better farms
than Barnet's and Crosby's folks have got
neither, but 'stead o' neighboring they must

pick their mean fusses and fight from generation to generation. My gran'ma'am used to say 't was just so with 'em when she was a girl — and she was one of the first settlers up this way. She al'ays would have it that Barnet's folks was the most to blame, but there 's plenty sides with 'em, as you know."

"There, 't is all mixed up, so 't is — a real tangle," answered Mrs. Powder. "I 've been o' both minds — I must say I used to hold for the Crosbys in the old folks' time, but I 've come round to see they ain't perfect. There! I 'm b'ilin' over with somethin' I 've got to tell somebody. I 've kep' it close long 's I can."

"Let 's get right to pickin', then," said Lyddy Bangs, "or we sha'n't budge from here the whole livin' afternoon," and the small thin figure and the tall stout one moved off together toward their well-known harvest-fields. They were presently settled down within good hearing distance, and yet the discussion was not begun. The cat curled herself for a nap on the smooth top of a rock.

"There, I have to eat a while first, like a young-one," said Mrs. Powder. "I always tell 'em that blueberries is only fit to eat

right off of the twigs. You want 'em full o'
sun; let 'em git cold and they 're only fit to
cook — not but what I eat 'em any ways
I can git 'em. Ain't they nice an' spicy?
Law, my poor knees is so stiff! I begin to
be afraid, nowadays, every year o' berryin'
may be my last. I don' know why 't should
be that my knees serves me so. I ain't
rheumaticky, nor none o' my folks was; we
go off with other complaints."

"The mukis membrane o' the knees gits
dried up," explained Lyddy Bangs, "an'
the j'ints is all powder-posted. So I 've be'n
told, anyways."

"Then they was ignorant," retorted her
companion, sharply. "I know by the feelin's
I have " — and the two friends picked in-
dustriously and discussed the vexed points
of medicine no more.

"I can't force them Barnets and Crosbys out o' my mind," suggested Miss Bangs
after a while, being eager to receive the
proffered confidence which might be forgotten. "Think of 'em, without no other
door-neighbors, fightin' for three ginerations
over the bounds of a lane wall. What if
't was two foot one way or two foot t'other,
let 'em agree."

" But that 's just what they could n't," said Mrs. Powder. " You know yourself you might be willin' to give away a piece o' land, but when somebody said 't wa'n't yours, 't was theirs, 't would take more Christian grace 'n I 've got to let 'em see I thought they was right. All the old Crosbys ever wanted, first, was for the Barnets to say two foot of the lane was theirs by rights, and then they was willin' to turn it into the lane and to give that two foot more o' the wedth than Barnets did — they wa'n't haggling for no pay ; 't was for rights. But Barnet's folks said " —

" Now, don't you go an' git all flustered up a-tellin' that over, Harri't Powder," said the lesser woman. " There ain't be'n no words spoke so often as them along this sidelin' hill, not even the Ten Command- ments. The only sense there 's be'n about it is, they 've let each other alone altogether, and ain't spoke at all for six months to a time. I can't help hoping that the war 'll die out with the old breed and they 'll come to some sort of peace. Mis' Barnet was a Sands, and they 're toppin' sort o' folks and she 's got fight in her. I think she 's more to blame than Barnet, a good sight ; but

Mis' Crosby 's a downright peace-making little creatur', and would have ended it long
ago if she 'd be'n able."

"Barnet's stubborn, too, let me tell you!"
and Mrs. Powder's voice was full of anger.
" 'T will never die out in his day, and he 'll
spend every cent lawing, as the old folks
did afore him. The lawyers must laugh at
him well, 'mongst themselves. One an' another o' the best on 'em has counseled them
to leave it out to referees, and tried to show
'em they was fools. My man talked with
judge himself about it, once, after he 'd been
settin' on a jury and they was comin' away
from court. They could n't agree; they
never could! All the spare money o' both
farms has gone to pay the lawyers and carry
on one fight after another. Now folks don't
know it, but Crosby's farm is all mortgaged; they 've spent even what Mis' Crosby
had from her folks. An' there 's worse behind — there 's worse behind," insisted the
speaker, stoutly. "I went up there this
spring, as you know, when Mis' Crosby was
at death's door with lung-fever. I went
through everything fetchin' of her round,
and was there five weeks, till she got about.
'I feel to'a'ds you as an own sister,' says

Abby Crosby to me. 'I'm a neighboring woman at heart,' says she; 'and just you think of it, that my man had to leave me alone, sick as I was, while he went for you and the doctor, not riskin' to ask Barnet's folks to send for help. I like to live pleasant,' says she to me, and bu'st right out a-cryin'. I knew then how she'd felt things all these years. — How are they ever goin' to pay more court bills and all them piles o' damages, if the farm's mortgaged so heavy?" she resumed. "Crosby's farm ain't worth a good two thirds of Barnet's. They've both neglected their lands. How many you got so fur, Lyddy?"

Lyddy proudly displayed her gains of blueberries; the pail was filling very fast, and the friends were at their usual game of rivalry. Mrs. Powder had been the faster picker in years past, and she now doubled her diligence.

"Ain't the sweet-fern thick an' scented as ever you see?" she said. "Gimme pasture-lands rather 'n the best gardins that grows. If I can have a sweet-brier bush and sweet-fern patch and some clumps o' bayberry, you can take all the gardin blooms. Look how folks toils with witch-grass and pusley and gets a starved lot o' poor sprigs, slug-eat, and all dyin' together in their front yards, when they might get better comfort in the first pasture along the road. I guess there's somethin' wild, that's never got tutored out o' me. I must ha' be'n made o' somethin' counter to town dust. I never could see why folks wanted to go off an' live out o' sight o' the mountings, an' have everything on a level."

"You said there was worse to tell behind," suggested Lyddy Bangs, as if it were only common politeness to show an appreciation of the friendly offering.

" I have it in mind to get round to that in proper course," responded Mrs. Powder, a trifle offended by the mild pertinacity. " I settled it in my mind that I was goin' to tell you somethin' for a kind of a treat the day we come out blueberryin'. *There!*" — and Mrs. Powder rose with difficulty from her knees, and retreated pompously to the shade of a hemlock-tree which grew over a shelving rock near by.

Lyddy Bangs could not resist picking a little longer in an unusually fruitful spot; then she hastened to seat herself by her friend. It was no common occasion.

Mrs. Powder was very warm ; and further evaded and postponed telling the secret by wishing that she were as light on foot as her companion, and deploring her increasing weight. Then she demanded a second sight of the blueberries, which were compared and decided upon as to quality and quantity. Then the cat, which had been left at some distance on her rock, came trotting toward her mistress in a disturbed way, and after a minute of security in a comfortable lap darted away again in a strange, excited manner.

"She 's goin' to have a fit, I do believe!" exclaimed Lyddy Bangs, quite disheartened, for the cat was Mrs. Powder's darling and she might leave everything to go in search of her.

"She may have seen a snake or something. She often gets scared and runs home when we 're out a-trarvelin'," said the cat's owner, complacently, and Lyddy's spirits rose again.

"I suppose you never suspected that Ezra Barnet and Ruth Crosby cared the least thing about one another ? " inquired the keeper of the secret a moment later, and the listener turned toward Mrs. Powder with a startled face.

"Now, Harri't Powder, for mercy's sakes alive!" was all that she could say; but Mrs. Powder was satisfied, and confirmed the amazing news by a most emphatic nod.

"My lawful sakes! what be they goin' to do about it?" inquired Lyddy Bangs, flushing with excitement. "A Barnet an' a Crosby fall in love! Don't you rec'lect how the old ones was al'ays fightin' and callin' names when we was all to school together? Times is changed, certain."

"Now, say you hope to die if ever you 'll tell a word I say," pursued Mrs. Powder. "If I was to be taken away to-morrow, you 'd be all the one that would know it except Mis' Crosby and Ezra and Ruth themselves. 'T was nothin' but her bein' nigh to death that urged her to tell me the state o' things. I s'pose she thought I might favor 'em in time to come. Abby Crosby she says to me, 'Mis' Powder, my poor girl may need your motherin' care.' An' I says, 'Mis' Crosby, she shall have it;' and then she had a spasm o' pain, and we harped no more that day as I remember."

"How come it about? I should n't have told anybody that asked me that a Barnet and a Crosby ever 'changed the time o' day, much less kep' company," protested the listener.

"Kep' company! pore young creatur's!" said Mrs. Powder. "They 've hid 'em away in the swamps an' hollers, and in the edge o' the growth, at nightfall, for the sake o' gittin' a word; an' they 've stole out, shiverin', into that plaguey lane o' winter nights. I tell ye I 've heard hifalutin' folks say that love would still be lord of all, but I never was 'strained to believe it till I see what that boy and girl was willin' to undergo. All the hate of all their folks is turned to love in them, and I could n't help a-watchin' of 'em. An' I ventured to send Ruth over to my house after my alpaccy aprin, and then I made an arrant out to the spring-brook to see if there was any cresses started — which I knew well enough there was n't — and I spoke right out bold to Ezra, that was at work on a piece of ditching over on his land. 'Ezra,' says I, 'if you git time, just run over to the edge o' my pasture and pick me a handful o' balm o' Gilead buds. I want to put 'em in half a pint o' new rum for Mis' Crosby, and there ain't a soul to send.' I knew he 'd just meet her coming back, if I could time it right gittin' of Ruth started.

He looked at me kind of curi's, and pretty quick I see him leggin' it over the fields with an axe and a couple o' ends o' board, like he'd got to mend a fence. I had to keep her dinner warm for her till ha'-past one o'clock. I don't know what he mentioned to his folks, but Ruth she come an' kissed me hearty when she first come inside the door. 'T is harder for Ezra; he ain't got nobody to speak to, and Ruth's got her mother if she is a Mis' Much-afraid."

"I don't know's we can blame Crosby for not wantin' to give his girl to the Barnets, after they've got away all his substance, his means, an' his cattle, like 't was in the Book o' Job," urged Lyddy Bangs. "Seems as if they might call it square an' marry the young folks off, but they won't nohow; 't will only fan the flame." Lyddy Bangs was a sentimental person; neighbor Powder had chosen wisely in gaining a new friend to the cause of Ezra Barnet's apparently hopeless affection. Unknown to herself, however, she had been putting the lover's secret to great risk of untimely betrayal.

The weather was most beautiful that afternoon; there was an almost intoxicating

freshness and delight among the sweet odors
of the hillside pasture, and the two elderly
women were serene at heart and felt like
girls again as they talked together. They
remembered many an afternoon like this;
they grew more and more confiding as they
reviewed the past and their life-long friendship. A stranger might have gathered only
the most rural and prosaic statements, and
a tedious succession of questions, from what
Mrs. Powder and Lyddy Bangs had to say to
each other, but the old stories of true love and
faithful companionship were again simply
rehearsed. Those who are only excited by
more complicated histories too often forget
that there are no new plots to the comedies
and tragedies of life. They are played
sometimes by country people in homespun,
sometimes by townsfolk in velvet and lace.
Love and prosperity, death and loss and
misfortune — the stories weave themselves
over and over again, never mind whether the
ploughman or the wit of the clubs plays the
part of hero.

The two homely figures sat still so long
that they seemed to become permanent
points in the landscape, and the small birds,
and even a wary chipmunk, went their ways

unmindful of Mrs. Powder and Lyddy Bangs. The old hemlock-tree, under which they sat discoursing, towered high above the young pine-growth which clustered thick behind them on the hillside. In the middle of a comfortable reflection upon the Barnet grandfather's foolishness or craftiness, Mrs. Powder gave sudden utterance to the belief that some creature up in the tree was dropping pieces of bark and cones all over her.

"A squirrel, most like," said Lyddy Bangs, looking up into the dense branches. "The tree is a-scatterin' down, ain't it? As you was sayin', Grandsir Barnet must have knowed well enough what he was about" —

"Oh, gorry! oh, git out! ow — o — w!" suddenly wailed a voice overhead, and a desperate scramble and rustling startled the good women half out of their wits. "Ow, Mis' Powder!" shrieked a familiar voice, while both hearts thumped fast, and Joel came, half falling, half climbing, down out of the tree. He bawled, and beat his head with his hands, and at last rolled in agony among the bayberry and lamb-kill. "Look out for 'em!" he shouted. "Oh, gorry! I thought 't was only an old last-year's hornet's nest — they 'll sting you, too!"

Mrs. Powder untied her apron and laid about her with sure aim. Only two hornets were to be seen; but after these were beaten to the earth, and she stopped to regain her breath, Joel hardly dared to lift his head or to look about him.

"What was you up there for, anyhow?" asked Lyddy Bangs, with severe suspicion. "Harking to us, I'll be bound!" But Mrs. Powder, who knew Joel's disposition best, elbowed her friend into silence and began to inquire about the condition of his wounds. There was a deep-seated hatred between Joel and Miss Bangs.

"Oh, dear! they've bit me all over," groaned the boy. "Ain't you got somethin' you can rub on, Mis' Powder?" — and the rural remedy of fresh earth was suggested.

"'T is too dry here," said the adviser. "Just you step down to that ma'shy spot there by the brook, dear, and daub you with the wet mud real good, and 't will ease you right away." Mrs. Powder's voice sounded compassionate, but her spirit and temper of mind gave promise of future retribution.

"I'll teach him to follow us out eaves-dropping, this fashion!" said Lyddy Bangs, when the boy had departed, weeping, "I'm more 'n gratified that the hornets got hold of him! I hope 't will serve him for a lesson."

"Don't you r'ile him up one mite, now," pleaded Mrs. Powder, while her eyes bore witness of hardly controlled anger. "He 's the worst tattle-tale I ever see, and we 've put ourselves into a trap. If he tells his mother she 'll spread it all over town. But I should no more thought o' his bein' up in that tree than o' his bein' the sarpent in the garden o' Eden. You leave Joel to me, and be mild with him 's you can."

The culprit approached, still lamenting. His ear and cheek were hugely swollen already, so that one eye was nearly closed. The blueberry expedition was relinquished, and with heavy sighs of dissatisfaction Lyddy Bangs took up the two half-filled pails, while Mrs. Powder kindly seized Joel by his small, thin hand, and the little group moved homeward across the pasture.

"Where 's your hat ? " asked Lyddy, stopping short, after they had walked a little distance.

"Hanging on a limb up by the wop's nest," answered Joel. "Oh, git me home, Mis' Powder ! "

III.

No one would suspect, from the look of the lane itself, that it had always been such a provoker of wrath, and even a famous battle-ground. While petty wars had raged between the men and women of the old farms, walnut-trees had grown high in air, and apple-trees had leaned their heavy branches on the stone walls and, year after year, decked themselves in pink-and-white blossoms to arch this unlucky by-way for a triumphal procession of peace that never came. Birds built their nests in the boughs and pecked the ripe blackberries; green brakes and wild roses and tall barberry-bushes flourished in their season on either side the wheel-ruts. It was a remarkably pleasant country lane, where children might play and lovers might linger. No one would imagine that this lane had its lawsuits and damages, its annual crop of briefs, and succession of surveyors and quarrelsome partisans; or that in every generation of owners each man must be either plaintiff or defendant.

The surroundings looked permanent enough. No one would suspect that a certain piece of wall had been more than once thrown down by night and built again, angrily, by day; or that a well-timbered corn-house had been the cause of much litigation, and even now looked, when you came to know its story, as if it stood on its long, straight legs, like an ungainly, top-heavy beast, all ready to stalk away when its position became too dangerous. The Barnets had built it beyond their boundary; it had been moved two or three times, backward and forward.

The Barnet house and land stood between the Crosby farm and the high-road; the Crosbys had never been able to reach the highway without passing their enemies under full fire of ugly looks or taunting voices. The intricacies of legal complications in the matter of right of way would be impossible to explain. They had never been very clear to any impartial investigator. Barnets and Crosbys had gone to their graves with bitter hatred and sullen desire for revenge in their hearts. Perhaps this one great interest, outside the simple matters of food and clothing and farmers' work, had taken the place to them of drama and literature and art. One could not help thinking, as he looked at the decrepit fences and mossy, warped roofs and buckling walls, to how much better use so much money might have been put. The costs of court and the lawyers' fees had taken everything, and men had drudged, in heat and frost, and women had pinched and slaved to pay the lane's bills. Both the Barnet and Crosby of the present time stood well enough in the opinion of other neighbors. They were hard-fisted, honest men; the fight was inherited to begin with, and they were stubborn enough to hold fast to the fight. Law Lane was as well known as the county roads in half a dozen towns. Perhaps its irreconcilable owners felt a thrill of enmity that had come straight down from Scottish border-frays, as they glanced along its crooked length. Who could believe that the son and daughter of the warring households, instead of being ready to lift the torch in their turn, had weakly and misguidedly fallen in love with each other?

Nobody liked Mrs. Barnet. She was a cross-grained, suspicious soul, who was a tyrant and terror of discomfort in her own household whenever the course of events ran counter to her preference. Her son Ezra was a complete contrast to her in disposition, and to his narrow-minded, prejudiced father as well. The elder Ezra was capable of better things, however, and might have been reared to friendliness and justice, if the Crosby of his youthful day had not been specially aggravating and the annals of Law Lane at their darkest page. If there had been another boy to match young Ezra, on the Crosby farm, the two might easily have fostered their natural boyish rivalries until something worse came into being; but when one's enemy is only a sweet-faced little girl, it is very hard to impute to her all manner of discredit and serpent-like power of evil. At least, so Ezra Barnet the younger felt in his inmost heart; and though he minded his mother for the sake of peace, and played his solitary games and built his unapplauded dams and woodchuck - traps on his own side of the fences, he always saw Ruth Crosby as she came and went, and liked her better and better as years went by. When the tide of love rose higher than the young people's steady heads, they soon laid fast hold of freedom. With all their perplexities, life was by no means at its worst, and rural diplomacy must bend all its energies to hinder these unexpected lovers.

Ezra Barnet had never so much as entered the Crosby house ; the families were severed beyond the reuniting power of even a funeral. Ezra could only try to imagine the room to which his Ruth had returned one summer evening after he had left her, reluctantly, because the time drew near for his father's return from the village. His mother had been in a peculiarly bad temper all day, and he had been glad to escape from her unwelcome insistence that he should marry any one of two or three capable girls, and so furnish some help in the housekeeping. Ezra had often heard this suggestion of his duty, and, tired and provoked at last, he had stolen out to the garden and wandered beyond it to the brook and out to the fields. Somewhere, somehow, he had met Ruth, and the lovers bewailed their trials with unusual sorrow and impatience. It seemed very hard to wait. Young Barnet was ready to persuade the tearful girl that they must go away together and establish a peaceful home of their own. He was heartily ashamed because the last verdict was in his father's favor, and Ruth forebore to wound him with any glimpse of the straits to which her own father had been reduced. She was too dutiful to leave the pinched household, where her help was needed more than ever; she persuaded her lover that they were sure to be happy at last — indeed, were not they happy now? How much worse it would be if they could not safely seize so many opportunities, brief though they were, of being together! If the fight had been less absorbing and the animosity less bitter, they might have been suspected long ago.

So Ruth and Ezra parted, with uncounted kisses, and Ezra went back to the dingy-walled kitchen, where his mother sat alone. It was hardly past twilight out of doors, but Mrs. Barnet had lighted a kerosene-lamp, and sat near the small open window mending a hot-looking old coat. She looked so needlessly uncomfortable and surly that her son was filled with pity, as he stood watching her, there among the moths and beetles that buffeted the lamp-chimney.

"Why don't you put down your sewing and come out a little ways up the road, mother, and get cooled off?" he asked, pleasantly; but she only twitched herself in her chair and snapped off another needleful of linen thread.

"I can't spare no time to go gallivantin',

like some folks," she answered. " I always have had to work, and I always shall. I see that Crosby girl mincin' by an hour ago, as if she 'd be'n off all the afternoon. Folks that think she 's so amiable about saving her mother's strength would be surprised at the way she dawdles round, I guess " — and Mrs. Barnet crushed an offending beetle with her brass thimble in a fashion that disgusted Ezra. Somehow, his mother had a vague instinct that he did not like to hear sharp words about Ruth Crosby. Yet he rarely had been betrayed into an ill-judged defense. He had left Ruth only a minute ago ; he knew exactly what she had been doing all day, and from what kind errand she had been returning ; the blood rushed quickly to his face, and he rose from his seat by the table and went out to the kitchen doorstep. The air was cool and sweet, and a sleepy bird chirped once or twice from an elm-bough overhead. The moon was near its rising, and he could see the great shapes of the mountains that lay to the eastward. He forgot his mother, and began to think about Ruth again ; he wondered if she were not thinking of him, and meant to ask her if she remembered an especial feeling of nearness just at this hour. Ezra turned to look at the clocks to mark the exact time.

"Yes," said Mrs. Barnet, as she saw him . try to discover the hour, "'t is time that father was to home. I s'pose, bein' mail-night, everybody was out to the post-office to hear the news, and most like he 's bawlin' himself hoarse about fall 'lections or something. He ain't got done braggin' about our gittin' the case, neither. There 's always some new one that wants to git the p'ints right from headquarters. I did n't see Crosby go by, did you?"

"He 'd have had to foot it by the path 'cross-lots," replied Ezra, gravely, from the doorstep. "He 's sold his hoss."

"He ain't!" exclaimed Mrs. Barnet, with a chuckle. "I s'pose they 're proddin' him for the money up to court. Guess he won't try to fight us again for one while."

Ezra said nothing; he could not bear this sort of thing much longer. "I won't be kept like a toad under a harrow," he muttered to himself. "I think it seems kind of hard," he ventured to say aloud. "Now he 's got to hire when fall work comes on, and " —

The hard-hearted woman within had long

been trying to provoke her peaceable son into an argument, and now the occasion had come. Ezra restrained himself from speech with a desperate effort, and stopped his ears to the sound of his mother's accusing voice. In the middle of her harangue a wagon was driven into the yard, and his father left it quickly and came toward the door.

"Come in here, you lout!" he shouted, angrily. "I want to look at you! I want to see what such a mean-spirited sneak has got to say for himself." Then changing his voice to a whine, he begged Ezra, who had caught him from falling as he stumbled over the step, "Come in, boy, an' tell me 't ain't true. I guess they was only thornin' of me up; you ain't took 'a shine' to that Crosby miss, now, have you?"

"No son of mine — no son of mine!" burst out the mother, who had been startled by the sudden entrance of the news-bringer. Her volubility was promptly set free, and Ezra looked from his father's face to his mother's.

"Father," said he, turning away from the scold, who was nearly inarticulate in her excess of rage — "father, I 'd rather talk to you, if you want to hear what I 've got to say. Mother 's got no reason in her."

"Ezry," said the elder man, "I see how 't is. Let your ma'am talk all she will. I 'm broke with shame of ye!"— his voice choked weakly in his throat. "Either you tell me 't is all nonsense, or you go out o' that door and shut it after you for good. An' ye 're all the boy I 've got."

The woman had stopped at last, mastered by the terror of the moment. Her husband's face was gray with passion; her son's cheeks were flushed and his eyes were full of tears. Mrs. Barnet's tongue for once had lost its cunning.

The two men looked at each other as long as they could; the younger man's eyes fell first. "I wish you would n't be hasty," he said; "to-morrow"—

"You 've heard," was the only answer; and in a moment more Ezra Barnet reached to the table and took his old straw hat which lay there.

"Good-by, father!" he said, steadily. "I think you 're wrong, sir; but I never meant to carry on that old fight and live like the heathen." And then, young and strong and angry, he left the kitchen.

"He might have took some notice o' me, if he 's goin' for good," said the mother spitefully; but her son did not hear this taunt, and the father only tottered where he stood. The moths struck against his face as if it were a piece of wood; he sank feebly into a chair, muttering, and trying to fortify himself in his spent anger.

Ezra went out, dazed and giddy. But he found the young horse wandering about the yard, eager for his supper and fretful at the strange delay. He unharnessed the creature and backed the wagon under the shed; then he turned and looked at the house — should he go in? No! The fighting instinct, which had kept firm grasp on father and grandfather, took possession of Ezra now. He crossed the yard and went out at the gate, and down the lane's end to the main road. The father and mother listened to his footsteps, and the man gave a heavy groan.

"Let him go — let him go! 't will teach him a lesson!" said Mrs. Barnet, with something of her usual spirit. She could not say more, though she tried her best; the occasion was far too great.

How many times that summer Mrs. Powder attempted to wreak vengeance upon Joel, the tattle-tale; into what depths of in-

termittent remorse the mischief-making boy
was resolutely plunged, who shall describe?
No more luncheons of generous provision;
no more jovial skirmishing at the kitchen
windows, or liberal payment for easy errands. Whenever Mrs. Powder saw Lyddy
Bangs, or any other intimate and sympathetic friend, she bewailed her careless con-
fidences under the hemlock-tree and detailed
her anxious attentions to the hornet-stung
eavesdropper.

"I went right home," she would say, sorrowfully; "I filled him plumb-full with as
good a supper as I could gather up, and I
took all the fire out o' them hornit-stings
with the best o' remedies. 'Joel, dear,'
says I, 'you won't lose by it if you keep
your mouth shut about them words I spoke
to Lyddy Bangs,' and he was that pious I
might ha' known he meant mischief. They
ain't boys nor men, they're divils, when
they come to that size, and so you mark my
words! But his mother never could keep
nothing to herself, and I knew it from past
sorrers; and I never slept a wink that night
— sure 's you live — till the roosters crowed
for day."

" Perhaps 't won't do nothin' but good!"

Lyddy Bangs would say, consolingly. " Perhaps the young folks 'll git each other a sight the sooner. They 'd had to kep' it to theirselves till they was gray-headed, 'less somebody let the cat out o' the bag."

"Don't you rec'lect how my cat acted that day!" exclaimed Mrs. Powder, excitedly. " How she was good as took with a fit! She knowed well enough what was brewin'; I only wish we 'd had half of her sense."

IV.

The day before Christmas all the long valley was white with deep, new-fallen snow. The road which led up from the neighboring village and the railroad station stretched along the western slope — a mere trail, untrodden and unbroken. The storm had just ceased; the high mountain-peaks were clear and keen and rose-tinted with the waning light; the hills were no longer green with their covering of pines and maples and beeches, but gray with bare branches, and a cold, dense color, almost black, where the evergreens grew thickest. On the other side of the valley the farmsteads were

mapped out as if in etching or pen-drawing;
the far-away orchards were drawn with a curious exactness and regularity, the crooked
boughs of the apple-trees and the longer
lines of the walnuts and ashes and elms came
out against the snow with clear beauty.
The fences and walls were buried in snow;
the farm-houses and barns were petty shapes
in their right-angled unlikeness to natural
growths. You were half amused, half
shocked, as the thought came to you of indifferent creatures called men and women,
who busied themselves within those narrow
walls, under so vast a sky, and fancied the
whole importance of the universe was belit-
tled by that of their few pent acres. What
a limitless world lay outside those play-
thing-farms, yet what beginnings of immor-
tal things the small gray houses had known!

The day before Christmas! — a festival
which seemed in that neighborhood to be of
modern origin. The observance of it was
hardly popular yet among the elder people,
but Christmas had been appropriated, nevertheless, as if everybody had felt the lack of
it. New Year's Day never was sufficient
for New England, even in its least mirthful

decades. For those persons who took true joy in life, something deeper was needed than the spread-eagle self-congratulations of the Fourth of July, or the family reunions of Thanksgiving Day. There were no bells ringing which the country-folks in Law Lane might listen for on Christmas Eve; but something more than the joy that is felt in the poorest dwelling when a little child, with all its possibilities, is born; something happier still came through that snowy valley with the thought of a Christmas-Child who "was the bringer-in and founder of the reign of the higher life." This was the greater Thanksgiving Day, when the whole of Christendom is called to praise and pray and hear the good-tidings, and every heart catches something of the joyful inspirations of good-will to men.

Ezra Barnet sat on a fallen tree from which he had brushed the powdery snow. It was hard work wading through the drifts, and he had made good headway up the long hill before he stopped to rest. Across the valley in the fading daylight he saw the two farms, and could even trace the course of Law Lane itself, marked by the well-known trees.

How small his own great nut-tree looked at
this distance! The two houses, with their
larger and smaller out-buildings and snow-
topped woodpiles, looked as if they had crept
near together for protection and companionship. There were no other houses within a
wide space. Ezra knew how remote the
homes really were from each' other, judged
by any existing sympathy and interest. He
thought of his bare, unnourished boyhood
with something like resentment; then he
remembered how small had been his par-
ents' experience, what poor ambition had
been fostered in them by their lives; even
his mother's impatience with the efforts he
had made to bring a little more comfort
and pleasantness to the old farm-house was
thought of with pity for her innate lack of
pleasure in pleasant things. Ezra himself
was made up of inadequacies, being born
and bred of the Barnets. He was at work
on the railroad now, with small pay; but he
had always known that there could be something better than the life in their farm-
house, while his mother did not. A different
feeling came over him as he thought whom
the other farm - house sheltered; he had
looked for that first, to see if it were stand-

ing safe. Ruth's last letter had come only the day before. This Christmas holiday was to be a surprise to her. He wondered whether Ruth's father would let him in.

Never mind! he could sleep in the barn among the hay; and Ezra dropped into the snow again from the old tree-trunk and went his way. There was a small house just past a bend in the road, and he quickened his steps toward it. Alas! there was no smoke in Mrs. Powder's chimney. She was away on one of her visiting tours; nursing some sick person, perhaps. She would have housed him for the night most gladly; now he must take his chances in Law Lane.

The darkness was already beginning to fall; there was a curious brownness in the air, like summer twilight; the cold air became sharper, and the young man shivered a little as he walked. He could not follow the left-hand road, where it led among hospitable neighbors, but turned bravely off toward his old home — a long, lonely walk at any time of the year, among woods and thickets all well known to him, and as familiar as they were to the wild creatures that haunted them. Yet Ezra Barnet did not find it easy to whistle as he went along.

Suddenly, from behind a scrub-oak that was heavily laden with dead leaves and snow, leaped a small figure, and Ezra was for the moment much startled. The boy carried a rabbit-trap with unusual care, and placed it on the snow-drift before which he stood waist-deep already. "Gorry, Ezry! you most scared me to pieces!" said Joel, in a perfectly calm tone. "Wish you Merry Christmas! Folks 'll be lookin' for you; they did n't s'pose you 'd git home before to-morrow, though."

"Looking for me?" repeated the young man, with surprise. "I did n't send no word" —

"Ain't you heard nothin' 'bout your ma'am's being took up for dead?"

"No, I ain't; and you ain't foolin' me with your stories, Joel Smith? You need n't play off any of your mischief onto me."

"What you gittin' mad with me about?" inquired Joel, with a plaintive tone in his voice. "She got a fall out in the barn this mornin', an' it liked to killed her. Most folks ain't heard nothin' 'bout it 'cause its been snowin' so. They come for Mis' Powder and she called out to our folks, as they brought her round by the way of Asa Pack-

er's store to git some opodildack or somethin'."

Ezra asked no more questions, but strode
past the boy, who looked after him a moment, and then lifted the heavy box-trap and
started homeward. The imprisoned rabbit
had been snowed up since the day before at
least, and Joel felt humane anxieties, else he
would have followed Ezra at a proper distance and learned something of his recep-
tion.

Mrs. Powder was reigning triumphant in
the Barnet house, being nurse, housekeeper,
and spiritual adviser all in one. She had
been longing for an excuse to spend at least
half a day under that cheerless roof for
many months, but occasion had not offered.
She found the responsibility of the parted
lovers weighing more and more heavily on
her mind, and had set her strong will at
work to find some way of reuniting them,
and even to restore a long-banished peace to
the farms. She would not like to confess
that a mild satisfaction caused her heart to
feel warm and buoyant when an urgent summons had come at last; but such was the
simple truth. A man who had been felling

trees on the farm brought the news, melancholy to hear under other circumstances, that Mrs. Barnet had been hunting eggs in a stray nest in the hay-mow, and had slipped to the floor and been taken up insensible. Bones were undoubtedly broken; she was a heavy woman, and had hardly recovered her senses. The doctor must be found as soon as possible. Mrs. Powder hastily put her house to rights, and, with a good round bundle of what she called her needments, set forth on the welcome enterprise. On the way she could hardly keep herself from undue cheerfulness, and if ever there was likely to be a reassuring presence in a sick-room it was Harriet Powder's that December day.

She entered the gloomy kitchen looking like a two-footed snow-drift, her big round shoulders were so heaped with the damp white flakes. Old Ezra Barnet sat by the stove in utter despair, and waved a limp hand warningly toward the bedroom door.

"She's layin' in a sog," he said, hopelessly. "I ought to thought to send word to pore Ezry — all the boy she ever had."

Mrs. Powder calmly removed her snowy outer garments, and tried to warm her hands over the fire.

"Put in a couple o' sticks of good dry wood," she suggested, in a soothing voice; and the farmer felt his spirits brighten, he knew not why. Then the whole-souled, hearty woman walked into the bedroom.

"All I could see," she related afterward, "was the end of Jane Barnet's nose, and I was just as sure then as I be now that she was likely to continner; but I set down side of the bed and got holt of her hand, and she groaned two or three times real desperate. I wished the doctor was there, to see if anything really ailed her; but I someways knowed there wa'n't, 'less 't was gittin' over such a jounce. I spoke to her, but she never said nothin', and I went back out into the kitchen. 'She 's a very sick woman,' says I, loud enough for her to hear me; I knew 't would please her. There was a good deal to do, and I put on my aprin and took right holt and begun to lay about me and git dinner; the men-folks was wiltin' for want o' somethin', it being nigh three o'clock. An' then I got Jane to feel more comfortable with ondressin' of her, for all she 'd hardly let me touch of her — poor creatur', I expect she did feel sore! — and then daylight was failin' and I felt kind o' spent, so

I set me down in a cheer by the bed-head
and was speechless, too. I knew if she was
able to speak she could n't hold in no great
spell longer.

"After a while she stirred a little and
groaned, and then says she, 'Ain't the doctor comin'?' And I peaced her up well 's
I could. 'Be I very bad off, Harri't?'
says she.

"'We 'll hope for the best, Jane,' says I;
and that minute the notion come to me how
I 'd work her round, an' I like to laughed
right out, but I did n't.

"'If I should lose me again, you must see
to sendin' for my son,' says she; 'his father 's
got no head.'

"'I will,' says I, real solemn. 'An' you
can trust me with anything you feel to say,
sister Barnet.'

"She kind of opened her eye that was
next to me and surveyed my countenance
sharp, but I looked serious, and she groaned
real honest. 'Be I like old Mis' Topliff?'
she whispered, and I kind o' nodded an' put
my hand up to my eyes. She *was* like her,
too; some like her, but not nigh so bad, for
Mis' Topliff was hurt so fallin' down the
sullar-stairs that she never got over it an'
died the day after.

"' Oh, my sakes!' she bu'st out whinin', 'I can't be took away now. I ain't a-goin' to die right off, be I, Mis' Powder?'

"' I ain't the one to give ye hope. In the midst of life we are in death. We ain't sure of the next minute, none of us,' says I, meanin' it general, but discoursin' away like an old book o' sermons.

"' I do feel kind o' failin', now,' says she. 'Oh, can't you do nothin'?' — and I come over an' set on the foot o' the bed an' looked right at her. I knew she was a dreadful notional woman, and always made a fuss when anything was the matter with her; could n't bear no kind o' pain.

"' Sister Barnet,' says I, 'don't you bear nothin' on your mind you 'd like to see righted before you go? I know you ain't been at peace with Crosby's folks, and 't ain't none o' my business, but I should n't want to be called away with hard feelin's in *my* heart. You must overlook my speaking right out, but I should want to be so used myself.'

"Poor old creatur'! She had an awful fight of it, but she beat her temper for once an' give in. 'I do forgive all them Crosbys,' says she, an' rolled up her eyes. I says to myself that wa'n't all I wanted, but I let her alone a spell, and set there watchin' as if I expected her to breathe her last any minute.

"She asked for Barnet, and I said he was anxious and out watchin' for the doctor, now the snow'd stopped. 'I wish I could see Ezra,' says she. 'I'm all done with the lane now, and I'd keep the peace if I was goin' to live.' Her voice got weak, and I did n't know but she was worse off than I s'posed. I was scared for a minute, and then I took a grain o' hope. I'd watched by too many dyin'-beds not to know the difference.

"'Don't ye let Barnet git old Nevins to make my coffin, will ye, Mis' Powder?' says she once.

"'He's called a good workman, ain't he?' says I, soothin' as I could. When it come to her givin' funeral orders, 't was more 'n I could do to hold in.

"'I ain't goin' snappin' through torment in a hemlock coffin, to please that old cheat!' says she, same 's if she was well, an' ris' right up in bed; and then her bruises pained her an' she dropped back on the pillow.

" ' Oh, I 'm a-goin' now! ' says she. ' I 've been an awful hard woman. 'T was I put Barnet up to the worst on 't. I 'm willin' Ezra should marry Ruthy Crosby; she 's a nice, pooty gal, and I never owned it till now I 'm on my dyin'-bed — Oh, I 'm a-goin', I 'm a-goin'! — Ezra can marry her, and the two farms together 'll make the best farm in town. Barnet ain't got no fight left; he 's like an old sheep since we drove off Ezra.' And then she 'd screech; you never saw no such a fit of narves. And the end was I had to send to Crosby's, in all the snow, for them to come over.

" An' Barnet was got in to hold her hand and hear last words enough to make a Fourth o' July speech; and I was sent out to the door to hurry up the Crosbys, and who should come right out o' the dark but Ezra. I declare, when I see him you could a-knocked me down with a feather. But I got him by the sleeve — ' You hide away a spell,' says I, ' till I set the little lamp in this winder; an' don't you make the best o' your ma's condition; 'pear just as consarned about her as you can. I 'll let ye know why, soon 's we can talk ' — and I shoved him right out an' shut the door.

"The groans was goin' on, and in come Crosby and Ruth, lookin' scared about to death themselves. Neither on 'em had ever been in that house before, as I know of. She called 'em into the bedroom and said she'd had hard feelin's towards them and wanted to make peace before she died, and both on 'em shook hands with her.

"'Don't you want to tell Ruth what you said to me about her and Ezry?' says I, whisperin' over the bed. ' 'Live or dead, you know 't is right and best.'

"'There ain't no half way 'bout me,' she says, and so there wa'n't. 'Ruth,' says she, out loud, 'I want you to tell pore Ezra that I gave ye both my blessin',' and I made two steps acrost that kitchen and set the lamp in the window, and in comes Ezra — pore boy, he did n't know what was brewin', and thought his mother was dyin' certain when he saw the Crosbys goin' in.

"He went an' stood beside the bed, an' his father clutched right holt of him. Thinks I to myself, if you make as edifyin' an end when your time really does come, you may well be thankful, Jane Barnet!

"They was all a-weepin', an' I was weepin' myself, if you 'll believe it, I 'd got

a-goin' so.   You ought to seen her take holt
o' Ruth's hand an' Ezra's an' put 'em together.   *Then* I 'd got all I wanted, I tell
you.   An' after she 'd screeched two or
three times more she begun to git tired ; the
poor old creatur' was shook up dreadful,
and I felt for her consid'able, though you
may not think it ; so I beckoned 'em out
into the kitchen an' went in an' set with her
alone.   She dropped off into a good easy
sleep, an' I told the folks her symptoms was
more encouragin'.

"I tell you, if ever I took handsome care
o' any sick person 't was Jane Barnet, before
she got about again ; an' Ruth she used to
come over an' help real willin'.   She got
holt of her ma'-in-law's bunnit one afternoon an' trimmed it up real tasty, and that
pleased Mis' Barnet about to death.   My
conscience pricked me some, but not a great
sight.   I 'm willin' to take what blame come
to me by rights.

"The doctor come postin' along, late that
night, and said she was doin' well, owin' to
the care she 'd had, and give me a wink.
And she 's alive yet," Mrs. Powder always
assured her friends, triumphantly — " and,
what 's more, is middlin' peaceable disposed.

She's said one or two p'inted things to me,
though, an' I should n't wonder, come to
think it over, if she mistrusted me just the
least grain. But, dear sakes! they never
was so comfortable in their lives; an' Ezra
he got a first-rate bargain for a lot o' Crosby's woodland that the railroad wanted, and
peace is kind o' set in amon'st 'em up in
Law Lane."

V.

When Ezra Barnet waked on Christmas
morning, in his familiar, dark little chamber under the lean-to roof, he could hardly
believe that he was at home again, and that
such strange things had happened. There
were cheerful voices in the kitchen below,
and he dressed hurriedly and went down-
stairs.

There was Mrs. Powder, cooking the
breakfast with lavish generosity, and beaming with good-nature. Barnet, the father,
was smiling and looking on with pleased an-
ticipation; the sick woman was comfortably
bolstered up in the bedroom. In all his life
the son had never felt so drawn to his
mother; there was a new look in her eyes as

he went toward her; she had lost her high
color, and looked at him pleadingly, as she
never had done before. "Ezry, come close
here!" said she. "I believe I'm goin' to
git about ag'in, after all. Mis' Powder says
I be; but them feelin's I had slippin' down
the mow, yesterday, was twice as bad as the
thump I struck with. I may never be the
same to work, but I ain't goin' to fight with
folks no more, sence the Lord 'll let me live
a spell longer. I ain't a-goin' to fight with
nobody, no matter how bad I want to. Now,
you go an' git you a good breakfast. I
ain't eat a mouthful since breakfast yesterday, and you can bring me a help o' anything Sister Powder favors my havin'."

"I hope 't will last," muttered Sister
Powder to herself, as she heaped the blue
plate. "Wish you all a Merry Christmas!"
she said. "I like to forgot my manners."

It was Christmas Day, whether anybody
in Law Lane remembered it or not. The
sun shone bright on the sparkling snow, the
eaves were dropping, and the snow-birds and
blue-jays came about the door. The wars of
Law Lane were ended.

MISS PECK'S PROMOTION.

MISS PECK had spent a lonely day in her old farm-house, high on a long Vermont hillside that sloped toward the west. She was able for an hour at noon to overlook the fog in the valley below, and pitied the people in the village whose location she could distinguish only by means of the church steeple which pricked through the gray mist, like a buoy set over a dangerous reef. During this brief time, when the sun was apparently shining for her benefit alone, she reflected proudly upon the advantage of living on high land, but in the early afternoon, when the fog began to rise slowly, and at last shut her in, as well as the rest of the world, she was conscious of uncommon depression of spirits.

"I might as well face it now as any time," she said aloud, as she lighted her clean kerosene lamp and put it on the table. "Eliza Peck! just set down and make it blazing clear how things stand with you, and what you 're going to do in regard to 'em! 'T ain't no use matching your feelin's to the weather, without you 've got reason for it." And she twitched the short curtains across the windows so that their brass rings squeaked on the wires, opened the door for the impatient cat that was mewing outside, and then seated herself in the old rocking-chair at the table end.

It is quite a mistake to believe that people who live by themselves find every day a lonely one. Miss Peck and many other solitary persons could assure us that it is very seldom that they feel their lack of companionship. As the habit of living alone grows more fixed, it becomes confusing to have other people about, and seems more or less bewildering to be interfered with by other people's plans and suggestions. Only once in a while does the feeling of solitariness become burdensome, or a creeping dread and sense of defenselessness assail one's comfort. But when Miss Peck was aware of the approach of such a mood she feared it, and was prepared to fight it with her best weapon of common-sense.

She was much given to talking aloud, as

many solitary persons are ; not merely talking to herself in the usual half-conscious way, but making her weaker self listen to severe comment and pointed instruction. . Miss Peck the less was frequently brought to trial in this way by Miss Peck the greater, and when it was once announced that justice must be done, no amount of quailing or excuse averted the process of definite conviction.

This evening she turned the light up to its full brightness, reached for her knitting-work, lifted it high above her lap for a moment, as her favorite cat jumped up to its evening quarters ; then she began to rock to and fro with regularity and decision. "'T is all nonsense," she said, as if she were addressing some one greatly her inferior— "'t is all nonsense for you to go on this way, Elizy Peck! you 're better off than you 've been this six year, if you only had sense to feel so."

There was no audible reply, and the speaker evidently mistook the silence for unconvinced stubbornness.

" If ever there was a woman who was determined to live by other folks' wits, and to eat other folks' dinners, 't was and is your lamented brother's widder, Harri't Peck — Harri't White that was. She's claimed the town's compassion till it's good as run dry, and she's thought that you, Elizy Peck, a hard-workin' and self-supportin' woman, was made for nothin' but her use and comfort. Ever since your father died and you've been left alone you've had her for a clog to your upward way. Six years you've been at her beck an' call, and now that a respectable man, able an' willing to do for her, has been an' fell in love with her, and shouldered her and all her whims, and promised to do for the children as if they was his own, you've been grumpin' all day, an' *I'd* like to know what there is to grump about!"

There was a lack of response even to this appeal to reason, and the knitting-needles clicked in dangerous nearness to the old cat's ears, so that they twitched now and then, and one soft paw unexpectedly revealed its white curving claws.

"Yes," said Miss Peck, presently, in a more lenient tone, "I s'pose 't is the children you're thinking of most. I declare I should like to see that Tom's little red head, and feel it warm with my two hands this minute! There's always somethin' hopeful

in havin' to do with children, 'less they come
of *too* bad a stock. Grown folks — well,
you can make out to grin an' bear 'em if
you must; but like 's not young ones 'll turn
out to be somebody, and what you do for
'em may count towards it. There 's that
Tom, he looks just as his father used to, and
there ain't a day he won't say somethin' real
pleasant, and never sees the difference betwixt you an' somebody handsome. I expect they 'll spile him — you don't know
what kind o' young ones they 'll let him play
with, nor how they 'll let him murder the
king's English, and never think o' boxin'
his ears. Them big factory towns is all for
eatin' and clothes. I 'm glad you was raised
in a good old academy town, if 't was the
Lord's will to plant you in the far outskirts.
Land, how Harri't did smirk at that man!
I will say she looked pretty — 't is hard
work and worry makes folks plain like me —
I believe she 's fared better to be left a widder with three child'n, and everybody saying
how hard it was, an' takin' holt, than she
would if brother had lived and she 'd had to
stir herself to keep house and do for him.
You 've been the real widder that Tom left
— you 've mourned him, and had your way

to go alone — not she!   The colonel's lady,"
repeated Miss Peck, scornfully — " that 's
what sp'ilt her.   She never could come down
to common things, Mis' Colonel Peck!
Well, she may have noble means now, but
she 's got to be spoke of as Mis' Noah Pigley all the rest of her days.   Not that I 'm
goin' to fling at any man's accident of
name," said the just Eliza, in an apologetic
tone.   " I did want to adopt little Tom,
but 't was to be expected he 'd object — a
boy 's goin' to be useful in his business, and
poor Tommy 's the likeliest.   I would have
'dopted him out an' out, and he shall have
the old farm anyway.   But oh dear me, he 's
all spoilt for farming now, is little Tom, unless I can make sure of him now and then
for a good long visit in summer time.

"Summer an' winter; I s'pose you 're
likely to live a great many years, Elizy,"
sighed the good woman.   " All sole alone,
too!   There, I 've landed right at the start-
in' point," — and the kitchen was very still
while some dropped stitches in a belated
stocking for the favorite nephew were ob-
scured by a mist of tears like the fog outside.   There was no more talking aloud, for
Miss Peck fell into a revery about old days

and the only brother who had left his little household in her care and marched to the war whence for him there was to be no return. She had remembered very often, with a great sense of comfort, a message in one of his very last letters. "Tell Eliza that she's more likely to be promoted than I am," he said (when he had just got his step of Major); "she's my superior officer, however high I get, and now I've heard what luck she's had with the haying, I appoint her Brigadier-General for gallantry in the field." How poor Tom's jokes had kept their courage up even when they were most anxious! Yes, she had made many sacrifices of personal gain, as every good soldier must. She had meant to be a school-teacher. She had the gift for it, and had studied hard in her girlhood. One thing after another had kept her at home, and now she must stay here — her ambitions were at an end. She would do what good she could among her neighbors, and stand in her lot and place. It was the first time she had found to think soberly about her life, for her sister-in-law and the children had gone to their new home within a few days, and since then she had stifled all power of proper reflection by hard

work at setting the house in order and getting in her winter supplies. " Thank Heaven
the house and place belong to me," she said
in a decisive tone. " 'T was wise o' father
to leave it so — and let her have the money.
She 'd left me no peace till I moved off if
I 'd only been half - owner; she 's always
meant to get to a larger place — but what
I want is real promotion."

The Peck farm-house was not only on a
by-road that wandered among the slopes of
the hills, but it was at the end of a long lane
of its own. There was rarely any sound at
night except from the winds of heaven or the
soughing of the neighboring pine-trees. By
day, there was a beautiful inspiriting outlook
over the wide country from the farm-house
windows, but on such a night as this the
darkness made an impenetrable wall. Miss
Peck was not afraid of it; on the contrary,
she had a sense of security in being shut
safe into the very heart of the night. By
day she might be vexed by intruders, by
night they could scarcely find her — her
bright light could not be seen from the road.
If she were to wither away in the old gray
house like an unplanted kernel in its shell,
she would at least wither undisturbed. Her

sorrow of loneliness was not the fear of mo-
lestation. She was fearless enough at the
thought of physical dangers.

The evening did not seem so long as she
expected — a glance at her reliable time-
keeper told her at last that it was already
past eight o'clock, and her eyes began to
feel heavy. The fire was low, the fog was
making its presence felt even in the house,
for the autumn night was chilly, and Miss
Peck decided that when she came to the end
of the stitches on a certain needle she would
go to bed. To-morrow, she meant to cut her
apples for drying, a duty too long delayed.
She had sent away some of her best fruit
that day to make the annual barrel of cider
with which she provided herself, more from
habit than from real need of either the
wholesome beverage or its resultant vinegar.
" If this fog lasts, I 've got to dry my apples by the stove," she thought, doubtfully,
and was conscious of a desire to survey the
weather from the outer doorway before she
slept. How she missed Harriet and the children ! — though they had been living with her
only for a short time before the wedding, and
since the half-house they had occupied in the
village had been let. The thought of bright-

eyed, red-headed little Tom still brought the warm tears very near to falling. He had cried bitterly when he went away. So had his mother — at least, she held up her pocket-handkerchief. Miss Peck never had believed in Harriet's tears.

Out of the silence of the great hillslope came the dull sound of a voice, and as Miss Peck sprang from her chair to the window, dropping the sleeping cat in a solid mass on the floor, she recognized the noise of a carriage. Her heart was beating provokingly; she was tired by the excitement of the last few days. She did not remember this, but was conscious of being startled in an unusual way. It must be some strange crisis in her life; she turned and looked about the familiar kitchen as if it were going to be altogether swept away. "Now, you need n't be afraid that Pigley's comin' to bring her back, Elizy Peck!" she assured herself with grim humor in that minute's apprehension of disaster.

A man outside spoke sternly to his horse. Eliza stepped quickly to the door and opened it wide. She was not afraid of the messenger, only of the message.

"Hold the light so 's I can see to tie this

colt," said a familiar voice; "it's as dark as a pocket, 'Liza. I'll be right in. You must put on a good warm shawl; 't is as bad as rain, this fog is. The minister wants you to come down to his house; he's at his wits' end, and there was nobody we could think of that's free an' able except you. His wife's gone, died at quarter to six, and left a mis'able baby; but the doctor expects 't will live. The nurse they bargained with 's failed 'em, and 't is an awful state o' things as you ever see. Half the women in town are there, and the minister's overcome; he's sort of fainted away two or three times, and they don't know who else to get, till the doctor said your name, and he groaned right out you was the one. 'T ain't right to refuse, as I view it. Mis' Spence and Mis' Corbell is going to watch with the dead, but there needs a head."

Eliza Peck felt for once as if she lacked that useful possession herself, and sat down, with amazing appearance of calmness, in one of her splint-bottomed chairs to collect her thoughts. The messenger was a good deal excited; so was she; but in a few moments she rose, cutting short his inconsequent description of affairs at the parsonage.

"You just put out the fire as best you can," she said. "We 'll talk as we go along. There 's plenty o' ashes there, I 'm sure; I let the stove cool off considerable, for I was meanin' to go to bed in another five minutes. The cat 'll do well enough. I 'll leave her plenty for to-morrow, and she 's got a place where she can crep in an' out of the wood-shed. I 'll just slip on another dress and put the nails over the windows, an' we 'll be right off." She was quite herself again now; and, true to her promise, it was not many minutes before the door was locked, the house left in darkness, and Ezra Weston and Miss Peck were driving comfortably down the lane. The fog had all blown away, suddenly the stars were out, and the air was sweet with the smell of the wet bark of black birches and cherry and apple-trees that grew by the fences. The leaves had fallen fast through the day, weighted by the dampness until their feeble stems could keep them in place no longer; for the bright colors of the foliage there had come at night sweet odors and a richness of fragrance in the soft air.

"'T is an unwholesome streak o' weather, ain't it?" asked Ezra Weston. "Feels like a dog-day evenin' now, don't it ? Come this time o' year we want bracin' up."

Miss Peck did not respond ; her sympathetic heart was dwelling on the thought that she was going, not only to a house of mourning, but to a bereft parsonage. She would not have felt so unequal to soothing the sorrows of her every-day acquaintances, but she could hardly face the duty of consoling the new minister. But she never once wished that she had not consented so easily to respond to his piteous summons.

There was a strangely festive look in the village, for the exciting news of Mrs. Elbury's death had flown from house to house —lights were bright everywhere, and in the parsonage brightest of all. It looked as if the hostess were receiving her friends, and helping them to make merry, instead of being white and still, and done with this world, while the busy women of the parish were pulling open her closets and bureau drawers in search of household possessions. Nobody stopped to sentimentalize over the poor soul's delicate orderliness, or the simple, loving preparations she had made for the coming of the baby which fretfully wailed in the next room.

" Here 's a nice black silk that never was touched with the scissors!" said one good dame, as if a kind Providence ought to have arranged for the use of such a treasure in setting the bounds of the dead woman's life.

"Does seem too bad, don't it? I always heard her folks was well off," replied somebody in a loud whisper; "she had everything to live for." There was great eagerness to be of service to the stricken pastor, and the kind neighbors did their best to prove the extent of their sympathy. One after another went to the room where he was, armed with various excuses, and the story of his sad looks and distress was repeated again and again to a grieved audience.

When Miss Peck came in she had to listen to a full description of the day's events, and was decorously slow in assuming her authority; but at last the house was nearly empty again, and only the watchers and one patient little mother of many children, who held this motherless child in loving arms, were left with Miss Peck in the parsonage. It seemed a year since she had sat in her quiet kitchen, a solitary woman whose occupations seemed too few and too trivial for her eager capacities and ambitions.

The autumn days went by, winter set in early, and Miss Peck was still mistress of the parsonage housekeeping. Her own cider was brought to the parsonage, and so were the potatoes and the apples; even the cat was transferred to a dull village existence, far removed in every way from her happy hunting-grounds among the snow-birds and plump squirrels. The minister's pale little baby loved Miss Peck and submitted to her rule already. She clung fast to the good woman with her little arms, and Miss Peck, who had always imagined that she did not care for infants, found herself watching the growth of this spark of human intelligence and affection with intense interest. After all, it was good to be spared the long winter at the farm; it had never occurred to her to dread it, but she saw now that it was a season to be dreaded, and one by one forgot the duties which at first beckoned her homeward and seemed so unavoidable. The farm-house seemed cold and empty when she paid it an occasional visit. She would not have believed that she could content herself so well away from the dear old home. If she could have had her favorite little Tom within reach, life would have been perfectly happy.

The minister proved at first very disappointing to her imaginary estimate and knowledge of him. If it had not been for her sturdy loyalty to him as pastor and employer, she could sometimes have joined more or less heartily in the expressions of the disaffected faction which forms a difficult element in every parish. Her sense of humor was deeply gratified when the leader of the opposition remarked that the minister was beginning to take notice a little, and was wearing his best hat every day, like every other widower since the world was made. Miss Peck's shrewd mind had already made sure that Mr. Elbury's loss was not so great as she had at first sympathetically believed; she knew that his romantic, ease-loving, self-absorbed, and self-admiring nature had been curbed and held in check by the literal, prosaic, faithful-in-little-things disposition of his dead wife. She was self-denying, he was self-indulgent; she was dutiful, while he was given to indolence — and the unfounded plea of ill-health made his only excuse. Miss Peck soon fell into the way of putting her shoulder to the wheel, and unobtrusively, even secretly, led the affairs of the parish. She never was deaf to the explanation of the wearing effect of brain-work, but accepted the weakness as well as the power of the ministerial character; and nobody listened more respectfully to his somewhat flowery and inconsequent discourses on Sunday than Miss Peck. The first Sunday they went to church together Eliza slipped into her own pew, half-way up the side aisle, and thought well of herself for her prompt decision afterward, though she regretted the act for a moment as she saw the minister stop to let her into the empty pew of the parsonage. He had been sure she was just behind him, and gained much sympathy from the congregation as he sighed and went his lonely way up the pulpit-stairs. Even Mrs. Corbell, who had been averse to settling the Rev. Mr. Elbury, was moved by this incident, but directly afterward whispered to her next-neighbor that "Lizy Peck would be sitting there before the year was out if she had the business-head they had all given her credit for."

It gives rise to melancholy reflections

when one sees how quickly those who have suffered most cruel and disturbing bereavements learn to go their way alone. The great plan of our lives is never really broken nor suffers accidents. However stunning the shock, one can almost always understand gratefully that it was best for the vanished friend to vanish just when he did; that this world held no more duties or satisfactions for him; that his earthly life was in fact done and ended. Our relations with him must be lifted to a new plane. Miss Peck thought often of the minister's loss, and always with tender sympathy, yet she could not help seeing that he was far from being unresigned or miserable in his grief. She was ready to overlook the fact that he depended upon his calling rather than upon his own character and efforts. The only way in which she made herself uncongenial to the minister was by persistent suggestions that he should take more exercise and " stir about out-doors a little." Once, when she had gone so far as to briskly inform him that he was getting logy, Mr. Elbury showed entire displeasure ; and a little later, in the privacy of the kitchen, she voiced the opinion that Elizy Peck knew very well that she never did think ministers

were angels — only human beings, like herself, in great danger of being made fools of.
But the two good friends made up their
little quarrel at supper-time.

"I have been looking up the derivation
of that severe word you applied to me this
noon," said the Reverend Mr. Elbury, pleasantly. "It is a localism; but it comes from
the Dutch word *log*, which means heavy or
unwieldy."

These words were pronounced plaintively,
with evident consciousness that they hardly
applied to his somewhat lank figure; and
Miss Peck felt confused and rebuked, and
went on pouring tea until both cup and sau-
cer were full, and she scalded the end of her
thumb. She was very weak in the hands
of such a scholar as this, but later she had
a reassuring sense of not having applied
the epithet unjustly. With a feminine reverence for his profession, and for his attain-
ments, she had a keen sense of his human
fallibility; and neither his grief, nor his
ecclesiastical halo, nor his considerate idea
of his own value, could blind her sharp eyes
to certain shortcomings. She forgave them
readily, but she knew them all by sight and
name.

If there were any gift of Mr. Elbury's which could be sincerely called perfectly delightful by many people, it was his voice. When he was in a hurry, and gave hasty directions to his housekeeper about some mislaid possession, or called· her down-stairs to stop the baby's vexatious crying, the tones were entirely different from those best known to the parish. Nature had gifted him with a power of carrying his voice into the depths of his sympathetic being and recovering it again gallantly. He had been considered the superior, in some respects, of that teacher of elocution who led the students of the theological seminary toward the glorious paths of oratory. There was a mellow middle-tone, most suggestive of tender feeling; but though it sounded sweet to other feminine ears, Miss Peck was always annoyed by it and impatient of a certain artificial quality in its cadences. To hear Mr. Elbury talk to his child in this tone, and address her as " my motherless babe," however affecting to other ears, was always unpleasant to Miss Peck. But she thought very well of his preaching; and the more he let all the decisions and responsibilities of every-day life fall to her share, the more she enjoyed life and told her friends that Mr. Elbury was a most amiable man to live with. And when spring was come the hillside farm was let on shares to one of Miss Peck's neighbors whom she could entirely trust. It was not the best of bargains for its owner, who had the reputation of being an excellent farmer, and the agreement cost her many sighs and not a little wakefulness. She felt too much shut in by this village life; but the minister pleaded his hapless lot, the little child was even more appealing in her babyhood, and so the long visit from little Tom and his sisters, the familiar garden, the three beehives, and the glory of the sunsets in the great, unbroken, western sky were all given up together for that year.

It was not so hard as it might have been. There was one most rewarding condition of life — the feast of books, which was new and bewilderingly delightful to the minister's housekeeper. She had made the most of the few well-chosen volumes of the farmhouse, but she never had known the joy of. having more books than she could read, or their exquisite power of temptation, the delight of their friendly company. She was oftenest the student, the brain-wearied member, of the parsonage-family, but she never made it an excuse, or really recognized the new stimulus either. Life had never seemed so full to her; she was working with both hands earnestly, and no half-heartedness. She was filled with reverence in the presence of the minister's books; to her his calling, his character, and his influence were all made positive and respectable by this foundation of learning on his library-shelves. He was to her a man of letters, a critic, and a philosopher, besides being an experienced theologian from' the very nature of his profession. Indeed, he had an honest liking for books, and was fond of reading aloud or being read to; and many an evening went joyfully by in the presence of the great English writers, whose best thoughts were rolled out in Mr. Elbury's best tones, and Miss Peck listened with delight, and cast many an affectionate glance at the sleeping child in the cradle at her feet, filled with gratitude as she was for all her privileges.

Mr. Elbury was most generous in his appreciation of Miss Peck's devotion, and never hesitated to give expression to sincere praise of her uncommon power of mind. He was led into paths of literature, otherwise untrod, by her delight ; and sometimes, to rest his brain and make him ready for a good night's sleep, he asked his companion to read him a clever story. It was all a new world to the good woman whose schooling and reading had been sound, but restricted ; and if ever a mind waked up with joy to its possession of the world of books, it was hers. She became ambitious for the increase of her own little library ; and it was in reply to her outspoken plan for larger crops and more money from the farm another year, for the sake of bookbuying, that Mr. Elbury once said, earnestly, that his books were hers now. This careless expression was the spark which lit a new light for Miss Peck's imagination. For the first time a thrill of personal interest in the man made itself felt, through her devoted capacity for service and appreciation. He had ceased to be simply himself ; he stood now for a widened life, a suggestion of added good and growth, a larger circle of human interests ; in fact, his existence had made all the difference between her limited rural home and that connection with the great world which even the most contracted parsonage is sure to hold.

And that very night, while Mr. Elbury had

gone, somewhat ruefully and ill-prepared, to his Bible class, Miss Peck's conscience set her womanly weakness before it for a famous arraigning. It was so far successful that words failed the defendant completely, and the session was dissolved in tears. For some days Miss Peck was not only stern with herself, but even with the minister, and was entirely devoted to her domestic affairs.

The very next Sunday it happened that Mr. Elbury exchanged pulpits with a brother-clergyman in the next large town, a thriving manufacturing centre, and he came home afterward in the best of spirits. He never had seemed so appreciative of his comfortable home, or Miss Peck's motherly desire to shield his weak nature from these practical cares of life to which he was entirely inadequate. He was unusually gay and amusing, and described, not with the best taste, the efforts of two of his unmarried lady-parishioners to make themselves agreeable. He had met them on the short journey, and did not hesitate to speak of himself lightly as a widower; in fact, he recognized his own popularity and attractions in a way that was not pleasing to Miss Peck, yet she was used to his way of speaking and unaffectedly glad to have him at home again. She had been much disturbed and grieved by her own thoughts in his absence. She could not be sure whether she was wise in drifting toward a nearer relation to the minister. She was not exactly shocked at finding herself interested in him, but, with her usual sense of propriety and justice, she insisted upon taking everybody's view of the question before the weaker Miss Peck was accorded a hearing. She was enraged with herself for feeling abashed and liking to avoid the direct scrutiny of her fellow-parishioners. Mrs. Corbell and she had always been the best of friends, but for the first time Miss Peck was annoyed by such freedom of comment and opinion. And Sister Corbell had never been so forward about spending the afternoon at the parsonage, or running in for half-hours of gossip in the morning, as in these latter days. At last she began to ask the coy Eliza about her plans for the wedding, in a half-joking, half-serious tone which was hard to bear.

"You're a sight too good for him," was the usual conclusion, "and so I tell everybody. The whole parish has got it settled for you; and there's as many as six think hard of you, because you 've given 'em no chance, bein' right here on the spot."

It seemed as if a resistless torrent of fate were sweeping our independent friend toward the brink of a great change. She insisted to the quailing side of her nature that she did not care for the minister himself, that she was likely to age much sooner than he, with his round, boyish face and plump cheeks. "They 'll be takin' you for his mother, Lizy, when you go amongst strangers, little and dried up as you 're gettin' to be a'ready; you 're three years older anyway, and look as if 't was nine." Yet the capable, clear-headed woman was greatly enticed by the high position and requirements of mistress of the parsonage. She liked the new excitement and authority, and grew more and more happy in the exercise of powers which a solitary life at the farm would hardly arouse or engage. There was a vigorous growth of independence and determination in Miss Peck's character, and she had not lived alone so many years for nothing. But there was no outward sign yet of capitulation. She was firmly convinced that the minister could not get on without her, and that she would rather not get on without him and the pleasure of her new activities. If possible, she grew a little more self-contained and reserved in manner and speech, while carefully anticipating his wants and putting better and better dinners on the parochial table.

As for Mr. Elbury himself, he became more cheerful every day, and was almost demonstrative in his affectionate gratitude. He spoke always as if they were one in their desire to interest and benefit the parish; he had fallen into a pleasant, home-like habit of saying " we " whenever household or parish affairs were under discussion. Once, when somebody had been remarking the too-evident efforts of one of her sister-parishioners to gain Mr. Elbury's affection, he had laughed leniently; but when this gossiping caller had gone away the minister said, gently, " We know better, don't we, Miss Peck ? " and Eliza could not help feeling that his tone meant a great deal. Yet she took no special notice of him, and grew much more taciturn than was natural. Her heart beat warmly under her prim alpacca-dress; she already looked younger and a great deal happier than when she first came to live at the parsonage. Her executive ability was made glad by the many duties that fell upon her, and those who knew her and Mr. Elbury best thought nothing could be wiser than their impending marriage. Did not the little child need Miss Peck's motherly care? did not the helpless minister need the assistance of a clear-sighted business-woman and good housekeeper? did not Eliza herself need and deserve a husband? But even with increasing certainty she still gave no outward sign of their secret understanding. It was likely that Mr. Elbury thought best to wait a year after his wife's death, and when he spoke right out was the time to show what her answer would be. But somehow the thought of the dear old threadbare farm in the autumn weather was always a sorrowful thought; and on the days when Mr. Elbury hired a horse and wagon, and invited her and the baby to accompany him on a series of parochial visitations, she could not bear to look at the home-fields and the pasture-slopes. She was thankful that the house itself was not in sight from the main road. The crops that summer had been unusually good; something called her thoughts back continually to the old home, and accused her of dis-

loyalty.   Yet she consoled herself by thinking it was very natural to have such regrets,
and to consider the importance of such a
step at her sensible time of life.   So it drew
near winter again, and she grew more and
more unrelenting and scornful whenever her
acquaintances suggested the idea that her
wedding ought to be drawing near.

Mr. Elbury seemed to have taken a new
lease of youthful hope and ardor.   He was
busy in the parish and very popular, particularly among his women-parishioners.   Miss
Peck urged him on with his good works, and
it seemed as if they expressed their interest
in each other by their friendliness to the
parish in general.   Mr. Elbury had joined
a ministers' club in the large town already
spoken of, and spent a day there now and
then, besides his regular Monday-night at-
tendance on the club-meeting.   He was pre-
paring a series of sermons on the history of
the Jews, and was glad to avail himself of a
good free-library, the lack of which he frequently lamented in his own village.   Once
he said, eagerly, that he had no idea of ending his days here, and this gave Miss Peck
a sharp pang.   She could not bear to think
of leaving her old home, and the tears filled

her eyes. When she had reached the shelter of the kitchen, she retorted to the too-easily ruffled element of her character that there was no need of crossing that bridge till she came to it; and, after an appealing glance at the academy-steeple above the maple-trees, she returned to the study to finish dusting. She saw, without apprehension, that the minister quickly pushed something under the leaves of his blotting-paper and frowned a little. It was not his usual time for writing — she had a new proof of her admiring certainty that Mr. Elbury wrote for the papers at times under an assumed name.

One Monday evening he had not returned from the ministers' meeting until later than usual, and she began to be slightly anxious. The baby had not been very well all day, and she particularly wished to have an errand done before night, but did not dare to leave the child alone, while, for a wonder, nobody had been in. Mr. Elbury had shown a great deal of feeling before he went away in the morning, and as she was admiringly looking at his well-fitting clothes and neat clerical attire, a thrill of pride and affection had made her eyes shine unwontedly. She was really beginning to like him very much.

For the first and last time in his life the minister stepped quickly forward and kissed her on the forehead. "My good, kind friend!" he exclaimed, in that deep tone which the whole parish loved; then he hurried away. Miss Peck felt a strange dismay, and stood by the breakfast-table like a statue. She even touched her forehead with trembling fingers. Somehow she inwardly rebelled, but kissing meant more to her than to some people. She never had been used to it, except with little Tom — though the last brotherly kiss his father gave her before he went to the war had been one of the treasures of her memory. All that day she was often reminded of the responsible and darker side, the inspected and criticised side, of the high position of minister's wife. It was clearly time for proper rebuke when evening came; and as she sat by the light, mending Mr. Elbury's stockings, she said over and over again that she had walked into this with her eyes wide open, and if the experience of forty years had n't put any sense into her it was too late to help it now.

Suddenly she heard the noise of wheels in the side yard. Could anything have happened to Mr. Elbury? were they bringing him home hurt, or dead even? He never drove up from the station unless it were bad weather. She rushed to the door with a flaring light, and was bewildered at the sight of trunks and, most of all, at the approach of Mr. Elbury, for he wore a most sentimental expression, and led a young person by the hand.

"Dear friend," he said, in that mellow tone of his, "I hope you, too, will love my little wife."

Almost any other woman would have dropped the kerosene lamp on the doorstep, but not Miss Eliza Peck. Luckily a gust of autumn wind blew it out, and the bride had to fumble her way into her new home. Miss Peck quickly procured one of her own crinkly lamplighters, and bent toward the open fire to kindle a new light.

"You 've taken me by surprise," she managed to say, in her usual tone of voice, though she felt herself shaking with excitement.

At that moment the ailing step-daughter gave a forlorn little wail from the wide sofa, where she had been put to sleep with difficulty. Miss Peck's kind heart felt the pathos of the situation; she lifted the little child and stilled it, then she held out a kindly hand to the minister's new wife, while Mr. Elbury stood beaming by.

"I wish you may be very happy here, as I have been," said the good woman, earnestly. "But Mr. Elbury, you ought to have let me know. I could have kept a secret" —and satisfaction filled Eliza Peck's heart that she never, to use her own expression, had made a fool of herself before the First Parish. She had kept her own secret, and in this earthquake of a moment was clearly conscious that she was hero enough to behave as if there had never been any secret to keep. And indignation with the Reverend Mr. Elbury, who had so imprudently kept his own counsel, threw down the sham temple of Cupid which a faithless god called Propinquity had succeeded in rearing.

Miss Peck made a feast, and for the last time played the part of hostess at the minister's table. She had remorselessly inspected the conspicuous bad taste of the new Mrs. Elbury's dress, the waving, cheap-looking feather of her hat, the make-believe richness of her clothes, and saw, with dire compassion, how unused she was to young children. The brave Eliza tried to make the best of things — but one moment she found herself thinking how uncomfortable Mr. Elbury's home would be henceforth with this poor reed to lean upon, a townish, empty-faced, tiresomely pretty girl; the next moment she pitied the girl herself, who would have the hard task before her of being the wife of an indolent preacher in a country town. Miss Peck had generously allowed her farm to supplement the limited salary of the First Parish; in fact, she had been a silent partner in the parsonage establishment rather than a dependent. Would the First Parish laugh at her now? It was a stinging thought; but she honestly believed that the minister himself would be most commiserated when the parish opinion had found time to simmer down.

The next day our heroine, whose face was singularly free from disappointment, told the minister that she would like to leave at once, for she was belated about many things, not having had notice in season of his change of plan.

" I 've been telling your wife all about the house and parish interests the best I can, and it 's likely she wants to take everything into her own hands right away," added the uncommon housekeeper, with a spice of malice; but Mr. Elbury flushed, and looked down at the short, capable Eliza appealingly. He knew her virtues so well that this announcement gave him a crushing blow.

"Why, I thought of course you would continue here as usual," he said, in a strange, harsh voice that would have been perfectly surprising in the pulpit. "Mrs. Elbury has never known any care. We count upon your remaining."

Whereupon Miss Peck looked him disdainfully in the face, and, for a moment, mistook him for that self so often reproved and now sunk into depths of ignominy.

"If you thought that, you ought to have known better," she said. "You can't expect a woman who has property and relations of her own to give up her interests for yours altogether. I got a letter this morning from my brother's boy, little Tom, and he's got leave from his mother and her husband to come and stop with me a good while — he says all winter. He's been sick, and they've had to take him out o' school. I never supposed that such stived-up air would agree with him," concluded Miss Peck, triumphantly. She was full of joy and hope

at this new turn of affairs, and the minister
was correspondingly hopeless. "I'll take
the baby home for a while, if 't would be
a convenience for you," she added, more
leniently. "That is, after I get my house
well warmed, and there's something in it
to eat. I wish you could have spoken to
me a fortnight ago; but I saw Joe Farley
to-day — that boy that lived with me quite
a while — he's glad to come back. He only
engaged to stop till after cider time where
he's been this summer, and he's promised to
look about for a good cow for me. I always
thought well of Joe."

The minister turned away ruefully, and
Miss Peck went about her work. She
meant to leave the house in the best of
order; but the whole congregation came
trooping in that day and the next, and she
hardly had time to build a fire in her own
kitchen before Joe Farley followed her from
the station with the beloved little Tom. He
looked tall and thin and pale, and largely
freckled under his topknot of red hair.
Bless his heart! how his lonely aunt hugged
him and kissed him, and how thankful he
was to get back to her, though she never
would have suspected it if she had not known

him so well. A shy boy-fashion of reserve
and stolidity had replaced his early demon-
strations, but he promptly went to the shelf
of books to find the familiar old " Robinson
Crusoe." Miss Peck's heart leaped for joy
as she remembered how much more she could
teach the child about books. She felt a
great wave of gratitude fill her cheerful soul
as she remembered the pleasure and gain of
those evenings when she and Mr. Elbury
had read together.

There was a great deal of eager discussion
in the village; and much amused scrutiny of
Eliza's countenance, as she walked up the
side aisle that first Sunday after the minister was married. She led little Tom by the
hand, but he opened the pew-door and ushered her in handsomely, and she looked smil-
ingly at her neighbors and nodded her head
sideways at the boy in a way that made them
suspect that she was much more in love with
him, freckles and all, than she had ever
been with Mr. Elbury. A few minutes later
she frowned at Tom sternly for greeting his
old acquaintances over the pew-rail in a way
that did not fit the day or place. There
was no chance to laugh at her disappointment; for nobody could help understanding

that her experience at the parsonage had been merely incidental in her life, and that she had returned willingly to her old associations. The dream of being a minister's wife had been only a dream, and she was surprised to find herself waking from it with such resignation to her lot.

"I'd just like to know what sort of a breakfast they had," she said to herself, as the bride's topknot went waving and bobbing up to the parsonage pew. "If ever there was a man who was fussy about his cup o' coffee, 't is Reverend Wilbur Elbury! There now, Elizy Peck, don't you wish 't was you a-setting there up front and feeling the eyes of the whole parish sticking in your back? You could have had him, you know, if you'd set right about it. I never did think you had proper ideas of what gettin' promoted is; but if you ain't discovered a new world for yourself like C'lumbus, I miss my guess. If you'd stayed on the farm all alone last year you'd had no thoughts but hens and rutabagys, and as 't is you've been livin' amon'st books. There's nothin' to regret if you did just miss makin' a fool o' yourself."

At this moment Mr. Elbury's voice gently

sounded from the pulpit, and Miss Peck sprang to her feet with the agility of a jack-in-the-box — she had forgotten her surroundings in the vividness of her revery. She hardly knew what the minister said in that first prayer; for many reasons this was an exciting day.

A little later our heroine accepted the invitation of her second cousin, Mrs. Corbell, to spend the hour or two between morning and afternoon services. They had agreed that it seemed like old times, and took pleasure in renewing this custom of the Sunday visit. Little Tom was commented upon as to health and growth and freckles and family resemblance; and when he strayed out-of-doors, after such an early dinner as only a growing boy can make vanish with the enchanter's wand of his appetite, the two women indulged in a good talk.

"I don't know how you viewed it, this morning," began Cousin Corbell; "but, to my eyes, the minister looked as if he felt cheap as a broom. There, I never was one o' his worshipers, you well know. To speak plain, Elizy, I was really concerned at one time for fear you would be over-persuaded. I never said one word to warp your judgment, but I did feel as if 't would be a shame. I" —

But Miss Peck was not ready yet to join the opposition, and she interrupted at once in an amiable but decided tone. "We 'll let by-gones be by-gones; it 's just as well, and a good deal better. Mr. Elbury always treated me the best he knew how; and I knew he wa'n't perfect, but 't was full as much his misfortune as his fault. I declare I don't know what else there was he could ha' done if he had n't taken to preaching; and he has very kind feelings, specially if any one 's in trouble. Talk of 'leading about captive silly women,' there are some cases where we 've got to turn round and say it right the other way — 't is the silly women that do the leadin' themselves. And I tell you," concluded Miss Peck, with apparent irrelevancy, "I was glad last night to have a good honest look at a yellow sunset. If ever I do go and set my mind on a minister, I m going to hunt for one that 's well settled in a hill parish. I used to feel as if I was shut right in, there at the parsonage; it 's a good house enough, if it only stood where you could see anything out of the windows. I can't carry out my plans o' life in any such situation."

" I expect to hear that you 've blown right off the top o' your hill some o' these windy days," said Mrs. Corbell, without resentment, though she was very dependent, herself, upon seeing the passing.

The church bell began to ring, and our friends rose to put on their bonnets and answer its summons. Miss Peck's practical mind revolved the possibility of there having been a decent noonday meal at the parsonage. "Maria Corbell!" she said, with dramatic intensity, "mark what I 'm goin' to say — it ain't I that 's goin' to reap the whirlwind; it 's your pastor, the Reverend Mr. Elbury, of the First Parish!"

MISS TEMPY'S WATCHERS.

THE time of year was April; the place was a small farming town in New Hampshire, remote from any railroad. One by one the lights had been blown out in the scattered houses near Miss Tempy Dent's; but as her neighbors took a last look out-of-doors, their eyes turned with instinctive curiosity toward the old house, where a lamp burned steadily. They gave a little sigh. "Poor Miss Tempy!" said more than one bereft acquaintance; for the good woman lay dead in her north chamber, and the light was a watcher's light. The funeral was set for the next day, at one o'clock.

The watchers were two of the oldest friends, Mrs. Crowe and Sarah Ann Binson. They were sitting in the kitchen, because it seemed less awesome than the unused best room, and they beguiled the long hours by steady conversation. One would think that neither topics nor opinions would hold out, at that rate, all through the long spring night; but there was a certain degree of excitement just then, and the two women had risen to an unusual level of expressiveness and confidence. Each had already told the other more than one fact that she had determined to keep secret; they were again and again tempted into statements that either would have found impossible by daylight. Mrs. Crowe was knitting a blue yarn stocking for her husband; the foot was already so long that it seemed as if she must have forgotten to narrow it at the proper time. Mrs. Crowe knew exactly what she was about, however; she was of a much cooler disposition than Sister Binson, who made futile attempts at some sewing, only to drop her work into her lap whenever the talk was most engaging.

Their faces were interesting, — of the dry, shrewd, quick-witted New England type, with thin hair twisted neatly back out of the way. Mrs. Crowe could look vague and benignant, and Miss Binson was, to quote her neighbors, a little too sharp-set; but the world knew that she had need to be, with the load she must carry of supporting an ineffi-

cient widowed sister and six unpromising
and unwilling nieces and nephews. The eldest boy was at last placed with a good man
to learn the mason's trade. Sarah Ann Binson, for all her sharp, anxious aspect, never
defended herself, when her sister whined
and fretted. She was told every week of her
life that the poor children never would have
had to lift a finger if their father had lived,
and yet she had kept her steadfast way with
the little farm, and patiently taught the
young people many useful things, for which,
as everybody said, they would live to thank
her. However pleasureless her life appeared
to outward view, it was brimful of pleasure
to herself.

Mrs. Crowe, on the contrary, was well to
do, her husband being a rich farmer and an
easy-going man. She was a stingy woman,
but for all that she looked kindly; and when
she gave away anything, or lifted a finger to
help anybody, it was thought a great piece
of beneficence, and a compliment, indeed,
which the recipient accepted with twice as
much gratitude as double the gift that came
from a poorer and more generous acquaintance. Everybody liked to be on good terms
with Mrs. Crowe. Socially she stood much

higher than Sarah Ann Binson. They were both old schoolmates and friends of Temperance Dent, who had asked them, one·day, not long before she died, if they would not come together and look after the house, and manage everything, when she was gone. She may have had some hope that they might become closer friends in this period of intimate partnership, and that the richer woman might better understand.the burdens of the poorer. They had not kept the house the night before; they were too weary with the care of their old friend, whom they had not left until all was over.

There was a brook which ran down the hillside very near the house, and the sound of it was much louder than usual. When there was silence in the kitchen, the busy stream had a strange insistence in its wild voice, as if it tried to make the watchers understand something that related to the past.

"I declare, I can't begin to sorrow for Tempy yet. I am so glad to have her at rest," whispered Mrs. Crowe. "It is strange to set here without her, but I can't make it clear that she has gone. I feel as if she had got easy and dropped off to sleep, and I'm more scared about waking her up than knowing any other feeling."

"Yes," said Sarah Ann, "it's just like that, ain't it? But I tell you we are goin' to miss her worse than we expect. She's helped me through with many a trial, has Temperance. I ain't the only one who says the same, neither."

These words were spoken as if there were a third person listening; somebody beside Mrs. Crowe. The watchers could not rid their minds of the feeling that they were being watched themselves. The spring wind whistled in the window crack, now and then, and buffeted the little house in a gusty way that had a sort of companionable effect. Yet, on the whole, it was a very still night, and the watchers spoke in a half-whisper.

"She was the freest-handed woman that ever I knew," said Mrs. Crowe, decidedly. "According to her means, she gave away more than anybody. I used to tell her 't wa'n't right. I used really to be afraid that she went without too much, for we have a duty to ourselves."

Sister Binson looked up in a half-amused, unconscious way, and then recollected herself.

Mrs. Crowe met her look with a serious face. "It ain't so easy for me to give as it is for some," she said simply, but with an effort which was made possible only by the occasion. "I should like to say, while Tempy is laying here yet in her own house, that she has been a constant lesson to me. Folks are too kind, and shame me with thanks for what I do. I ain't such a generous woman as poor Tempy was, for all she had nothin' to do with, as one may say."

Sarah Binson was much moved at this confession, and was even pained and touched by the unexpected humility. "You have a good many calls on you"—she began, and then left her kind little compliment half finished.

"Yes, yes, but I've got means enough. My disposition's more of a cross to me as I grow older, and I made up my mind this morning that Tempy's example should be my pattern henceforth." She began to knit faster than ever.

"'T ain't no use to get morbid: that's what Tempy used to say herself," said Sarah Ann, after a minute's silence. "Ain't it strange to say 'used to say'?" and her own voice choked a little. "She never did like to hear folks git goin' about themselves."

"'T was only because they're apt to do it

so as other folks will say 't was n't so, an'
praise 'em up," humbly replied Mrs. Crowe,
"and that ain't my object. There wa'n't a
child but what Tempy set herself to work
to see what she could do to please it. One
time my brother's folks had been stopping
here in the summer, from Massachusetts.
The children was all little, and they broke
up a sight of toys, and left 'em when they
were going away. Tempy come right up
after they rode by, to see if she could n't
help me set the house to rights, and she
caught me just as I was going to fling some
of the clutter into the stove. I was kind of
tired out, starting 'em off in season. 'Oh,
give me them!' says she, real pleading; and
she wropped 'em up and took 'em home with
her when she went, and she mended 'em up
and stuck 'em together, and made some young
one or other happy with every blessed one.
You 'd thought I 'd done her the biggest
favor. 'No thanks to me. I should ha'
burnt 'em, Tempy,' says I."

"Some of 'em came to our house, I
know," said Miss Binson. "She 'd take a
lot o' trouble to please a child, 'stead o'
shoving of it out o' the way, like the rest of
us when we 're drove."

" I can tell you the biggest thing she ever gave, and I don't know 's there 's anybody left but me to tell it. I don't want it forgot," Sarah Binson went on, looking up at the clock to see how the night was going. " It was that pretty-looking Trevor girl, who taught the Corners school, and married so well afterwards, out in New York State. You remember her, I dare say ? "

" Certain," said Mrs. Crowe, with an air of interest.

" She was a splendid scholar, folks said, and give the school a great start ; but she 'd overdone herself getting her education, and working to pay for it, and she all broke down one spring, and Tempy made her come and stop with her a while, — you remember that ? Well, she had an uncle, her mother's brother, out in Chicago, who was well off and friendly, and used to write to Lizzie Trevor, and I dare say make her some presents ; but he was a lively, driving man, and did n't take time to stop and think about his folks. He had n't seen her since she was a little girl. Poor Lizzie was so pale and weakly that she just got through the term o' school. She looked as if she was just going straight off in a decline. Tempy, she cosseted her up a while, and then, next thing folks knew, she was tellin' round how Miss Trevor had gone to see her uncle, and meant to visit Niagary Falls on the way, and stop over night. Now I happened to know, in ways I won't dwell on to explain, that the poor girl was in debt for her schoolin' when she come here, and her last quarter's pay had just squared it off at last, and left her without a cent ahead, hardly ; but it had fretted her thinking of it, so she paid it all ; they might have dunned her that she owed it to. An' I taxed Tempy about the girl's goin' off on such a journey till she owned up, rather 'n have Lizzie blamed, that she 'd given her sixty dollars, same 's if she was rolling in riches, and sent her off to have a good rest and vacation."

"Sixty dollars ! " exclaimed Mrs. Crowe. "Tempy only had ninety dollars a year that came in to her ; rest of her livin' she got by helpin' about, with what she raised off this little piece o' ground, sand one side an' clay the other. An' how often I 've heard her tell, years ago, that she 'd rather see Niagary than any other sight in the world ! "

The women looked at each other in si-lence ; the magnitude of the generous sacri-

fice was almost too great for their compre-
hension.

" She was just poor enough to do that ! "
declared Mrs. Crowe at last, in an abandon-
ment of feeling. " Say what you may, I
feel humbled to the dust," and her companion ventured to say nothing. She never had
given away sixty dollars at once, but it was
simply because she never had it to give. It
came to her very lips to say in explanation,
"Tempy was so situated ; " but she checked
herself in time, for she would not break in
upon her own loyal guarding of her dependent household.

" Folks say a great deal of generosity,
and this one's being public-sperited, and
that one free-handed about giving," said
Mrs. Crowe, who was a little nervous in the
silence. " I suppose we can't tell the sorrow it would be to some folks not to give,
same's 't would be to me not to save. I
seem kind of made for that, as if 't was what
I 'd got to do. I should feel sights better
about it if I could make it evident what I
was savin' for. If I had a child, now, Sarah Ann," and her voice was a little husky,
— " if I had a child, I should think I was
heapin' of it up because he was the one

trained by the Lord to scatter it again for
good. But here's Crowe and me, we can't
do anything with money, and both of us like
to keep things same 's they 've always been.
Now Priscilla Dance was talking away like
a mill-clapper, week before last. She 'd
think I would go right off and get one o'
them new-fashioned gilt-and-white papers
for the best room, and some new furniture,
an' a marble-top table. And I looked at
her, all struck up. ' Why,' says I, ' Priscilla, that nice old velvet paper ain't hurt a
mite. I should n't feel 't was my best room
without it. Dan'el says 't is the first thing
he can remember rubbin' his little baby fingers on to it, and how splendid he thought
them red roses was.' I maintain," continued
Mrs. Crowe stoutly, " that folks wastes
sights o' good money doin' just such foolish
things. Tearin' out the insides o' meetin'-
houses, and fixin' the pews different ; 't was
good enough as 't was with mendin' ; then
times come, an' they want to put it all back
same 's 't was before."

This touched upon an exciting subject to
active members of that parish. Miss Binson and Mrs. Crowe belonged to opposite parties, and had at one time come as near hard

feelings as they could, and yet escape them. Each hastened to speak of other things and to show her untouched friendliness.

"I do agree with you," said Sister Binson, "that few of us know what use to make of money, beyond every-day necessities. You 've seen more o' the world than I have, and know what 's expected. When it comes to taste and judgment about such things, I ought to defer to others;" and with this modest avowal the critical moment passed when there might have been an improper discussion.

In the silence that followed, the fact of their presence in a house of death grew more clear than before. There was something disturbing in the noise of a mouse gnawing at the dry boards of a closet wall near by. Both the watchers looked up anxiously at the clock; it was almost the middle of the night, and the whole world seemed to have left them alone with their solemn duty. Only the brook was awake.

"Perhaps we might give a look up-stairs now," whispered Mrs. Crowe, as if she hoped to hear some reason against their going just then to the chamber of death ; but Sister Binson rose, with a serious and yet satisfied countenance, and lifted the small lamp from the table. She was much more used to watching than Mrs. Crowe, and much less affected by it. They opened the door into a small entry with a steep stairway; they climbed the creaking stairs, and entered the cold upper room on tiptoe. Mrs. Crowe's heart began to beat very fast as the lamp was put on a high bureau, and made long, fixed shadows about the walls. She went hesitatingly toward the solemn shape under its white drapery, and felt a sense of remonstrance as Sarah Ann gently, but in a business-like way, turned back the thin sheet.

"Seems to me she looks pleasanter and pleasanter," whispered Sarah Ann Binson impulsively, as they gazed at the white face with its wonderful smile. "To - morrow 't will all have faded out. I do believe they kind of wake up a day or two after they die, and it 's then they go." She replaced the light covering, and they both turned quickly away; there was a chill in this upper room.

"'T is a great thing for anybody to have got through, ain't it?" said Mrs. Crowe softly, as she began to go down the stairs on tiptoe. The warm air from the kitchen

beneath met them with a sense of welcome
and shelter.

"I don' know why it is, but I feel as
near again to Tempy down here as I do up
there," replied Sister Binson. "I feel as if
the air was full of her, kind of. I can sense
things, now and then, that she seems to say.
Now I never was one to take up with no
nonsense of sperits and such, but I declare I
felt as if she told me just now to put some
more wood into the stove."

Mrs. Crowe preserved a gloomy silence.
She had suspected before this that her companion was of a weaker and more credulous
disposition than herself. "'T is a great
thing to have got through," she repeated,
ignoring definitely all that had last been
said. "I suppose you know as well as I
that Tempy was one that always feared
death. Well, it's all put behind her now;
she knows what 't is." Mrs. Crowe gave a
little sigh, and Sister Binson's quick sym-
pathies were stirred toward this other old
friend, who also dreaded the great change.

"I 'd never like to forgit almost those last
words Tempy spoke plain to me," she said
gently, like the comforter she truly was.
"She looked up at me once or twice, that

last afternoon after I come to set by her, and let Mis' Owen go home; and I says, 'Can I do anything to ease you, Tempy?' and the tears come into my eyes so I could n't see what kind of a nod she give me. 'No, Sarah Ann, you can't, dear,' says she; and then she got her breath again, and says she, looking at me real meanin', 'I'm only a-gettin' sleepier and sleepier; that's all there is,' says she, and smiled up at me kind of wishful, and shut her eyes. I knew well enough all she meant. She'd been lookin' out for a chance to tell me, and I don' know's she ever said much afterwards."

Mrs. Crowe was not knitting; she had been listening too eagerly. "Yes, 't will be a comfort to think of that sometimes," she said, in acknowledgment.

"I know that old Dr. Prince said once, in evenin' meetin', that he'd watched by many a dyin' bed, as we well knew, and enough o' his sick folks had been scared o' dyin' their whole lives through; but when they come to the last, he'd never seen one but was willin', and most were glad, to go. ''T is as natural as bein' born or livin' on,' he said. I don't know what had moved him to speak that night. You know he wa'n't

in the habit of it, and 't was the monthly
concert of prayer for foreign missions anyways," said Sarah Ann; " but 't was a great
stay to the mind to listen to his words of experience."

" There never was a better man," responded Mrs. Crowe, in a really cheerful
tone. She had recovered from her feeling
of nervous dread, the kitchen was so comfortable with lamplight and firelight; and
just then the old clock began to tell the hour
of twelve with leisurely whirring strokes.

Sister Binson laid aside her work, and
rose quickly and went to the cupboard.
" We 'd better take a little to eat," she explained. " The night will go fast after this.
I want to know if you went and made some
o' your nice cupcake, while you was home
to-day ? " she asked, in a pleased tone ; and
Mrs. Crowe acknowledged such a gratify-
ing piece of thoughtfulness for this humble
friend who denied herself all luxuries.
Sarah Ann brewed a generous cup of tea,
and the watchers drew their chairs up to
the table presently, and quelled their hun-
ger with good country appetites. Sister Binson put a spoon into a small, old-fashioned
glass of preserved quince, and passed it to

her friend. She was most familiar with the house, and played the part of hostess. "Spread some o' this on your bread and butter," she said to Mrs. Crowe. "Tempy wanted me to use some three or four times, but I never felt to. I know she'd like to have us comfortable now, and would urge us to make a good supper, poor dear."

"What excellent preserves she did make!" mourned Mrs. Crowe. "None of us has got her light hand at doin' things tasty. She made the most o' everything, too. Now, she only had that one old quince-tree down in the far corner of the piece, but she'd go out in the spring and tend to it, and look at it so pleasant, and kind of expect the old thorny thing into bloomin'."

"She was just the same with folks," said Sarah Ann. "And she'd never git more 'n a little apernful o' quinces, but she'd have every mite o' goodness out o' those, and set the glasses up onto her best-room closet shelf, so pleased. 'T wa'n't but a week ago to-morrow mornin' I fetched her a little taste o' jelly in a teaspoon; and she says 'Thank ye,' and took it, an' the minute she tasted it she looked up at me as worried as could be. 'Oh, I don't want to eat that,' says she.

'I always keep that in case o' sickness.' 'You 're goin' to have the good o' one tumbler yourself,' says I. 'I 'd just like to know who 's sick now, if you ain't!' An' she could n't help laughin', I spoke up so smart. Oh, dear me, how I shall miss talkin' over things with her! She always sensed things, and got just the p'int you meant."

"She did n't begin to age until two or three years ago, did she?" asked Mrs. Crowe. "I never saw anybody keep her looks as Tempy did. She looked young long after I begun to feel like an old woman. The doctor used to say 't was her young heart, and I don't know but what he was right. How she did do for other folks! There was one spell she was n't at home a day to a fortnight. She got most of her livin' so, and that made her own potatoes and things last her through. None o' the young folks could get married without her, and all the old ones was disáppointed if she wa'n't round when they was down with sickness and had to go. An' cleanin', or tailorin' for boys, or rug-hookin', — there was nothin' but what she could do as handy as most. 'I do love to work,' — ain't you heard her say that twenty times a week?"

Sarah Ann Binson nodded, and began to clear away the empty plates. "We may want a taste o' somethin' more towards mornin'," she said. "There's plenty in the closet here; and in case some comes from a distance to the funeral, we'll have a little table spread after we get back to the house."

"Yes, I was busy all the mornin'. I've cooked up a sight o' things to bring over," said Mrs. Crowe. "I felt 't was the last I could do for her."

They drew their chairs near the stove again, and took up their work. Sister Binson's rocking-chair creaked as she rocked; the brook sounded louder than ever. It was more lonely when nobody spoke, and presently Mrs. Crowe returned to her thoughts of growing old.

"Yes, Tempy aged all of a sudden. I remember I asked her if she felt as well as common, one day, and she laughed at me good. There, when Dan'el begun to look old, I couldn't help feeling as if somethin' ailed him, and like as not 't was somethin' he was goin' to git right over, and I dosed him for it stiddy, half of one summer."

"How many things we shall be wanting to ask Tempy!" exclaimed Sarah Ann

Binson, after a long pause. "I can't make up my mind to doin' without her. I wish folks could come back just once, and tell us how 'tis where they've gone. Seems then we could do without 'em better."

The brook hurried on, the wind blew about the house now and then; the house itself was a silent place, and the supper, the warm fire, and an absence of any new topics for conversation made the watchers drowsy. Sister Binson closed her eyes first, to rest them for a minute; and Mrs. Crowe glanced at her compassionately, with a new sympathy for the hard-worked little woman. She made up her mind to let Sarah Ann have a good rest, while she kept watch alone; but in a few minutes her own knitting was dropped, and she, too, fell asleep. Overhead, the pale shape of Tempy Dent, the outworn body of that generous, loving-hearted, simple soul, slept on also in its white raiment. Perhaps Tempy herself stood near, and saw her own life and its surroundings with new understanding. Perhaps she herself was the only watcher.

Later, by some hours, Sarah Ann Binson woke with a start. There was a pale light of dawn outside the small windows. Inside the kitchen, the lamp burned dim. Mrs. Crowe awoke, too.

"I think Tempy'd be the first to say 't was just as well we both had some rest," she said, not without a guilty feeling.

Her companion went to the outer door, and opened it wide. The fresh air was none too cold, and the brook's voice was not nearly so loud as it had been in the midnight darkness. She could see the shapes of the hills, and the great shadows that lay across the lower country. The east was fast growing bright.

"'T will be a beautiful day for the funeral," she said, and turned again, with a sigh, to follow Mrs. Crowe up the stairs. The world seemed more and more empty without the kind face and helpful hands of Tempy Dent.

A VILLAGE SHOP.

I.

Madam Jaffrey in her later years always sat at one of her front parlor windows in the winter afternoons. But one day, many years ago, she was not there, and passers-by missed her kindly greeting or the smiling nod of invitation with which she was apt to favor her intimate acquaintances. One could not help being uneasy at her absence; she was an older woman than her years and like a piece of her own frail china. She had seen much trouble, but there never was a braver heart.

As you went by on the flagstoned pavement, you could see the south parlor at a glance. The delightful old-fashioned room was flooded with sunlight. If you lingered for a moment, you could look through and beyond the room itself, and see the old garden pear-trees whose fruit all Grafton knew. Where could Madam Jaffrey be? and where was Miss Esther Jaffrey this February after-noon ?

The two ladies are sitting in an upper chamber together, and suffering the first pangs of a great disappointment. All Grafton knows the story of their pinching econo-mies, and the cheerful sacrifice of their own comfort, and that these have been reckoned as nothing in their pride and joy at further-ing the interests of Leonard Jaffrey, the only son and last hope of his house and name. Perhaps if the good unworldly women had known the increased expense of a college education, as compared with the prim figures in ancient family account books, they would have lacked courage for even this darling project of their hearts, but from the time of the boy's babyhood there had never been any question of his being sent to Harvard College. The Jaffrey men had all been graduates. Famous old Marlborough Jaf-frey, the first of them in the colonies, was an Oxford student who forsook his scholar's gown for a new-world enterprise, and though money grew scarcer as the last of his grand-sons grew older, the brave ladies looked forward hopefully to the days when their sacrifices would be returned to them fourfold. They thought of Leonard Jaffrey's ancestry as if it were a solvent bank of distinctions and emoluments in which he had a noble credit account. If he could not represent the actual wealth of old Marlborough, — for this, in their poverty, might have been most alluring, — he could at least reëmbody the shade of his grandfather, the great jurist, or, failing him, there had been well-salaried and devout clergymen. His own father had chosen this career lovingly and died young, but already famous ; in the collateral branches of the family tree hung plenty of well-ripened fruit. But it appeared sometimes as if Leonard had descended not from these but from some less worthy infusion of sap ; some heedless alliance which had been quickly overlooked and ignored had yet left its corrupting and perverting influence in the Jaffrey blood. This young scholar was a very Jaffrey to look at ; you could make up his somewhat characterless face from the features of the family portraits — a nose here, an eye-brow there, a lock of waving brown hair from his wistful-eyed father in gown and bands. Yet he had not the spirit of the Jaffreys, this Leonard who was the last of them, and it was only in sad and disheartened reveries that his sister was forced to acknowledge this melancholy deficiency. If she had been the son! she often said to herself with a surging thrill of pride and daring. If she had been the son how she could work and win her way, and not be the least of those who had borne the Jaffrey name unsullied! But she was only a woman, and the Jaffreys were more provincial than they used to be — a Jaffrey of Grafton could not lead public opinion in unfeminine directions; she was not a social reformer but fiercely conservative at heart. She had denied herself everything that could be denied, but treated her mother like a queen in exile, and so with sinking heart and dwindling hopes they came at last to this day when a letter had arrived from Leonard to say that he had finally forsaken any intention of exercising his profession. His general studies would more than fill his time, and he had conscientious scruples against preaching the dogmas of the faith in which he had been reared and trained. And the two women knew that there was to be no such thing as persuading him to change his mind. The Jaffreys had always won their fame by their power of decision. Leonard had said I will not! and could hang back with all the steadfastness with which his ancestors had said I will! and then pushed forward to their goals.

Now the acknowledgment must be made that he had disappointed all hopes from the first. From the day that Miss Jaffrey with eager, elder-sisterly forethought had looked through the list of his classmates and rejoiced to find a Quincy, a Boylston, a Winthrop, or a Gardiner, and gladly planned for the resuming of old family alliances and friendship, only to find her brother uninterested and even reluctant; from the day when she sadly acknowledged that Leonard saw the world through strange eyes and was indifferent to the old home standards, she had been driven back inch by inch to the very stronghold of her opinions. She only held to her own instincts and the Jaffrey code all the more fiercely because there was a traitor on the very throne. Something must be allowed for the natural rebellion of a young man to petticoat government, but the fact remained that Leonard Jaffrey was indifferent to worldly honor, careless of the world's needs or its demands, in no wise public-spirited, and a strange bird altogether to have been hatched in the ambitious Jaffrey nest.

Fortunately the already aged and fading mother was not forced to stay long in this world to bewail the blasting of her hopes, and make futile excuses for her wrongheaded boy. By the time he came home from his theological school with a collection of miscellaneous volumes for which he must have practiced economies only second in severity to those which had kept him a student at all, Madam Jaffrey had but time to see him once or twice in her darkened room; to whisper that she forgave him her disappointment and respected his conscientiousness. Leonard vaguely understood these expressions, but her death touched him deeply. Let us hope that he regretted his inability to win either gain or glory to lay at her feet, and saw at last in one swift flash of light, his own torpor, and the burden he had let this patient mother carry. He was only made more silent by the loss and change in his home, and there was a more impenetrable barrier than ever set up between him and his sister Esther. She was the eldest of a large family of children of whom all had died but Leonard and herself, and their

relationship was somehow unequal; not that
of a brother and sister who have constantly
seen life from somewhere near the same
angle. He was only too well aware of her
noble rectitude and loyalty and her uncommon powers of mind, even of her good looks,
which seemed to increase instead of paling
with the march of years — but he felt her
generosity like a chain of steel, and the
memory of her sacrifices and her opinion of
his course burnt him like living coals. Perhaps he thought it wiser not to undertake a
career in which he foresaw inevitable failure,
perhaps it was simply that the natural indolence and love of a book-worm's life filled
his whole horizon. He went away directly
after his mother's funeral, for he could bear
neither the sight of the empty rooms, nor
the weight of his sister's stately courtesy,
which only covered that sullen disapproval of
himself that lay beneath. But to this sister
he was still a Jaffrey, and however carefully
she avoided meeting his eyes, she was able
to speak of him serenely to her acquaintances, and to acknowledge without hesitation that he intended to lead the life of a
student henceforth, and instead of following
his profession had decided to become a man

of letters. She liked to repeat the words,
"a man of letters;" yes, Leonard was a
Jaffrey and had a Jaffrey's right. But
those who knew the household best puzzled
their brains to know by what means it was
to be sustained. The Jaffrey lands had
shrunk to the limits of the old pear-tree
garden and a strip of decaying wharf-prop-
erty by the river; the Jaffrey fortune had
been spent almost to the last farthing in
uncomplaining furtherance of the scholar's
welfare. Here he was, stranded in the old
house with as much energy as a barnacle,
looking already close upon middle-age from
his lack of physical activity; the most unproductive man of letters in New England,
with no apparent value either social or commercial. A step farther and he would only
have become what the canny Scotsmen call
"a stickit minister."

II.

There were enough of the old people left
in Grafton twenty or thirty years ago to
suffer an acute attack of pain and misgiv-
ing, when the news was whispered to and
fro under the elms that Miss Esther Jaffrey

intended to keep a ladies' shop. The immediate reason for it was so aggravating that a great deal of unkind comment flew about the indignant town; there was an unusual visiting from house to house, and some of Miss Jaffrey's own friends were heard to say sorrowfully that it would be more than they could bear to see her stand to serve them behind the counter. Her grandfather the judge's office, her granduncle's ministerial study; her own father's study, and the place that knew his youthful hopes, the writing of his famous and saintly sermons, and the burning of much midnight oil; what a degradation it seemed to put the old room to this new use. Besides this, had it not been the counting-room of Marlborough Jaffrey, the great colonial merchant? Here he had kept the papers of those busy two hundred-ton ships which had earned his fortune; here he lived his long and noted life, and defied wind and weather, time and tide, as he pushed forward his bold enterprises through half a score of distant seas. From the small-paned windows he could look far down the broad tide-river which seemed to dutifully dispatch its lazy waters toward the ocean and draw them back again twice a day

in deference to his fleet of packets and gun-
dalows, deep-laden with their out-bound or
incoming cargoes. Those were rich and glorious days for Grafton, but nobody had made
any money since. Not only the merchant's
own descendants but everybody else had lived
on the remains of their ancient fortunes,
except for the yearly produce of the farms
and a barely sufficient local system of petty
commerce. The farms, the few large houses
in the village, even the high-steepled church
itself, had been paid for with money that had
come in the Jaffrey ships. But it is long
since anybody had chosen the business of
sailor — there are only a few slippery old
sticks of oak timber left in the river-mud,
and the fortunes have all dwindled away.
The embargo gave a killing blow to the
prosperity of Grafton, and spendthrifts and
foolish men and women and the wear of
time have been undermining the once secure
investments ever since. The worst punishment fell upon the town's pride when no
sooner had the news been told of a certain
Mary Destin's giving up her business in
small wares, than it was also known that
Miss Esther Jaffrey had made definite arrangements to become her successor. Miss

Esther Jaffrey, like Hawthorne's Miss Pyncheon, had become reduced to the keeping of a shop. The bulwarks of social safety were broken down, and public opinion was ready to reproach the former owner of the business, since it was vaguely believed that if Mary Destin had not planned to go westward to live with a married sister, this catastrophe would have been averted. Her good sense in making the change was loudly questioned; there was a general feeling as if she had somehow involved another's ruin, that she ought to have remained in her own lot and place.

III.

Since we looked in at the parlor windows many things have happened, but there is no apparent difference in the room itself except that Madam Jaffrey has gone away. It is two weeks now since she died, and they have been two bitterly anxious weeks to the lonely daughter who has seen the small hours of nearly every night, and has wondered what her future could be until her brain has been fairly burning, and her eyes fixed wide open in a sleeplessness that seemed to drain her very soul of its strength. Nobody knew her sorrows now, save herself; there was no longer any incentive for keeping them back lest some one else might sorrow the more. She had nobody to keep cheerful for now, since her mother died. Loyal Betty, the one maid-servant, was dim and dull of wits, except in her own province, and she and Miss Jaffrey plodded their frugal way together with little conscious thought of each other. Betty's hero was Mr. Leonard, and yet she was taught by instinct to be silent about him before her younger mistress, even in the days when Madam Jaffrey took joy in telling of his poor triumphs and that noble future apparently now more remote than ever. Betty had been a great resource to the boy's mother; Betty saw no reason why the most improbable successes might not come to pass.

The house seemed very much too large nowadays, and it was a poor mockery when it was set in order, as if for guests, during the early summer. Some of the furnishings were already threadbare, but the old timbers were live-hearted, and the long purses of its earlier inhabitants had shaped it with the soundest and best wood and fabric of their day. Little need be spent on it for years to come, but this was a starved and sorry life compared with the earlier abundance, the luxury, the cheerful company, the busy maids and men of an earlier time. Just when the need of getting into debt came now like a crouching tiger into Esther Jaffrey's well-trodden path, the deliverance was also there, a melancholy alternative, but welcomed by her with all a Jaffrey's pride in independence and self-respect. It was indeed sad to think of shop-keeping at her age, and under the shadow of her family tree, but it would be much sadder to have no shop to keep, no way to look for deliverance from her poverty. Before the good people of Grafton had ceased gasping, and had half reviewed the resources of friends, and fitting employments which surely belonged to their leader, the goods of Mary Destin had become those of Esther Jaffrey, and the small projecting room next the sunny parlor which had been counting-house and study by turns — this historic room which opened handily to the street was insulted by a stained wood counter and meagre show-cases, with boxes of thread and needles, and whalebone and edgings and all the minor wares that home-keeping women need in their daily work of mending and making. Miss Jaffrey's shop! would it ever seem right to say it — could one ever mention its resources unconsciously, or dare to suggest better bargains? Mary Destin was a cheerful gossip and a born tradeswoman; she had gone away contented with the value of an ancient silver-set diamond ring safely pinned into her pocket. And yet Miss Jaffrey had not ceased to be a lady because she had begun to keep a shop. As one woman after another ventured in to make a necessary purchase after the first awed week, they found her more friendly and sympathetic than ever. She was ready to talk across the counter, to take a bit off her prices when she heard a lofty hint of the article being too expensive. She only listened with wistful eagerness when a story was told that a former resident of Grafton had given the old town a vast sum of money for a public library. The Jaffreys' day was almost over, but no jealousy of any new patrons seemed to be in her generous heart. In fact Miss Jaffrey now first became really known to some of the Grafton people who had wished through envy and conscious inferiority to take pennyworths out of her high reputation. They could not help being pleased with her lovely bearing, and her serene acceptance of her altered fortunes. And so the enterprise of her later life began with the sympathy and blessing of all who knew her. The familiar white-lettered black boxes of ships' papers that had belonged to rich old Marlborough Jaffrey were still perched in line on a high upper shelf that corniced the room. All his descendants had been proud to keep them there. Ship Esther, Brig Marlborough, Brig Brasenose, Ship Palatine, Ship Pactolus; how well Miss Jaffrey knew the long row; they were almost like funereal coffers that held the ashes of her ancestors.

During the second week after the shop was opened Mr. Leonard Jaffrey came home. He had already sent some of his books, and dimly expected to find them neatly placed on the shelves; now he brought more, and as he drew near the old house he looked with eagerness at the study windows as if there must be his true home henceforth. He had already planned the disposition of his treasures with rare enthusiasm; but he was suddenly aware of strange shapes and colors behind the familiar small panes. Could Esther have let the room to a stranger? He grew dizzy for a moment with uncharacteristic wrath, then he was smitten, let us hope, with regret. When the trunks were carried into the wide hall, and he stood uncertain what to do, feeling for once the weak man he was from his lack of force and strange inadequacy, Miss Jaffrey made her appearance. She was singularly gentle toward him, indeed was not she his protector and defender, had not she solved the puzzling problem of their being clothed and fed? And the sister and brother kissed each other with a softening remembrance of the mother who had loved them both and been patient with them, and from that day forward the shop was never discussed, or in any way berated.

IV.

It sometimes appeared as if nature had destined Leonard Jaffrey for a reservoir of learning. He was absolutely without any original thoughts or gifts, he was unproductive from the beginning, yet with unquenched appetite he devoured the wisdom and imagination that were stored between his book covers. Unsated, unflagging, unforeseeing, he became at last a perfectly unavailable treasury of other people's knowledge, like some lake that has no outlet. Yet there surely must have been an invisible exhauster of his hoards to correspond to the lake's evaporations; not speech, for he grew silent and withdrew more and more into himself as years went by. Miss Jaffrey was much the gainer by her increased facility for intercourse with all sorts and conditions of women, but the brother seemed to have let his individuality ooze out to the dry pages of his books as if they were a species of treacherous blotting paper, and destined in time to completely absorb him. He never asked his sister for money, but she spared him what she could. Was not that one cause of the shop? Sometimes he looked at her very wistfully as he put the price of her self-sacrifice slowly into his pocket, and vaguely called up a feeble ghost of his purpose to more than make things up to her by and by. But when his pockets clung together for very leanness, and some longed-for pile of dusty volumes was slipping out of his grasp with every hour, he even found himself greedily gazing at the shining silver tea-service of which he and Miss Esther were the sole heirs. Packed away in the sideboard were useless porringers and tankards — yes, he was quite capable of selling the whole of the Jaffrey plate in these moments of anguish and limitation. He was a book-miser at last. It was a mercy that he lived in Grafton, for the vicinity of book-stores and ragged companies of volumes on corner stalls of the great towns would either have made him mad or a hardened offender against justice.

As the years slipped by he gained some little reputation as a scholar, quite unworthily, for he was too firmly grafted into his position as idle accumulator and reader to exercise his stunted powers of thought. He was only a personified memory with no gift at combination and association; an encyclopædia, a very rag-bag of true and worthless knowledge; and the easy life which made no continuous demands upon him seemed to hold no inspiration in any of its lights or shadows. The library slowly grew, the man himself really dwindled, yet he was thought a much wiser and more awesome person than the resolute and gentle sister who kept her petty shop as intently as that famous grandfather had managed his shipping. She was secretly glad to spend what energy she could upon the slow little business, and tried to fancy that she was by nature a business woman. Yet she at first insisted upon the old family custom of reading aloud, and so upon sharing as much of her brother's evenings as possible. Sometimes she was interrupted, but as a rule her own evening leisure was respected, and the solitary lamp.on the shop counter hinted that no errands except those of urgent necessity were expected or provided for.

If the brother was glad that their mother had not lived to be wounded by the sound of the tinkling shop-bell, Miss Jaffrey was rejoiced that she had never been forced to surrender all hope of her son's gaining distinction. But toleration and good breeding kept a harmonious atmosphere in the old house, and on summer Sundays, when there were strangers in the village, admiring neighbors still pointed out Mr. and Miss Jaffrey as the most interesting figures in the congregation.

For a long time there was little change in the quiet old village, but there came a day when everybody acknowledged that Grafton was waking up. It has already been hinted that a large sum of money was left in trust for the building of a public library. The old academy, well endowed and famous along the line of its earlier history, seemed to take a new lease of life, and as in days of the past, a successful teacher drew round him the brightest boys and girls of the neighboring towns. There were more and more people, too, who discovered the beauties of the wide tidal river and its wooded banks; and from the neighboring resorts on the sea-shore near by, increasing numbers of summer idlers came inland like birds of passage to linger for a while in the shade of the great Grafton elms. The time-honored repose of the village seemed permanently broken, and not the least attractive figure was this stately Miss Jaffrey who had achieved the dignity of self-sacrifice in willingly supporting her learned brother. It was considered a true romance when the village people discovered this aspect of the shopkeeping through the help of others. They were delightfully eager to enlarge upon the old-time majesty of the Jaffreys and the slow succession of its assailments. Lookers-on could only guess at the self-denial which made it possible for the dear lady to do her part in giving for the good of church or state, or to carry forward, even in simplest

fashion the old-time hospitalities and gen-
erosities of the house. But what she gave
she gave royally, and with that cheerfulness
which the Lord himself loves. The bright
young people were a great pleasure to gray-
haired, dignified Miss Esther, as they went
flitting about the streets in their gay gowns,
or lingered in her shop with sweet sympathetic looks. Some found their way into the
parlor and learned to know the rest of the
fine old house, and were even graciously en-
tertained at tea to their hearts' delight and
admiration. More than one descendant of
the house's old acquaintances carried away
to Boston a glowing description of this fine
gentlewoman, in her nobly equipped dwelling, and the pathetic unworthy business of
her life. The brother did not lose charm
from the fact that he was seldom seen and
was still in middle life, with the manly
beauty of the painted Jaffreys on the walls.
But as winter took the place of summer, and
these gay guests disappeared like butterflies,
the village seemed more familiar again, and
as if it had turned over for another nap.
The walls of the new library were rising,
Miss Jaffrey liked to hear the clink of the
masons' hammers, and one day thought sor-

rowfully that she was growing old and there
was no one to follow herself and Leonard in
the Jaffrey house. There was one comfort,
he had not gathered his books for nothing,
she would urge him to decide to leave them
to the town by and by when Death called
him away for his sins to a bookless world.
She herself had not been worthy the name
of Jaffrey, there was no reason why anybody
should remember her; but she had kept her
house generously and her shop honestly.
" Perhaps I had to be punished for my
pride," she thought, at the wistful remembrance of a proud and hopeful girlhood.
The elder ladies of Grafton were fond of
saying to each other with gentle emphasis,
" You know, Miss Jaffrey understands what
ladies care for ! " This was the gift of her
ancestry then — a delicate power of selecting
linen, cambric, or soft ribbons? Was there,
beside, a trained capacity and usable force
which some persons of less illustrious de-
scent found themselves without? She was
the chief literary authority of the town,
though it was acknowledged that her brother
was more available for serious questioning.
The old-fashioned book-club had its headquarters in the shop, and the best talk and

best influence in Grafton resided under Miss
Jaffrey's roof, — in truth her own ladylike,
apologetic little head-dress thatched it in.
Yet, alas, there were some new shops now
in the new part of the town. Miss Jaffrey
had a mere trifle of money for the rainy days
of her fast approaching age, and yet she
had been careful and wise and self-denying
all the way. She was almost proud of the
bookworm overhead instead of being indignant with him; she never reproached her
brother, it would have broken her heart if
he had gone to shopkeeping. "Yes, Leonard is a man of letters," she used to say
with smiling indulgence. "One cannot expect business gifts in him with all the rest."
She began to dream now of his making a
proper marriage. It was partly for this that
she planned her summer tea-parties.

That winter brought new problems.
Betty was really old, and for the first time in
her life fell ill. Miss Jaffrey overworked
herself and had to close the shop for many
days together, and at last hired an inadequate young girl to tend it in her place in
order to serve Betty, herself. But Betty
was only enraged at such officiousness, and

the shop was quickly put into dire disorder.
Miss Jaffrey was in real distress for a time;
but after a while the clouds blew over, and
she was left with a miserable fear of the
repetition of such dark days. Several of her
best patrons and most valued friends had
died; time was fast assailing her security as
a business woman. What had she to look
forward to but dependent poverty, the sharp-
est sorrow that old age can bring to a
woman of her nature. Yet Leonard did
not suspect these anxieties. He ate his methodical breakfast and took his methodical
walk and made his accurate notes in a
clerkly hand, catalogued and re-catalogued
his books, and lived his peaceful life.
Sometimes he noticed that his sister had
changed in outward looks, but it never occurred to him to ask the reason. They
walked into church on Sunday with widely
different feelings — the woman's heart crying for help and, for the second time, driven
to despair; the man comfortable, unappre-
hensive, and ready to quibble with the cler-
gyman about the emphasis of a Greek word
or incorrect quotation from one of the early
fathers. Miss Jaffrey climbed to the garret
once to look at a disused set of heavy ma-

hogany chairs; if worst came to worst, she would write presently to a young summer friend who had delicately suggested her ardent desire to buy such fine old furniture. Leonard would not miss the chairs. As they sat opposite each other at tea-time, Leonard being also a silent ·sufferer for more books, the tea-urn winked and blinked at first one and then the other, as if conscious of its solid worth. It was secure in the belief that its owners were capable of starving before their empty plates rather than sell it to a stranger.

V.

One winter day a man came driving slowly up the wide Grafton street under the leafless branches of the elms. For some time before there had been no other passerby, and the people who sat at their windows looked out with mingled relief and curiosity at the small old-fashioned sleigh and heavy, slow-stepping horse. It was certainly very dull in Grafton in winter weather, and in a cold clear day like this when the snow on the house roofs refused to melt, as every one said, " in the eye of the sun," there was little going abroad. Several house-bound women, eager for something new to think about, flattened their foreheads against the cold window panes to see where John Grant was going. He was a rich farmer from a comfortable home of his own two or three miles below on the river shore, a widower these dozen years, and well known in the village.

"He's turnin' up by Miss Jaffrey's shop," said one observer. "I hope he's goin' to buy her out, I'm sure. Time was that most all the farmer's folks used to trade with her, but they've been tolled off to the new stores down by the factory, and she must find it dreadful poor pickin'. Hard, ain't it? but then she might make some effort to keep up with the times, and get some sort o' fancy wares."

Miss Jaffréy herself was sitting in her sunny parlor trying to busy herself with some mending; there was little making to do now, the year round. She gladly saw John Grant stop and fasten his horse, then a shadow dimmed her eyes as she laid down her work and went toward the shop to meet him. There was no fire there; for three days she had done almost no business, and she could not waste the firewood. Brief errands could be done in spite of the cold; she would trust to the forbearance of her customers, and she had just been almost congratulating herself that no one had yet appeared. In mild weather the place of business could easily be warmed by the parlor fire, but John Grant might be chilled after his drive. With ready hospitality she only waited until he had knocked the last lump of snow off his sturdy boots and shut the shop door behind him, before she asked him to come into the parlor to warm himself.

The kindly pitying heart of the man grew very sad as he looked at his hostess; standing before her half-empty shelves, he hesitated a minute as if it might be kinder to ignore the cold, then he saw how thin and gray she looked, for the quaint, three-cornered shawl round her thin shoulders was not preventing one shiver after another. He followed her somewhat bashfully into the next room and unbuttoned his coat without speaking, though he bowed with sober dignity as Miss Jaffrey placed a chair for him before the Franklin stove. It was quite another atmosphere in every respect from that in the shop, but while the eyes of the portraits and the presence of a lady were trying at first to his composure, they quickly confirmed him in his secret purpose.

"I called to see you on a little private business, Miss Jaffrey," said good, sensible John Grant, after they had decorously considered the weather. "I am going to ask a great favor at your hands." Miss Jaffrey looked anxious at first, then relieved. The Jaffreys liked to grant favors much better than to receive them, and she felt strangely at the world's mercy in these days.

"I shall be very glad if I can do anything to serve you," she said, simply.

"I hope you will not think I mean to presume too far," the plain man said, with grave deference, and almost courtesy, entirely different from his cheerful farmer's manner. "You know that I have only one girl at home? She was the baby when her mother died, a little child following me about, hardly above my knee, and I could n't seem to do without her for long at a time, so I have n't taken the thought I should about her education till here she is a young woman. She has taken what schooling she could get in our district, and she 's a great hand for story-books, reads everything she can get. And I see all too plain that she shows some lack of woman's care. I'm well enough off to send her to some o' the smart boarding schools, but I can't seem to make up my mind to it. Some young fellow'll be picking her off," — this with a wise twinkle of his eye at Miss Jaffrey, — " but I mean to keep her while I can. Now, there's this good teacher at the academy and all the chance she really needs. If you could see your way to taking her and giving her a little good advice and letting her have the profit of seeing how a lady like you behaves herself, I should be — well, more obliged to you than I've got words to say."

There was a moment of silence before Miss Jaffrey gave her answer. The speaker grew a little anxious, and feared that he had been, as he first suggested, presuming. There had long been cordial relations between the Jaffreys and the farm by the river. It was his grandmother's pride to tell how the Madam Jaffrey of her day brought gay parties to eat strawberries and cream, and had once done the gracious favor of showing all her own treasures of china to the admiring farmer's wife. Courtesy and mutual regard and dependence there had always been, but this sort of equality, never; and yet the shop and the unstemmed flood of poverty and anxiety remained. The petitioner had truly meant a kindness to Miss Jaffrey as well as a favor to himself; his pretty Nelly was good enough for any household.

Miss Jaffrey turned from the half-moon table where she had been fingering her sewing work in an aimless fashion. "I should indeed be very glad to have her come, if" — shyly, "you think she will be contented. We are a sober pair, my brother and I, but he will be able to aid with her studies. I will not try to conceal from you that it will be a great help to me; I have been anxious lately about" — but the sentence was never ended. "She has a sweet young face."

The father's heart was quickly touched. He could hardly have told why the simple occasion affected him so much. He had already noticed that the fire was made of chilly bits of the old pear-trees which had been broken by winter winds, and determined to send an honest load of his own wholehearted rock-maple wood for Nelly's benefit as well as the Jaffreys'. The certainty of the old house's poverty, and an empty cellar beneath made him warmly resolve to provi-

sion it as for a siege. All his generous lav-
ishness should work its will. Miss Jaffrey's
grandfather, the judge, had saved his own
grandfather from ruin, and he ought to have
been seeing what he could do for this poor
lady in her pinched housekeeping. It was
hard to come down from a delightful level of
talk about Nelly's needs and prospects and
insistence upon paying a good price for board
in view of her rare advantages, but at last,
when the interview was ended, John Grant
bought Miss Jaffrey's entire stock of fine
handkerchiefs by way of a gift for his daughter. It was such bleak weather in the shop
that he tried to shorten the process of sale
by stuffing them into his deep coat pocket,
but Miss Jaffrey insisted upon wrapping
them with proper precision and figuring
their cost on a bit of paper which she would
have him audit with care. Her own fingers
stiffened all too easily at the least chill.
Could it be possible that Miss Jaffrey went
hungry now and then to make her scanty
larder hold out the longer? Oh, good John
Grant, you were an angel that day, in disguise of your worn fur cap and warm, faded
old coat with its big buttons! And Miss
Jaffrey sat in the winter sunshine and cried

as the old sleigh bells jingled away again out of hearing. Now she had surely seen her darkest day, and things could never be so hard and trying again.

In the twilight brother Leonard came down, unusually fretful, because his lamp held no oil, and he had been obliged to lay by his work. "Betty told me that we had no more, but I could not send for any," said the patient sister. "I have a little money now, however; Mr. Grant has been a good customer."

"I do not see any objection," Leonard Jaffrey gave kind assurance, after the new plan had been detailed with not a little apprehension. "Nelly Grant has a pretty face like a spring flower," he added, with unexpected sentiment, this elderly bookworm whom nobody suspected of knowing one young parishioner from another in the old Grafton church.

Betty alone was daunted at the prospect. "There's no knowing what work she and her mates will make trapesing through the house," the bent old woman grumbled. "I thought 't was time to end this playin' of keepin' shop," she added to herself later. "We should all have starved pretty soon,

like a nest of frozen mice. An' see if I
don't hint round an' spy if they ain't got
some o' them big pippin apples at the farm,
now, that old madam used never to be without. They do make proper dumplings and
sliced pies."

VI.

Mr. Leonard Jaffrey stood behind a closed
upper window one rainy April day, indulg-
ing himself in a fit of complete idleness.
His sister still regarded him as a youngish
man, but he had long since passed the time
when one could justly call him anything but
middle-aged. There was a becoming lustre
of whitening locks against the original dark
brown of his hair, and his complexion was
like a girl's in its freshness and unmanly absence of any traces of exposure to wind and
weather. Student life had evidently agreed
with his constitution of body as well as mind.
He smiled placidly as he looked out across
the brown-budded pear-trees, and noted the
hour on the steeple clock of the old academy. Everywhere in Grafton the Jaffreys
might be reminded of their ancestors, for
the needs of church and state had always

been liberally considered as long as there was any money to give. Judge Jaffrey had handsomely endowed the ancient parish, and had given the very steeple clock itself to which his great-grandson now listened as it struck three. It seemed a fitting return of such favors on the part of the family that a poor boy who had grown rich in the western country should have chosen a public library as his monument. Grafton as a town was not especially dependent upon literature, but when the last of the Jaffreys proved to be a scholar, public notice was naturally taken of it, and the old-time favors would now be suitably returned. But the last of the Jaffreys gave the question no definite thought as he cast a sidewise glance at the new library's roof, and contemptuously reminded himself that there would probably never be a collection of books under it which would afford him much interest. Trivial modern volumes of transient worth were all that his fellow-townspeople might be expected to select. It did not naturally occur to this learned gentleman that his own duty lay in the direction of wise counsel and devoted interest; to him the practical affairs of life or any sense of personal obligation were as foreign as the problems of astronomy to a blind man. Through the recent struggles of his own family life, through years and years while Miss Jaffrey had crept painfully along the narrow path between want and tolerable comfort, he had been as unconscious of her makeshifts and anxieties as if he had been an Indian brave whose round-shouldered squaw existed for nothing but to carry tent-poles on her back, and to provide their necessary food. Yet he was sublimely conscious of much tenderness of heart, and proper interest in the human race. His world was a book world, not peopled with material shapes. While he stood at the window one could not help being struck by the neatness and quaintness of his attire, for the clothes he wore expressed a man who rightfully belonged to an earlier generation. He might have been the despair of a fashionable tailor, with that almost instantaneous process of assimilating his garments to the out-of-date spirit underneath. There was an odor of old leather books about his overcoat when he stood meekly in the Grafton post-office, or conscientiously drifted with the crowd toward the place of voting on town meeting days. As one glanced about the room upon which his back was turned that cloudy afternoon, it presented a curious appearance, and it was impossible not to be reminded of certain shell - fish whose covering thickens with age. No wonder that a suggestion of brown leather bindings followed him in his rare progresses into the outer world, for here there were hundreds shelved in crowded lines, piled in small toppling precipices against the wainscoted walls, and stacked in sliding hillocks here and there on the uncarpeted floor. Leonard Jaffrey himself could find his way among them, even in the dark, like a soft-pawed pussy cat; the noise of a fallen book was the only sound that roused his anger. There was apparent danger for a stray visitor, as if in time this floor and walls of experienced volumes would suddenly close in and stifle the room's occupant. The mahogany bedstead was furnished with a wooden canopy draped with faded blue damask, and armful after armful of books, for which there was no other lodging, had been stowed away on the top, next the ceiling. The apparent method of reaching them at such an inconvenient height was by climbing the slender, carved mahogany posts, but it would be difficult to fancy the dignified owner sliding carefully down to the floor after a season of reference and review of his celestial authors. A discerning eye might have shrewdly noticed one evil-disposed work which had slipped out from its pile on the burdened tester until it seemed to be wickedly just holding itself back until it could drop fatally upon Mr. Jaffrey's head just as he intended to retire for the night. There was truly something evil in the way it bravely held its dangerous weight high in air, or risked the possibility of gathering more dust.

The scholar at the window leaned closer against the sash as if something attracted his attention. Those who were quick enough to look over his shoulder could have caught a glimpse of a young girl who went with flitting step along the sidewalk next the old garden. The fence was unfortunately of solid boarding, and was far from being transparent, even after many years of necessary wear and moss growing. At the top it was cut in sharp points, and the girlish face moved quickly past in full view. The watcher drew back into the shelter of the window shutter, but his face had noticeably brightened. As he went back to his seat beside the table which held his writing materials,

it was impossible to resist the suspicion that
this was not the first time that he had seen
Nelly Grant on her way home from her afternoon lessons at the academy.

A few moments later there was heard the
familiar groaning creak of the old front
door, and the noise of its decided closing.
Mr. Leonard Jaffrey half rose from his
wooden arm-chair, which was made altogether
of serviceable slender rungs, then he regret-
fully sank back again with an almost bashful
look upon his face. He waited listening intently, but he was not gratified by the sound
of approaching footsteps. It seemed as if
the mist which had followed an earlier rain
were making the old bedroom-library almost too dark and dismal to be borne, and
he drummed on the table fretfully with his
familiar penholder.

Miss Jaffrey greeted her young housemate with a cordial smile of welcome as she
came in, rosy and smiling, from the street.
Nelly was very much of a little lady, and,
with the help of numerous visits to the
farm, had managed to be perfectly happy in
the imposing Jaffrey house. She inquired
now whether her father had made his appearance while she had been at school, and

heard that nothing had been seen of him with hardly a shade of disappointment. "I told him to stop for me if he came over this afternoon," she explained; "but I don't believe he cares about bringing me back so early in the morning in this rainy weather." She was kneeling on the window-seat and looking eagerly up and down the deserted street. "You must go and take off your damp clothes," advised Miss Jaffrey quietly. "I don't want to send you home with a cold;" but the healthy country-girl only laughed, and made no other reply. "What do the school-girls want with so much of that narrow tape?" asked the elder woman timidly; for Nelly had fallen into a deep revery, as she still knelt in the window.

"Oh, it's a notion about a kind of stiff little trimming; they sew it together in pointed patterns. I'm sure I never should have patience to do it. Why, have they been here for some?" asked the young lodger with eager interest; for she had already learned to share in the satisfaction that followed a day of good sales.

"Yes, they came like a flock of pigeons an hour or two ago," answered Miss Jaffrey. "I happened to have a box full of narrow tapes put aside, of the very best quality too, and they pounced upon them gladly. I think I have had those little tapes ever since I kept the shop at all ” — she added by way of reminiscence — “ dear, dear ! how many years it has been now, yet I somehow always think of it as a new thing, and the bell always startles me a little.”

“ I suppose it has been a good deal of company to you,” replied Nelly with a vagueness in her tone that implied her intention of changing the subject. “ I ’m so confused about my mental philosophy lesson Miss Jaffrey,” she announced with sudden bravery. “ I wonder if Mr. Leonard would explain it a little ? ”

“ Perhaps you would do as well to wait until the evening now,” the mistress answered respectfully. “ He never likes to be interrupted.”

“ I must study my Latin then,” said the girl, with something like a pout. “ He always says that I may come up at any time, and if he is too busy he will say so. I don’t see any sense in mental philosophy, any way. I like things that belong to out-of-doors.”

“ I dare say you are right about asking him now,” said Miss Jaffrey after a mo-

ment's pause. Her brother's learned exposi-
tion of the Baconian philosophy the evening
before in that pleasant parlor had been to
her very dull and unrewarding, but she was
only a plain, uninstructed woman whose
choice of reading ranged through the hum-
bler level of fiction rather than among the
mandates of the philosophers. The young
girl gathered her books with alacrity and
went up the wide hall-staircase. There was
one step that announced her coming by a
peculiar creaking sound, and when Leonard
Jaffrey heard it, he fairly ran to open his
door.

Miss Jaffrey was possessed by an unusual
spirit of thankfulness when she was again
left alone. Life had been so much easier
for them all since Nelly Grant became a
member of the household; they all seemed
revivified by her fresh young life. She was
a mannerly child, surely, and had been so
considerate about making extra trouble, and
forcing her own companions and personal
concerns into undue prominence. It was
good for Leonard to have this new interest
to draw him away from his books. He
really had seemed in excellent spirits of late,
and lost the elderly look that he had begun

to wear. "What an advantage his society is to that girl who knows nothing of the world!" thought the admiring sister as she creased down the edges of a collar. Leonard had really for once noticed that he needed a new article of raiment, and had even advised a slight modernizing change in the old collar pattern. Dear, unworldly Miss Esther Jaffrey — where were your woman's wits!

In spite of Leonard's variation and deflection from his sister's ideal of the last of the Jaffreys, she still looked forward confidently to some less and less possible change. In one of the great camphor-wood packing chests lay a silk Geneva gown of which the folds grew sharper and the texture more limp year by year, but Miss Jaffrey touched it tenderly every spring and fall in her careful housekeeping as if the day might still come when Leonard would soberly deck himself in the ancestral garment. But the Geneva gown had long ago been too narrow for his plump back; it was cut for a slender, dutiful ascetic.

Sometimes Miss Jaffrey folded her hands in her lap and looked at her brother with pleased wonder at his vast learning. She tried to make it real to herself that he could read Greek and Hebrew and was way-wise in the most perplexing by-paths of ancient history. She was blessed with the gift of reverence, was Miss Jaffrey, like many another woman of her generation. She would have found it convenient if Leonard could have bestirred his feeble muscles enough to drive a nail straight or grapple with a rusty screw, but she never reproached him, and learned to use a hammer herself instead. With Nelly Grant's veneration for the scholar, her own pride and pleasure bloomed afresh. She was thankful to have her brother get a glimpse of fresh young life; it was in every way desirable to give him a little change from his books and creaking pen.

It was plain that Mr. Leonard Jaffrey himself was by no means averse to such refreshment. He became unwontedly agreeable, and lost a good deal of the dull expression of countenance and heaviness of motion which were the result of a good appetite and dangerous lack of exercise. As the spring days grew longer and brighter, and the snow disappeared and the early frogs piped loud and clear in the river marshes, Nelly besought her tutor and governor to take a walk after tea down the river road. She wanted to talk about her lessons, she said, and she hated to be shut up in the house all the time, now that the pleasant weather had come. It was such tiresome work studying, but she liked to have people tell her things that one ought to know. And Mr. Jaffrey amiably accepted her invitation, and took a stalwart ancestral walking stick from behind the hall door, smiling all the time at Nelly's girlish opinions of life.

Somebody jingled the shop door-bell impatiently for the second time and scuffed her feet about on the clean floor, and Miss Jaffrey obeyed the summons as if she were in a dream. She had watched the two figures depart up the street under the budding elms with a strange feeling of bewilderment, as if the air she breathed there at the parlor window held a kind of dull intoxication. She was vaguely afraid that poor little Nelly might grow over-fond of her stately companion, but the fear was driven away during an interview with a loquacious customer. Leonard would gravely discourage any silly feeling that a young girl might have. Miss Jaffrey smiled; for herself she would as soon fall in love with her brother's great dictionary as with himself. With all his worth, he was not her idea of a lover — and the dear soul blushed as if she were as young at heart as Nelly herself. Besides, the Jaffrey dignities sailed as high as the moon over the head of society in general, and Nelly did not even belong to Grafton society, dear fresh-faced little country-girl! The shop-bell jingled again and again. All feminine Grafton seemed to be in need of pins and needles. One or two of the women who lived along the street said meaningly that they had seen Miss Jaffrey's brother go by a little while before. But Miss Jaffrey responded with very little interest, as she counted out change or buttons for her curious customers. At that moment the scholar and his young admirer were strolling in the odorous dampness beside a long row of willows made shadowy by the twilight. "I get into such a hurry for the flowers to come at this time of the year," said the girl impulsively. "To my thought there is no flower so sweet as a youthful face," said Mr. Leonard Jaffrey. "You have made a constant spring in our quiet lives." And Nelly blushed as bright as any rose of the June for which she was waiting.

A spirit of eager youth drove away all the shadows and haunting ghosts from the Jaffrey house in that bright May weather. The young girls of the academy flitted in and out of the doorway, at first awed by the atmosphere of stateliness and fading grandeur so foreign to their more prosaic modern lives. Nelly was very popular among her classmates, and had a way of asking them to the farm by twos and threes to spend the Saturdays and holidays of term time. They felt much more at their ease in such surroundings, and secretly admired their hostess because she was so completely unawed and at home with severe Miss Jaffrey and her hermit brother. Miss Jaffrey was patient and affable in her place of business, but it was quite another matter when she rose to receive you in her parlor with that grand manner and simple welcome. The old house was always pleasant in the spring, and its mistress now found herself unusually cheerful and hopeful. She hardly dared to look forward to the time when her young housemate must disappear, not only with her gay young train, but with her generous contribution to the slender revenues of the housekeeping. There was a delightful reminis-

cence of the past in all the intercourse with
the farm. John Grant himself had been
reared in all the ancient spirit of respect
and even reverence for the Jaffreys, and
never ceased to show it or to acknowledge
Miss Esther's kindness and condescension
to Nelly. But he had a great respect for
the Grants, too, and looked upon them as
people who never need be ashamed of themselves or their forefathers in any company,
being people who paid their debts and did
their duty in the place to which it had
pleased God to call them. And John Grant
the rich farmer and honest selectman of
Grafton was as proud of his pretty girl as if
she were a princess. He gave himself great
credit for having hit on the best of all plans
for bringing her social gain and pleasure in
her last year at school. He was as fond of
the old place as any man could be of his
home, and hated the thought of leaving it
for a night; but in the early autumn, after
the crops were under cover, he meant to take
Nelly a journey to New York, perhaps even
to Washington and Mount Vernon, that
Mecca of every old-fashioned American's
pilgrimage. Once he was for a moment
possessed of a glowing thought that it would

be well to invite Miss Esther Jaffrey to
make one of this adventurous party, but his
good judgment rebelled. That would be
taking a social liberty : with whatever appreciation of kindness, Miss Jaffrey would
be sure to instantly decline. It was not
John Grant's habit to ask favors that must
be refused, but he was none the less loyal
to the first lady of Grafton.

VII.

Spring came to Grafton like an unan-
nounced young guest who steals into a dull
dismantled house and surprises the inhabitants with a charming gayety and laughing
voice, with a disorderly litter of fresh flowers and greenery all about the bare prosaic
rooms. Nelly herself might have personified in advance the welcome change of
season, and nobody greeted the coming of
spring with more joy than the young girl,
who went singing up and down the stairs,
and brought in Mayflowers and anemones
until Miss Jaffrey seriously announced that
there was no longer an empty china mug
or flower glass in the closets.

New England people are never quite sure

that they may not have another snow-storm until a certain day of movable date when the sun shines and the dry ground settles itself with a determination not to be mistaken. This day usually comes early in May, and gives conclusive evidence that winter is fairly gone. It is not a day when one can comfortably exert one's self, it is too much like summer. Only yesterday the east wind may have been full of shivers, but now Miss Jaffrey and Betty were busy in the upper part of the house, suffering more or less from the heat and from the cares of spring housekeeping. The fragrant air was blowing through the rooms, even Mr. Leonard had opened his window a little way, and propped it by a too thin book that was slowly bending together under the weight of the heavy sash.

The unseasonable heat did not end with the close of day, but a summer-like evening followed, lighted by a full moon. Everybody was out-of-doors, and though Miss Jaffrey was tired after her busy care-taking, she was kept in the shop until long after eight. The academy girls were weaving a fine romance about her of late, and liked to come to buy her wares. In June would be

the great exhibition day, and their hearts
were already more concerned about their
white gowns and their outward decoration
than about the improvement of their un-
scholastic minds. They hushed their chat-
ter and put on a more decorous and def-
erential manner as they came into Miss
Jaffrey's presence, but they smiled at each
other, and understood a great many things
without speech, the elder woman and the
gay girls.   Miss Jaffrey was very glad
when her revenues were all collected; the
long street was empty at last and silent,
the young people had all gone home, and
when the last garrulous neighbor had disappeared it was a great satisfaction to step
from behind the counter and close the shop
door and put the strong cross-bar in the
sockets.   When the light was out and the
two or three chairs were pushed back
against the wall, Miss Jaffrey gave a deep
sigh, and thought that she would just look
at the evening paper and then go to bed.
She was really very tired. Almost always
when there was a busy evening Nelly took
pleasure in coming in to help her. To be
sure their nearest approach to a misunder-
standing had followed a gentle reminder

that the parlor, not the shop, was the place for Nelly to receive and entertain her friends, and there had been a subsequent day or two of cloudy weather. The shop was much less demanding in a social way than the rest of the house, one must confess. But Nelly was busy with her lessons nowadays, and quite solemn and cheerful by turns about the approaching end of her school life. Mr. Leonard was obliged to render a vast deal of assistance. Either Nelly was stupid with her book or he was beginning to squander his time. Miss Jaffrey felt a sense of uneasiness as she stepped into the parlor. There was no light there yet, though it was so late in the evening, and she stumbled against a strayed footstool. The glass door that led into the old garden was wide open, — somebody had taken the trouble to force back the heavy inner shutter that was always drawn across the lower part of it in cold weather. Miss Jaffrey went to the door-sill and looked out. It was ridiculous in the girl to behave as if summer were already here, she would take cold in the dampness.

There was wonderful beauty in the familiar outlook, and Esther Jaffrey forgave the careless young offender as she herself yielded to the temptation. The air was deliciously soft and warm, there was a caressing sweetness in the fragrance of the old pear-trees which were standing like white ghosts of themselves all in full bloom in the moonlight. The box was sending up its heavy quaint odor — the lines of its winter-faded leafage led straight down the old path where the mistress of the house had walked to and fro on many nights like this. She stepped outside the house and stood under the first St. Michael's pear-tree, and drew a long breath close to its lowest branch. "How the old things keep on blooming!" she thought, with a rush of feeling at the remembrance of her own faded youth.

Two figures leaning close together came out of the shadows beyond a high syringa thicket. Miss Jaffrey's heart stood still. They were lovers, they were whispering to each other, and the man held the woman to his heart and kissed her. Leonard Jaffrey and Nelly Grant! the moonlight made them look the same age. Leonard's late spring-time was in full glory of flowering and delight.

"What does this mean?" cried Esther

Jaffrey in a voice that seemed strange to her own ears. " Nelly, you must go in at once. Leonard! Leonard! are you beside yourself ? "

"Somebody dearer than myself," answered Leonard with a famous burst of sentiment and valor. " Esther, you must be first to know how happy I am " — but Miss Jaffrey turned away and followed Nelly into the house with stately steps. Nelly had disappeared, and the sister waited for her brother to come in. It seemed as if they could see the indignant eyes of the family portraits through the dark.

"Go to your room, Leonard; I am tired out. I leave you to think what you have been doing in your thoughtlessness. Nelly must leave us at once," said Miss Jaffrey in the same hard voice, and the convicted listener meekly obeyed. There seemed little use in bolting the doors of the old Jaffrey house now that its pride and honor had fallen, but the mistress patiently went her nightly round, and was careful to follow all her time-honored customs of care-taking before she wearily climbed the stairs.

In three rooms that night were three wide-awake and troubled persons. Nelly cried

bitterly for a whole half hour at the woeful
ending of her new joy. Miss Jaffrey sat in
the moonlight, still and pale as if she were
made of wood. Mr. Leonard Jaffrey fell
asleep long before the first hour of the vigil
was past, but he was enough alive to the
gravity of the occasion not to go to bed. He
sat in the study chair by the table; it might
have been that the dangerously pendent volume on his bed's canopy could not refrain
from letting itself be the instrument of cap-
ital punishment.

It seemed very late in the night when the
scholar was roused from pleasant dreams by
a rap at his door. Before he could fairly
open his eyes, Miss Jaffrey entered, carrying
the last end of her candle in a tall silver
candlestick, and she placed this on the table
and stood looking at him, while he rubbed
his eyes and tried to remember what was the
matter and then to appear heroic. On the
whole it was a gratification to find that he
was disturbed enough not to go to bed, but
his sister relented sufficiently to say that he
might as well have been there, it was very
foolish to run the risk of getting cold at his
age.

"We are only as old as our hearts are,"

said Leonard, still looking upon himself as the successful lover, but his voice sounded like that of a whimpering boy.

"Be still, Leonard!" cried the over-wrought woman. Her own loveless life cried out suddenly, fired as it was by a piteous jealousy that was hard to bear. She saw her brother at last without the least disguise of sentiment. No hope was there any longer, of professorship, or pulpit; she had abased her pride and starved and forbidden the hopes of her own life for *this.*

"I thought that we must talk about Nelly as soon as possible," she said presently, in a stumbling, weak way. "I feel as if we have broken the trust of having her here, and John Grant will be free to blame us both" —

"Esther," said the culprit, leaving his chair somewhat stiffly, "I am engaged to marry his daughter. I do not see why you think our loving each other so disgraceful. The Jaffreys" —

"Don't, Leonard!" and Miss Jaffrey steadied herself by the table. "We must put all that by. What right have you to ask that young girl to marry you? What have you to give her? Are you going to let

John Grant support you? He is a clear-headed, right-minded man, and you have not a cent, unless I give it you; we have been nearer beggary in our lives than you have ever known. It would not be like you to think what John Grant will say."

"I shall stand before him as an honest man and a gentleman. I wish you would go to bed, Esther, and let things take their course. We are no poorer than we ever have been. I wonder that Nelly loves me, but she does, and she loves you. I have some work, very valuable data and that sort of thing, which I mean to prepare for publication. There may be duties in connection with the academy," murmured Mr. Leonard Jaffrey with some confidence.

"There is the shop," replied his sister, looking gray and old. "I have very few dollars laid aside after all these years. You must go to John Grant's to live," she said savagely, as if she meant it for a taunt. "No doubt he will remember that you are a Jaffrey."

"It would be too far from the post-office," said the placid, literal man, taking a step or two toward the door, which was slowly swinging open, released as if for a ghost's entrance by its worn latch, and then Miss Jaffrey, disheartened and shivering with excitement, left the room without another word. She was powerless with all her clever energy and loyal steadfastness before this purposeless creature of indolent drifting and lifelessness. Ah, well; she had often tortured herself in past years by wondering what would become of him if she died first; his future was secure now, even Betty would take his part and rejoice in the luxury that this marriage would make permanent.

VIII.

The pear-trees opened their blossoms all night, the maples and lilacs and syringas swelled their buds and showed fresh tips of green by morning. There were bluebirds and robins at work in the garden and singing high in the elms all along the Grafton street. It was a terrible ordeal for the three members of the family to meet each other at breakfast-time, but high tragedy is impossible by daylight, however suitable it may appear at night. Nelly Grant looked frightened and heavy - eyed and a little sulky;

Miss Jaffrey was thin and old, but most appealing, with a gentle stateliness that won the young girl's heart all over again. The lover looked and appeared exactly as usual.

"Nelly," said Esther Jaffrey, and she held out her hand to the girl. "Nelly, I have been very much grieved and worried, but I do not mean to be unkind. You are very young, a great deal younger than my brother and me, and you must not think of — this any more until your father has heard of it. My brother will talk with him as soon as possible, and you must be reasonable; there are so many things which make me think it would be unwise " — and then the good woman turned to the breakfast-table, and tried to behave as if nothing had happened. It was not a repast which was afterward remembered as having been cheerful or convivial, but it was brief and things were at least made no worse. Nelly helped Miss Jaffrey wash the china and silver afterward; she noticed curiously for the first time the handsome crest that was engraved on the silver cream-pitcher, and looked up to find her companion's eyes fixed upon her with unwonted coldness. The crest did not mean half so much to Nelly as one might have thought or wished, and was not in the least connected with her simple ambitions. Alas, how Miss Jaffrey's heart was aching! She had never been ashamed before as she was ashamed now. The Jaffreys were to be John Grant's dependents, unless he was sensible enough to cast them off and accuse them indignantly of lack of care for his daughter and her best interests. Alas, alas! If Nelly would only go to school it would be more possible to think what should be done; but it was a long hour from eight to nine, and Leonard would not even go to his study and take himself out of the way. If Miss Jaffrey had understood that the lovers were hoping to have a few words alone together, I do not think that she was in a frame of mind to have granted the opportunity.

There came a loud knock at the front door just as Nelly was coming down-stairs with her school-books. She looked rueful when she saw her father, and was startled into a fear that Miss Jaffrey had already summoned him, and that Lynch-law was to be served upon her love. But the other selectmen of the town were with him, and she waited on the stairs while they solemnly deposited their hats on the straight-backed mahogany chair by the parlor door and disappeared, then she flew out to school without even a greeting to her father, who started to call her back, and then remembered the important business in hand.

"We have come to see your brother on business this morning," said the spokesman, turning to Miss Jaffrey, though the brother was also in the room. "You are acquainted with the fact that the selection of a librarian for the new library built under our supervision, together with that of the committee, rests in our hands. We have said nothing of the time of decision, for fear that outside influence would be brought to bear. We don't feel as if we had any right to pass by such a distinguished lover of learning and a member of our most noted family, and now request Mr. Jaffrey to consider and accept. There will be arduous work in selecting the books and getting the thing going," said the selectman, relaxing from the effort of his previously composed speech, and beginning to grow red in the face and damp as to his skin, "but I can tell you there 's money enough to pay the bills, and for clerk-hire too, if he wants it. The regular salary at present, besides expenses, will be a thousand dollars a year."

Miss Jaffrey and her brother looked at each other; he at least was triumphant. "I accept this mark of confidence with profound thanks," said Leonard, bowing handsomely to the selectmen. "I shall feel that my long years of study have been in the providence of God a special training for the position."

Miss Jaffrey was dizzy and unnerved; she bade the selectmen good-morning, for they were in haste with morning calls at that season of the year, being busy farmers. The new librarian ushered them out with great politeness and closed the hall-door gently. Then he stopped a moment to reflect, and presently hurried back on tiptoe with a pompous smile. Miss Esther still stood where he had left her.

" I am very glad and proud, brother," she said with effort, and the great man was unexpectedly a little chilled.

" Esther," he answered amiably, as if he had something to forgive her, "I have always had confidence that the time would come when I should be able to repay your kindness. You must be done with the shop now. We " —

"*Never!*" said the pale old woman, but in spite of this, her heart felt curiously light. At that moment the shop-bell tinkled impatiently, and Miss Jaffrey went in, stately as a princess, to wait upon an early customer.

MÈRE POCHETTE.

I.

THE French Canadian village of Bonaventure seemed to have strayed away from its companions and lost itself in the interminable wilderness that lies between the settlements of the Eastern States and the St. Lawrence country. For many years the community was self-centred and the nearest market-town too far away to be of consequence. A visionary *seigneur*, an aerial, castle-building Frenchman who never took the trouble to leave his own château except to taste the joys of Paris, had sent out a colony to this new possession, but it dwindled away and did not flourish. The factor was proved a cheat at last, and the old count shrugged his shoulders, smiled, and resigned himself. Some of the disappointed settlers retraced the trail to the great river, but a few remained; they had their gardens and their pigs and chickens. Life might be far worse elsewhere.

The lumbermen came by and by with
their long axes; the old *seigneur's* timber
made rich other men than his heirs, while
Bonaventure flourished for a season with
new prosperity. The rough road over which
the great logs were hauled to a distant stream
proved a permanent thoroughfare, and now
and then a stranger came and stayed. The
mother-church sent a pastor to teach and
pray among these neglected children, and a
sharp spire, in glistening armor of tin, rose
above the later growth of spruces and maples that had hastened to conceal the great
stumps of the vanished pines. The first log
huts were one by one replaced by the high-
roofed houses of regulation shape and size
which one may see in Beauport, in Lorette,
in a hundred other villages of the French
régime. This was a small town, this Bonaventure, but it valued itself even more than
was necessary in later years. The hereditary
owners of the petty estates were apt to look
with suspicion upon any new-comers, and
when it was ascertained that a man called
Joseph Pochette from the neighborhood of
Quebec had bought the Rispé house and
land, with a piece of outlying forest, there
was a bitter arraignment of such proceed-

ings. Mère Poulette, who kept the village shop in her front room, was particularly angry, though one would have believed her ready to welcome a new customer. "Some crime has forced him to abandon his birthplace," she exclaimed, and glared round upon the startled company.

But Joseph himself, a good fellow enough, quickly pacified the neighborhood, especially as he died of fever within a year or two after his appearance in Bonaventure society. His funeral was a satisfactory one, but Mère Pochette had already drawn down upon herself the dislike of her associates. She was wickedly proud and independent, a blackhearted schemer who cared only to grow rich; and when she went by the houses with her fatherless baby in her arms, she won no compassion, for she asked none, and all hearts were on the defensive. Even the fact that old Poulette had not succeeded in making a good bargain with widow Manon for her woodland was not lost sight of, for had not this stranger the soul of an aristocrat under her peasant's clothes.

At last there was another change at Bonaventure; one day the surveyors came with their chains and compasses, and before any-

body could take time to fairly consider such
an innovation the new railroad was pushing
its way northward through the swamps and
forests. Now the piece of worthless waste
which Manon would not sell to Poulette —
the obstinate woman! — was sold to the company at an excellent price. It was all a
piece of luck, but the indignant chorus of
the little shop could not forgive such an out-
rage. As time went on, however, Providence
seemed to repay her for her behavior. Her
only child made an unfortunate match with
a foreigner, though it was well known that
Mère Pochette meant to buy the chit a rich
husband. Then she was presently burdened
with an orphan grandchild, and the chorus
chattered and sing-songed their satisfaction.
It took a stalwart character to keep its own
way with almost an aspect of serenity; there
was no light task in facing the dislike and
distrust of one's townspeople, though as
Mère Pochette grew richer and, if the truth
must be told, prouder and more powerful
year by year, her neighbors were civil enough
to her face and even obsequious, the worst
of them, whatever they might have said in
winter evenings behind her back. She had
devoted all her energies to securing a gener-

ous dowry for her daughter. The mistaken
girl had disregarded this provision, had
thwarted her mother's wishes, and had suffered enough, God knows! Now Mère Pochette's object in life was the wise ordering
of the little granddaughter, and when, by
and by, she was enviably settled in life, the
sneering by-standers might say what they
chose. This noble worldly ambition made
Mère Pochette glad to work early and late
and to toil and save. She would put her
grandchild where all the village might not
touch her. A career of pride and happiness
should be put into little Manon's future.

The neighbors were apt to look suspiciously at little Manon, the granddaughter,
as she went by their houses with quick, light
footsteps. She was of mixed race at any
rate. Her father was a young engineer from
the States who had married this old Manon
Pochette's handsome daughter, and they had
held their heads too high, the fools! and
shaken the dust of the little village off their
feet. It was the way of the world; one April
day their ribbons were flying, and they
laughed aloud together and never cared to
cast a look behind them at old friends; the
next spring a letter came, and the priest read

it to the widow, that her daughter Jeanne was
dead.   Presently the young engineer, broken
and spent by chills and fever and hard fortune, came creeping back with a cough and
a white scared face and an ailing motherless
baby to the high-roofed cottage.   Old Manon blessed herself, and waved her thrifty
hands in dismay.   She rolled her eyes and
made grimaces, and became eloquent in
patois sentences which her son-in-law did not
even try to translate for himself.   Then she
mounted to her garret and came down presently with the dusty cradle.   The wailing
child was fumbled and tumbled and smoth-
ered in coverings that seemed to have been
waiting for it, and the waning fire in the
high, square stove was rekindled, though the
May sun shone in benignantly.   The young
man coughed less often for a blissful hour;
he sank into an angular chair at the chimney
corner, and hid his face in his hands and
cried silently.

The little house had seemed as full of
romance as a scene at a play, the year before; he had not concerned himself with the
rest of the *habitants* of Bonaventure; they
were only the tawdry stage crowd that weeps
and exclaims in perfunctory unison while the

hero and heroine suffer real pains and know
true joys just behind the footlights. Now
the sentiment and the amusement had faded
out entirely. The garden of his life had suddenly been blackened by the most chilling of
frosts; it was late spring here in old Manon's
plain house, she was a stout, unsympathetic
old French Canadian; and as he had come
from the railway station tired to death with
his long journey and finding even the baby a
heavy burden, he had not been blind or deaf
to the unspoken jeers and curious glances
which were ready for him at almost every
house. He had once been a hero in his
petty fashion; the men of the village had
been obliged to obey him for a short three
months; he had disdained the women, all
except the pretty creature who had become
his wife. Whether he had regretted his
marriage nobody would ever know. It was a
dangerous experiment to carry her among
young girls whose training and schooling
had been of a better sort, but now there
was nothing sweeter or sadder to think of
than the days when they had been deep in
love. Poor Jeanne! her grave was left
alone in an unsheltered western burying-
ground. He could not see even that low

sandy mound again, and now that he had in despair begged and borrowed his way hither to bring little Manon to her grandmother, he felt that the great mystery of death would soon be made plain to him. The few men who remembered him on this new railroad had been very kind, and for a few hours his reinstatement to a semblance of his former position and relationship had brought back something of his old good comradeship and vigor. He even criticised the finish of the work which had been done since he went away, and discussed it with an acquaintance who was now an official of the company and journeying prosperously to the terminus at Quebec. A kind-hearted woman had helped him to take care of the baby; he had seen her eyes fill with tears at his bungling attempt to undress it the night before, but he could not cry himself. He had sometimes looked at the little trimming of the baby's dress for a half hour at a time, he remembered so well the tune his wife had sung as she sewed it on, and held and shaped it with her fingers, months ago. It seemed like years already, though the baby's short life almost linked that time to this.

.   .   .   .

The fire crackled in the box-stove, the little child was sound asleep in the great cradle; old Manon, the grandmother, stepped heavily to and fro, and now and then put a bowl or a plate on the kitchen-table. She muttered something about her poor little one, and clasped her hands ostentatiously, and seemed to consider the question of prayer, but gave a savage glance at the poor son-in-law instead, and went on her slow rounds about the room. He noticed that she looked ten years older than she had the year before, but it hardly surprised him, all the rest of the world was so changed, and then he looked wistfully at the plump bed in the corner, and longed to lie there and forget his weariness in sleep. He and Jeanne had run away to be married; her mother would not hear to the match, because this would-be son-in-law was not a Catholic. When he looked up at the mantel shelf, however, his own letter that told the stern mistress of the house of her daughter's death was displayed beside the brass candlestick and the little picture of St. Joseph which had been blessed by the archbishop. After all, was it not something to have a literate son-in-law?

In the next house and the house beyond, the neighbors were talking, and watching by turns the door which the traveler had lately entered. " It is well that Manon Pochette has made the round of the blessed stations of the cross every morning these many years," said the fierce dame who sat in her little shop across the way. "The saints warned her, she will be poor indeed and incapable, without their help, to bring up an infant of no gifts; a perfectly deplorable occasion, my friends," and she looked from one to another, while a doleful neighbor closed her eyes and groaned loudly. It was a great while since anything so interesting had happened in Bonaventure.

" He has been robbed of his haughty behavior," continued the first speaker. " A wicked pride indeed, but an abased manner of return to an insulted house. He will not toss pennies now to good Justin Poulette, who has indeed a safe subsistence, but spends nothing for fine clothes " —

" She threw them at his face," said doleful old Marie Binet sharply. " She had reason. If he treated Jeanne wickedly he now has his reward. She had an amiable appearance, but Mère Pochette clothed her like a doll, and the devil tempted her. She had not the look of a child whom one may believe either good or beautiful," and Marie Binet gazed at her acquaintances for confirmation. This was venturing too far. Marie was known to the initiated to be a thief and a liar, and she feigned not to notice a smile of derision while she took her basket of potatoes and went her way. She had her revenge; at the moment she closed the inhospitable door, and began to mutter a refreshing imprecation, Manon Pochette beckoned and called her eagerly from across the way. The audience within the little shop watched her from the window with envious eyes. Manon Pochette was one who kept her own secrets, she never had been one of the chosen company of gossips.

But this must be a dire emergency, for presently Marie reappeared without her basket. Somebody must go for Father David; the son-in-law had a few moments before slipped from his chair and become a dead weight of insensibility upon the floor; they had borne him to the bed; who could tell whether he might not be dead already?

"*Marche! marche!*" said Marie importantly, stamping her foot and raising her voice as if her betters were nothing but dilatory horses, and while some one hurried away to find his reverence, the rest followed her over to the Pochette kitchen.

In a few hours more the excitement was over and night had fallen. The young man's face was peaked and white, and his body was lying at its slender length, thin and forsaken of the poor warmth that life had lately kept. Manon was sitting by his side, rocking to and fro and keeping watch by herself. She had lighted some sacred candles which she had long been hoarding, and they were burning at the sleeper's head in the brass candlesticks. The priest had come in time, thank God! the despised son-in-law had opened his eyes and looked around bewildered for a moment. He had assented to, and even welcomed the offices of the church; they must have been to him a last and only provision against the evils that might be waiting for him and his. The baby was christened too; the father had already whispered, with an appealing look, that she was named Manon. Late in the night a waning moon rose solemnly above the level line of the horizon, and looked long at the few whitewashed houses with their high roofs. She

shone into the eastern windows all along the
row. The whole flat country was lying in
shadow; this faded moon at last looked into
one window that was apart from the rest, as
if she had an errand there. Manon was old
and tired, she would have no watchers, but
she had ceased her prayers and fallen asleep,
and the dead man's face wore a look of in-
effable peace. The candles were almost
burnt out, the poor baby cried sometimes in
a faint unexpectant way, and the moon hid
herself under the edge of a great cloud.

II.

Out of this nourishing of sorrow and
misfortune, like a plant that blooms best in
a hard cold soil, grew little Manon. Her
childhood was not a pleasant one in its surroundings, indeed a less vigorous nature
would have been stunted by the narrow life
and lack of sympathy. Bonaventure was a
selfish parish in spite of the lovely influence
of the old priest, Father David, who, worn
out with his service to a stolid flock, at length
lay down his terrestrial body to rest in the
tawdry burying-ground, while his spiritual

body went away to its own inheritance. The
new priest had come to the parish half un-
wittingly; it was a poor cure, and his house
and church were plain and uninviting. They
could give him no pedestal of worldly pride
and power. The new part of the village
grew steadily; over at the other side of
the railroad there were repair shops and
supplies of wood for the trains, and in that
quarter Bonaventure expanded itself. The
new parishioners were a somewhat lawless
set and distinct from the old residents; the
little priest was not man enough to control
them or to lift them up in the arms of his
faith. He moved about among them conscious of the dignity of the church, bland
and double, but an inoffensive creature in
the main, who wished things were better,
but also wished other people to take the
trouble of making them so.

Manon Pochette's house was still the last
one at that end of the row; she owned a
good bit of land just beyond it, and if you
crossed that you came to a swamp; the house
itself stood a good deal higher, and overlooked the wide country that stretched away
to the westward. Behind it was all the
eastern country, and from the low ridge there

was also a grand view of the railroad that carried idle people to and fro on the face of the earth.

To Manon·Pochette's mind the railroad was quite unnecessary except for carrying her wares and her neighbors to the market-twon. As for the passengers, they always seemed the same persons who went to and fro in the hurrying trains, for some foolish reason. She never went into a car herself, the saints defend it, no! She had duties in life, and a vocation, with a piece of land far too large for an old woman to till, and beside, there was the grandchild, who grew like a young fowl, with an unforeseen and impossible appetite into the bargain. The mother, Jeanne, had been no care at all; she had seemed to take care of herself entirely when one compared her with this one, who was a terrible child of desires and eagernesses. All Mère Manon's grievances against the young people had vanished long ago; it was fate that had been hard upon her, not they, and the good Lord had taken them to himself, poor children! Old Manon had said many a prayer for them in the bleak church of a winter morning, and had appeased her conscience by the number of masses she had caused Father David and Father Pierre to say for the good of such innocent souls. Yet occasionally, as she leaned on the heavy hoe to take a minute's rest as she worked among her cabbages, the old Adam in her nature got the better of such pious views of her affliction, and she grumbled to herself about that foolish infant, that ungrateful child, her daughter, or that worthless beggarly heretic, her son-in-law. But she kept their black wooden crosses in good order in the church-yard, and their memories came to her like pale ghosts beside the actual presence and constant demands of her young granddaughter.

III.

Little Manon was made up of puzzles and contradictions; the old peasant woman was more and more distressed and gratified by them day by day. She was glad to have the neighbors see that her grandchild was better than theirs — in fact she had always maintained a social advantage in Bonaventure corresponding to her residence on the highest point of the ridge. She overlooked Julie Partout and Marie Binet and Mère

Poulette disdainfully in more ways than one,
but she was exasperated all the same by little Manon's vagaries and differences from
her own standard.

The child was devoted to church-going —
she cried when she was very young to go
with her grandmother to mass, and her eyes
grew large and her face grew grave, when
she sat or knelt before the altar and looked
at its poor decorations of candles and gild-
ing and the votive offerings of faded artificial flowers and tinsel work that were arranged upon a smaller altar at the side.
Poor child, it was not because she was satisfied with this cheap splendor, but rather that
she caught the hint it gave of better glories,
that she liked to be in church. She gave
it no thought, as a bird sings in a cage and
praises the bit of sunshine at the garret
window, when it has never in all its life
spread wings to the current of a great wind
or gone swiftly through the bright noonday
air to a woodland nest. The grandmother,
who knew the human nature of the trans-
planted Frenchmen and women of her limited Canadian existence; who could tell at
once the value of a sheep or even a horse,
and the weight of a pig; who was shrewd

at gardening and clever at housekeeping;
who knew when she was lied to, or when
her dearest friend cheated her at a bargain;
old Manon, who was never stingy to the
priest, or behindhand at her devotions, who
thought herself entirely acquainted with
things of this world and sure of a respect-
ably high seat in heaven beside, — this same
old Manon was baffled at last and confessed
herself unable to understand her granddaughter. The only thing to be said was
that Manon the less was made of different
stuff.

Sometimes it seemed to the priest, who
knew the story of the child's parentage only
through the medium of the romancing vil-
lagers, that the vigor of the young father
and mother had been transferred to little
Manon — that their lives had been checked
and blasted to enrich this one descendant.
He was given to sentimentalizing a little, was
Father Pierre, the parish priest, and he felt
a great lack of excitement of the best sort in
Bonaventure. Sometimes he told himself
that he would see to it that little Manon had
some schooling. She should go to the school
of the Sacred Heart; she might surely have
a year or two first with the good gray nuns;

she must not be left to her own devices in
this hole of a place. Nobody seemed to
know much of the child's father. He had
told old Mère Pochette that he had neither
brothers nor sisters, but Father Pierre soon
discovered that the good woman did not like
to be questioned about her son-in-law. She
had felt a certain contempt for him because
he came from the States; besides, it was indeed a monstrous cowardice that he should
have died so miserably and so young, and
have made neither place nor fortune for
himself in the world. "They should have
waited for my consent," old Manon assured
herself. "I could not properly hold out always against them if he had been a good
man. He was a perfectly stupid pig not to
make sure of the wardrobe and dowry he
might have been certain I would give to
Jeanne. What was my wealth for if not for
my one daughter?" she would scold sadly,
pulling hard and fast at the weeds; but now
it would not be long before young Manon,
the little aggravation, would be finding herself a man. But if all the powers of heaven
would kindly aid, Manon at least should
have a respectable wedding before the high
altar, and should drive with her husband

and the wedding party as far across the
country as the season would allow. Old Manon was herself reared in Quebec, and her
hard brown face grew rosy and tender for one
moment as she thought of the train of caléches that followed her on her wedding-day.
The tall ungainly vehicles ; the shouts of the
guests ; the red-coated soldiers who stopped
in the narrow streets to see them pass ; the
miles of houses and the tall poplars of the
Beauport road, — the thought of it all came
back with a greater glory year by year.
" He was a good man to me from that day,"
said the widow to herself ; " he might have
done better than to bring me to this rat-hole
and leave me here ; but it was a good bit of
land and of an enormous cheapness, and he
knew that well. If the Lord had pleased to
let us remain together, and work in the same
world and watch each other grow old, like
the rest of the neighbors ! It was best so
if he must have one of us ; a woman can
work on the land, but a man is a simpleton
in his house. Joseph and Mary aid me with
these innocent cabbages that they may hold
up their heads ; the Lord send us rain, for
my poor bones will fail me to bring water
to the crops a day longer," and Manon

stopped to carefully bless herself as she knelt
at her work.   Little Manon was of no great
use in the garden, and she was frequently berated because she had not been a grandson
instead of a granddaughter.   She was apt not
to be very efficient in the house, but it was
not for lack of power or of discretion.   She
was idle and straying, and liked the fresh
air and the sunshine.   She was fond of visiting the priest's housekeeper of an afternoon,
and sometimes Father Pierre himself beckoned her into his own parlor, and gave her
lumps of sugar or well-dried figs from the
drawer of his writing-table.   She had her
mother's beauty and her father's persuasive
ways, but when she was in pain or her grandmother scolded her, little Manon grew pale
and pinched, and looked as her father did
that night he came back defeated and dying
to Bonaventure.   Old Manon was always
particularly aggrieved when she caught this
painful, surprising likeness, and began to
talk about her own sorrows in a wailing pet-
ulant tone that sent the young girl from the
house to seek elsewhere for comfort.

IV.

In this village, where the days dragged so slowly, the years had a way of vanishing unaccountably. Old Manon had never succeeded in getting her establishment quite to rights again, after the intrusion of the young engineer and his baby. She had made up her mind that certain changes and arrangements would be necessary, and she was an uncommonly executive person, as everybody knew. Suddenly one became aware that little Manon was grown up, and that there was danger of a lover. She was not old enough nor wise enough to think of such things, but elderly people always say that of girls, as if they themselves had waited for their husbands until the year before. Manon was unexpected in her choice; her grandmother was so conscious of her kinship to an unknown mass of strange, rich, willful, clever, and vagrant foreigners who belonged to the States, that she had vaguely looked forward to the appearance of a hero who should claim Manon's idle hand; a man, however, who had wealth and power, and who would be a son-in-law, indeed! But one

spring night the silly girl had come saunter-
ing home later than usual, laughing softly
and chattering like a swallow with young
Charles Pictou, of whom no one could say
anything good. A terror to the school-
mistress, a rebel at home and abroad; a.
youth who liked nothing but leading his dog
through the world, or lounging about the
railroad station to see the roaring engines
and the gaping strangers. Charles Pictou,
indeed! and Manon's light-heartedness was
promptly quenched by a vigorous box of her
pretty ears as soon as she had entered the
house. " Pick these beans, quickly," said
the cross old woman. "Am I to die of toil?
You would starve like the beasts if I were
not here to earn the bread for your foolish mouth." And in that moment a fierce
championship arose in little Manon's heart
for the lad whose whistle could even then be
heard distinctly, as if he were waiting outside,
longing to defend her in her distress.

That summer the crops were bad, and all
Canada was poor and complaining. The
lumber-yards were deserted, the rain spoiled
the grain, the fishermen were in distress, and
aid was to be sent to them in the forlorn
gulf villages. Once in a while some enter-

prising family had gone to the States, and indefinite rumors of their splendid prosperity had journeyed back along the straight shining lines of the railroad; but soon it became a common event, and the old women knitted in their doorways, and saw the younger neighbors go proudly away to seek their fortunes. The elder Manon was more contemptuous. " It is all one, here or there," she said to the priest's housekeeper; " the good-for-nothing expect to find a country where larks go to the oven and cook themselves, and apples fall sugared from the trees." She surveyed the paltry possessions of the emigrants with pity, and wished their owners good luck with compassion. " I am one who remains behind," she said stiffly, and shook her head until her flat black hat shuddered from a sense of its insecurity.

The autumn shut down dark and rainy; every few days some pale-faced sisters of mercy or of charity, in their quaint out-of-date garb, went flitting from house to house of the Bonaventure settlement, begging alms for the love of Mary and of Jesus, for some sufferers or for the impoverished church. The remote villages were in danger of famine. It was the worst harvest ever known, and in spite of reports that work was hard to find in the States, the trains were fuller than ever of emigrants. Bonaventure was tided over any great distress, in common with most of the railway settlements, but some of its inhabitants thought they were miserable because other people were, and at best life was neither too rich nor too comfortable. In the Western States there were whole farms given away; in the East there were mills where even the children could earn great wages. The little place was in a ferment, the quiet habitants had never been so excited and restless. The old women croaked, they were condemning some persons for going, and others for staying. Father Pierre laid down his mass-books and tried to calm his people, but those who remembered his predecessor spoke often of the benignant presence of Father David, and openly reminded each other of his value to the parish. The fiery French nature began to show itself unpleasantly, and households were divided against themselves.

The gloomy weather continued, the winter drew near. Little Manon and old Manon went their separate ways, for the young girl

was disobedient and would not listen to her
grandmother's objections and commands.
She and Charles Pictou loved each other
dearly, and were only wondering how they
could manage to marry. He also was an
orphan, and the aunt with whom he had
lived was but a poor woman, and lately had
gone away with her five thin children to the
States. Of late years he had helped to support the household, for he earned a bit of
money now and then; but now he was growing older and he would work his fingers to
the bones for Manon if there were anything
to do. He was full of hope, he would have
gone away afoot long ago if it had not been
for Manon. The grandmother had talked a
great deal in these last days about sending
her to school at a nunnery in Quebec, and
the young girl knew what it meant; she
knew, too, that while everybody else was poor
there were loose bricks in their chimney that
covered shining money. Sometimes she
wondered if it would be wrong to steal some
of it to give to Charles, so that he might go
away to make a home where they could live
together. Father Pierre had never liked
young Pictou, the lad's shrewd eyes had seen
more than was necessary, and lately Charles

had stayed away from mass. But as for the housekeeper, she was on Manon's and her lover's side, and sometimes when the priest sat with her grandmother, Manon slipped over to the great house and took revenge in confiding her dear secrets to so kind a friend as old Josephine. Josephine's little room was like a nun's with its bare boards and its worn crucifix, and pictures of various suffering saints. The good soul had once cherished a certainty that she had a vocation, and told Father Pierre that she must join a sisterhood of great sanctity and benevolence, but the priest had persuaded himself and her that she was wrong. He could not imagine where he should supply her place; surely this also was a vocation, and Josephine was a most careful cook. Life in Bonaventure must not become any more difficult.

But in the face of disapproval at home and distress abroad, the young people fairly flaunted their contentment and happiness. They were sure that Charles would somehow get to the States, and that he would soon become able to send for Manon or to come for her. "The old tyrant is right," Charles said magnanimously. "She knows I should be able to take care of you, and so I should indeed. But she might show some confidence in me," and he stamped his foot and twirled the tassel of his raveled red worsted belt.

V.

The sweet sad day came at length, without note or warning. Josephine herself, after scores of prayers and misgivings, had ventured to offer Charles a liberal assistance from her slender savings, and he was off like a falcon, after a few hurried kisses and promises to his sweetheart. He ran to the next station, five miles away, to catch an express train which did not stop at Bonaventure, and the girl with tearful eyes went down to the village, to the place where the street crossed the track, to catch a last glimpse of her lover. She wished that Charles had been able to say a prayer in the church, but she would do that for him. Her woman's heart shrank from the strangeness and dangers which he might meet, but she longed to go with him; she would have braved sorrow and want if she could have gone with him to the States. It seemed very lonely in the old cottage, when she returned ; she passed her grandmother, who sat in the doorway looking surly and dismal, without a word. The sky was covered with low-lying gray and silver-white clouds, the black spruce woods stretched away cold and thin to the level horizon. It was almost winter weather, and she was alone and felt unsheltered in that great flat landscape with its threadbare coat. She hoped that she need not go down to the station again for a long time to come. She had not seen Charles on the train, there was such a roar and dustiness as the train rushed by and a crowd of young men; one of those with the red sashes must have been Charles himself; had shouted adieu, or sung noisily. She felt as if every one of them were laughing at her own secret, and hated the strange faces that stared at her for one miserable moment before they were swept out of sight. Charles was a thousand times more skillful than the other lads of Bonaventure ; he could surely make his way, but to what temptations might he not yield, and only yesterday they had been together, and separation had seemed almost impossible ; at that hour the States had seemed as remote as Heaven.

VI.

Now that Manon's heart had gone away from Canada, she seemed more a foreigner than ever. All her thoughts and hopes had gone to the States with her lover, and the short days seemed long and dreary. In the house she tried to serve her grandmother well, she hardly cared to go out-of-doors at all, and sat near the fire, sewing, or picking beans with a far-away look in her eyes that made her companion more and more angry. They had said nothing to each other about Charles since their first fierce battles earlier in the year. The provincial life was very dull at best. One has only to look at the transplanting of the French peasants, child-ish, mercurial, and full of traditions and grievances, from their ancient civilization to this untamed wilderness — only to think of their being carried by a sort of social inertia over the roughness of their changed condi-tions, to understand the incongruities of Canadian life in the remote settlements. By the time Manon was grown there were few *fêtes* and but little revelry and amuse-ment of any description. The young men

soon hardened into stolid farmers, who discussed the politics of the province and scru-
tinized the behavior of their English rulers
with more or less inapprehension. They
grew stupid and heavy; they drank gin
and bad beer; some of the wives had a hard
time of it, and one would hardly recognize
their relationship to the merry vine-growers
and soldiers who had been their ancestors.
Old Manon Pochette preserved many of the
old customs; she was more a French peasant
and less a Canadian than her neighbors,
but young Manon, who had been seeing life
of late through a glamour and dazzle of happiness, sat listlessly in the clean bare cottage,
and wished herself away. There was a col-
ored print of a saint with a bleeding heart,
which the grandmother had bought from a
peddler. Manon had hated it once with
its woebegone look, but now she looked to
it often for sympathy and companionship.
The brass candlesticks still decorated the
high shelf above the stove. The same angular chairs and tables which thrifty Joseph
Pochette had made himself stood in order
around the room.

The chief thing to be hoped for was a
letter, but none came from young Pictou;

perhaps the noisy company he had joined on the train had beguiled him, and he had already forgotten Bonaventure. He had promised to send a letter to Josephine's care at the priest's house, but presently she was found one day in tears and shook her head dismally when Manon asked the often repeated question. The girl's sharp eyes discovered that some enemy had guessed her simple plot, and went away to pray, not for patience but for vengeance. Later, as she entered the house, she found old Marie Binet warming herself by the stove. The drifts were deep out-of-doors and the girl came in softly enough in her great snow boots, but her grandmother feigned not to hear her. "He was a good-for-nothing" she was grumbling; "he will never return, and at last I have nothing to fear. I had already directed Father Pierre to advance the price of a ticket from me, when that trembling fool Josephine forestalled the plan."

Manon stood on the threshold and the old women quailed at the sight of her angry eyes. "Come in from the snow," growled the mistress of the house, "my old bones ache already, and you will like to see me bent double."

"Another year," and she had quite re-
gained her self-possession, — "another year
and I will go to the shrine of La Bonne Ste.
Anne. It will be a pretty tour for thee, too,
Manon," she added in a softer tone, but Manon's ears had become deaf. "Another year,"
she was saying to herself; " I may be dead
then, and if not, to go with a groaning procession of cripples ! God forbid!" and tears
filled Manon's eyes, and even fell down upon
the well-scoured floor. "Where is my letter?" she said suddenly, and turned fiercely
upon her grandmother.

Old Manon was equal to so slight an occasion. Father Pierre himself was deep in
this intrigue, which gave it a certain dignity
and value. "Letter!" she repeated, "you
never had a letter in your life, and why
should I covet it who cannot read even my
mass-book? Ungrateful, listen to me! Next
year you shall go to Quebec and see fine
things; to Lorette church, and to the chapel
of the Seminary, where are blessed relics.
That is all the world; when one has seen
Quebec, one knows everything. I have a
little money saved from my poor garden,"
she added amiably by way of explanation to
old Marie, who nodded sagely. " It is some-

thing to pray for — Quebec!" Marie responded devoutly, but the foolish girl would not listen, she was pressing her forehead against the cold window-pane and staring out into the starlit night. What fools she and Charles had been! Of course Father Pierre had taken the letter from the post and given it to her grandmother. Old Manon fairly chuckled with satisfaction, and went on chattering with her guest. After this startling episode, they spoke a quaint dialect, clipping their thin words, and dwelling lightly on the objectionable letters. Such language belonged to the lips and not the heart, one would say who listened and did not understand.

Marie did not mean to stay any longer than she could help; she was too anxious to give herself the pleasure of reporting such a bit of news elsewhere. Some persons would take the lovers' part, and there might be a fine discussion presently, in the little shop across the way. Manon Pochette was in most things a shrewd woman; one cannot tell why she chose to make a confidant of the least reliable of her neighbors.

Manon the younger grew more and more angry that night and longed more and more to find her hoped-for letter. If she could only hold it in her hand, she believed that she could easily wait for daylight and read it aloud then over and over, until she knew it by heart. She lay in bed beside her grand-mother with wide open eyes until she heard the familiar long-drawn breaths that be-longed to sound sleep. Then she crept out softly, and went like a mouse about the room ; she felt in the capacious pocket, in a little box that was under a loose board in the floor. Her heart beat fast as she unwound the long cord that fastened it, but there was no letter anywhere. The old woman was growing deaf lately, and could not have heard such gentle movements, but it seemed a perilous enterprise, and proved to be a dis-appointing one. If Manon only knew where to write to her lover, or if she only knew how to follow him, it would be enough, but she cried herself to sleep that night and the next night and the next. Before many weeks were spent, Father Pierre went away suddenly and a stranger came to take his place.

VII.

The winter months passed by, there was sickness in the village of Bonaventure, and everybody longed for the spring. Manon had grown thin and pale; she could not eat, she would not smile, her life was spoiled at its outset, and Josephine, who had meant to be a friend to the young people, bewailed her indiscretion and wished that she had tried to keep young Pictou at home. There was plenty of work now at the station; they had even brought some young men from elsewhere, and Charles might have been well established, if only he had gained a little patience. "We that fight for ourselves make enemies of Heaven," she sighed, and tried to make amends with prayers and piteous confessions of her sins. As for the letters, they had long ago been read and laughed over and burnt in the priest's room, and Father Pierre had given old Manon a generous glass of wine. Josephine had seen it through the keyhole. She never told little Manon of that; she would not lower the child's reverence for the priest and for sacred things. Father Pierre had always hated Charles; alas for that poor human nature that even his holy calling could not lift above the earth and its weaknesses.

When Mère Pochette looked at her young housemate, and in spite of herself could not help pitying the dull eyes that had once been so bright, and the faded cheeks, she forgave herself her share in the sad change; for was not she thinking always that every day added something to her possessions, and that by and by she would find a suitable young man, and would go frankly to him and announce the magnitude of little Manon's dowry. All the lads gave shy glances at her, the pretty simpleton! There must be thriving grandsons of her old Quebec acquaintances by this time; she would fling her money east and west at the wedding, and then work on among her vegetables until her time for departure came. "All, yes, she shall have all," the old woman muttered once in a while, and blessed herself at the thought.

At last her plans began to take definite shape, since it was plain something must be done. The neighbors need not scowl at her, for was not she meaning to make the long-talked-of journey to Quebec as soon as the first fine weather came, and her garden was

made and planted? That would pay Manon
for all her fancied grievances, and as the
winter waned the glories of that expedition
pictured themselves brighter and brighter.
Manon should find a rich husband there for
a certainty, of a description and with such
amiable qualities. She herself would indeed
like to see the old city again and those of
her friends who were left. Manon would
think no more of that foolish, handsome
beggar lad who had forgotten her after all;
she had nothing else but him to think of
in Bonaventure, but in Quebec she would
quickly console herself. "For what have I
slaved myself all these years?" the old woman would demand angrily of Marie. "I
have a right to forbid her marriage with a
worthless lad, and I only step in to keep her
from her mother's fate—my good Jeanne,
who was thrown away to a vagabond."

But when the early spring came, little
Manon had lost her strength and her youthful spirit altogether. She cared nothing
for the stories about Quebec, which were at
last paraded desperately. She sat all day
in the doorway, watching the long trains
come across the plain and go away into the
dim distance of the north. The clouds of

spring hung low, and when sometimes a clear band of light was left above the western horizon, she grew hopeful and gazed at it as if some blessed vision might appear there for her reassurance. It seemed as if the child of misfortune and sorrow must have disappointment for her inheritance. The neighbors scolded to each other about old Manon Pochette's vast wealth, and repeated their conviction over and over that she would soon only have herself to hoard it for, if she did not take care.

One night there came a summons to the grandmother that Father Henri, the new priest, desired her to remain at the church after early mass next morning. Mère Pochette obeyed somewhat unwillingly; she was shy of this stranger, and angry beside that indulgent Father Pierre had been superseded. He had carried more than one of her secrets out of harm's way, that was a comfort; and she did not mean to take another spiritual adviser so far into her confidence.

She left her granddaughter sleeping, and sighed a little as she stood by the bedside looking at the sad face of the young creature who was after all the dearest thing in the

world. Once or twice lately the thought
had crossed her mind that the first thing to
be thought of in Quebec was a good doctor.
More than one silly girl had pined away
and faded out of this world like the April
snow-drifts — for nothing but love's sake;
while if only young Pictou's presence would
cure little Manon, nobody knew where to
find him. Perhaps Father Pierre would
remember, but where was he?

Early mass was over, the sun was well
above the horizon, and began to shine warmly into the bare church, and the tarnished
finery of the altar glittered and looked quite
splendid. It might be that the new priest
meant to beg for a great sum of money for
the restoration of the church; some one had
said he had this much at heart, and Manon's face was black for a moment with resentment. She was truly very anxious now
about the sick girl at home. As she knelt
at her prayers her thoughts kept wandering
homeward instead of to a vague heaven, and
a great throne to which the Bonaventure
altar was a plaything. What would life be
worth if little Manon should die? Such an
event would make her own prayers and good
works worse than useless, for it was her own

short-sightedness that had brought this grief. There were only a few old people left in the church, who had nothing else to do and could take their time at their rosaries ; the altar boys had scuffled in the vestry and gone away, leaving their tumbled and torn ecclesiastical raiment on the floor. Father Henri had flushed angrily when he caught sight of them, and quickly opened the door to call the young rascals back, but a moment afterward he gently shut it, and came out into the church tall and slender, with a grave sweet face, stopping to kneel before the altar as he passed before it to where old Manon Pochette seemed to be diligently praying. She was watching him through a narrow crack of her eyelids, but she bowed her head as he approached and pressed the small worn crucifix to her breast. The slender cord broke, the beads separated and fell with a patter like hail upon the floor. " Do not gather them now," said Father Henri hurriedly, but somehow the old woman did not dare to look higher than the frayed hem of his long black gown. It was scant and made of poor material, she observed, and the thought seemed like a reprieve that she would make him a present of a new one at

Easter.   Easter was late that year, and
there would still be time.   Josephine would
know the proper means to use and the cost
of such a benevolence.

She rose to her feet and followed the
good man; they made obeisance together
side by side as they crossed to the vestry
door.   The old parishioners regarded this
with interest, and wondered what was going
to happen, taking counsel of each other in
loud whispers as the door was shut.   Mère
Pochette's heart was quaking; she watched
the priest while he picked up the small vest-
ments and half smiled as he heard the owners' merry voices outside.   Then he turned
and took a letter from his pocket.   "I
bring good news to you and yours," he said
courteously; and Manon the elder, who had
feared some dire calamity,—the loss of her
savings or the death of young Pictou for a
certainty,—found herself growing faint and
dizzy.   "Sit down, my child," said the
priest.   "You are no doubt fasting.   Listen,
I will read this letter."

Once to hear such news would have given
Manon a fancied foretaste of Heaven; now
she heard it without excitement, almost
with disappointment.   Her poor grandchild's

father had been one of a respectable family, and now a sum of money equal to the old Canadian's own fortune had fallen to the poor sick girl at home. The lawyer had been at some trouble to trace the heir. Father Henri volunteered to answer the communication, and with some surprise at the manner in which it had been received he turned away. He had much business on hand that day, there was a visit to be made to a dying person miles away down one of the long muddy roads of Bonaventure parish.

But old Manon had fallen upon her knees; she was weeping sorely and begging for a blessing. She had sinned; she was avaricious and stony-hearted; the good God was punishing her already with the pains of hell, and taking her one treasure to himself.

Father Henri listened with dismay. " I am cursed by this wealth," she groaned, and groveled upon the floor at his feet. He knew that the young girl was ill, but in that bleak country one learns to take such dispensations without surprise; the tender creatures are kindly gathered to the dear saints, and taken up from this blighting and evil world.

"Listen," said Manon Pochette, at last regaining her composure and standing before the priest determinedly. "Listen, you must find for me this Charles Pictou before it is too late. I cannot let this my child die with hatred in her heart toward me. I am an old woman; I have had my way long enough, and it brings me only sorrow and shame. I will send him money. I will treat him as my own son. I will tell him all, for I burnt the letters that he wrote to Manon long ago. If he has taken another in her place, the punishment will be mine." Was this the hard-faced woman who had looked scornfully in even Father Henri's face? He closed his saintly eyes and said a prayer as he stood before her, and raised his hands as if to call down mercy upon the stricken gray head. "I will talk with you this evening," he promised, and they parted silently.

Little Manon had waked and arisen, and presently she crept feebly to the window to watch for her grandmother. She wondered what kept her so long away. The big black hats of the neighbors had reappeared in the short street, and the day was begun as usual. The men were off to their work, and the

children were gathering around the school-
house. The sun was bright and clear, and
the girl felt strengthened and cheered by it.
She heard the cars presently; perhaps Charles
might yet come back, though she had almost
ceased to look for such a happiness. She
grew hungry, she became tired with the ex-
ertion of crossing the room, she was so weak
that the tears began to flow down her thin
cheeks. " My grandmother cares nothing
for me, nothing," she mourned; " she is bar-
gaining with old Philippe, the gardener;
every year she is less generous; " but at that
moment Mère Pochette was kneeling in passionate grief at Father Henri's feet in the
chilly vestry.

At last she approached, and little Manon
was filled with wonder at her look. "You
must get well in this good weather," she
said; " we will go soon to Quebec, and you
shall have the one you love best for company. Forgive me at last, my child," but
the sick girl could not comprehend the full
meaning of such words, though the speaker
stood there appealing, repentant, the square,
sensible business woman who could be
cheated by no one. And now little Manon
rose and put her arms close about the weep-

ing grandmother's neck. Only yesterday faithless Marie Binet had announced that this neck should in the name of justice be encircled by a halter.

The train from the States was just out of sight that very morning — its long plume of smoke had hardly drifted away in the clear air before a handsome young man came lightly up the street. He did not stop at any of the drinking shops near the station, as most men did, but he hurried toward the older village on the ridge above — the straight, uniform row of ancient French houses, and from several of these eager eyes followed him to the end of the settlement. Then the various housekeepers rushed out to confer with each other upon the astonishing event of young Charles Pictou's incomprehensible return. It was like unneighborly old Mère Pochette to have sent for him without giving anybody the pleasure of knowing it, but at that moment she was thanking blessed Mary and Joseph, her patron saints, for this miracle straight from the skies. It was seldom at any rate that an emigrant returned so soon. Charles had a prosperous air already, and the whole village was in commotion that morning, while Father Henri was called to a noble feast the moment he returned from his errand of consolation.

The young habitants, who still wore red worsted belts with tassels, looked at their former neighbor's fine clothes with admiration. He was earning good wages with prospect of advance, but he had become too miserable at the strange silence. He was not so very far away, and had taken his first chance to see little Manon again. He had sent letters to prudent Father Pierre, but that worthy had kept silence, being at any rate at a great distance from Bonaventure over seas.

So Manon's strength came back again in this sunshine of happiness, and the lovers presently were married and lived their simple lives together. The world was a comfortable place enough without going to Quebec, but the occasion of Mère Pochette's grandchild's wedding could be marked by nothing less than such a journey, and she saw her children lead their procession of caléches, with immense complacency, living her own youthful joys over again in their behalf, as one returns in autumn to the meadows where one has gathered the flowers of spring.

Old Manon bore a vast bundle when she

returned to Bonaventure, and took from it
proudly a handsome cassock for Father
Henri.   The good man was at his devotions,
but she gave it to Josephine and lingered
for a few moments to have a friendly talk.
She had brought Josephine herself a remembrance of less value. "He is a blessed
saint, this father," the stayer at home said.
" He speaks no harsh word, but goes before
us like a holy shepherd! " and the housekeeper blessed herself as devoutly as she
could have blessed the priest himself.   The
ancient holiday maker could not linger; her
shrewd eyes had detected a grievous neglect
of her young cabbages on the part of their
guardian, old Philippe. He had not expected her home so soon, the pig! Presently the round black hat made its appearance among the weeds, a new and imposing
great black bonnet having been laid aside,
and one would find it hard to believe that
Mère Pochette had taken so great a journey.

The neighbors came one by one without
fear or reproach and leaned over the railing
of the garden. They were all very good-
natured, for had not one of their own Bonaventure lads secured the old miser's money
after all ? The high-roofed white house was

lonely that night; the upper casements were wide open, and the color of little Manon's deserted red geraniums could be seen in the bright moonlight. Little Manon herself, rich and happy, had gone away to the States.

Works of Fiction

PUBLISHED BY

HOUGHTON, MIFFLIN AND COMPANY,

4 PARK ST., BOSTON; 11 E. 17TH ST., NEW YORK.

Thomas Bailey Aldrich.

Story of a Bad Boy. Illustrated. 12mo $1.50
Marjorie Daw and Other People. 12mo 1.50
Marjorie Daw and Other Stories. Riverside Aldine
    Series. 16mo 1.00
Prudence Palfrey. 12mo 1.50
The Queen of Sheba. 12mo 1.50
The Stillwater Tragedy. 12mo 1.50

Hans Christian Andersen.

Complete Works. In ten uniform volumes, crown 8vo.
A new and cheap Edition, in attractive binding.
The Improvisatore; or, Life in Italy 1.00
The Two Baronesses 1.00
O. T.; or, Life in Denmark 1.00
Only a Fiddler 1.00
In Spain and Portugal 1.00
A Poet's Bazaar 1.00
Pictures of Travel 1.00
The Story of my Life. With Portrait 1.00
Wonder Stories told for Children. Illustrated . . . 1.00
Stories and Tales. Illustrated 1.00
    The set 10.00

William Henry Bishop.

Detmold: A Romance. "Little Classic" style. 18mo 1.25
The House of a Merchant Prince. 12mo 1.50
Choy Susan, and other Stories. 16mo 1.25
The Golden Justice. 16mo 1.25

Björnstjerne Björnson.

Works. *American Edition*, sanctioned by the author,
    and translated by Professor R. B. Anderson, of the
    University of Wisconsin.
The Bridal March, and Other Stories. 16mo . . . 1.00

Captain Mansana, and Other Stories. 16mo . . . $1.00
Magnhild. 16mo 1.00
Complete Works, seven volumes in three. 12mo.
    The set 4.50

Alice Cary.

Pictures of Country Life. 12mo 1.50

John Esten Cooke.

My Lady Pokahontas. 16mo 1.25

James Fenimore Cooper.

Complete Works. New *Household Edition*, in attrac-
    tive binding. With Introductions to many of the
    volumes by Susan Fenimore Cooper, and Illustra-
    tions. In thirty-two volumes, 16mo.

Precaution.	The Prairie.
The Spy.	Wept of Wish-ton-Wish.
The Pioneers.	The Water Witch.
The Pilot.	The Bravo.
Lionel Lincoln.	The Heidenmauer.
Last of the Mohicans.	The Headsman.
Red Rover.	The Monikins.
Homeward Bound.	Miles Wallingford.
Home as Found.	The Red Skins.
The Pathfinder.	The Chainbearer.
Mercedes of Castile.	Satanstoe.
The Deerslayer.	The Crater.
The Two Admirals.	Jack Tier.
Wing and Wing.	The Sea Lions.
Wyandotté.	Oak Openings.
Afloat and Ashore.	The Ways of the Hour.

(Each volume sold separately.)

Each volume 1.00
The set 32.00

New Fireside Edition. With forty-five original Illustra-
    tions. In sixteen volumes, 12mo. The set . . . 20.00
(Sold only in sets.)

Sea Tales. New *Household Edition*, containing Intro-
    ductions by Susan Fenimore Cooper. Illustrated.
    First Series. Including —

The Pilot.	The Red Rover.
The Water Witch.	The Two Admirals.
Wing and Wing.	

Second Series. Including —

The Sea Lions.	Afloat and Ashore.

Jack Tier.   Miles Wallingford.
The Crater.
    Each set, 5 vols. 16mo $5.00
Leather-Stocking Tales. New *Household Edition*, containing Introductions by Susan Fenimore Cooper. Illustrated. In five volumes, 16mo.
The Deerslayer.   The Pioneers.
The Pathfinder.   The Prairie.
Last of the Mohicans.
    The set 5.00
Cooper Stories; being Narratives of Adventure selected from his Works. With Illustrations by F. O. C. Darley. In three volumes, 16mo, each 1.00

Charles Egbert Craddock.

In the Tennessee Mountains. 16mo 1.25
The Prophet of the Great Smoky Mountains. 16mo . 1.25
Down the Ravine. Illustrated. 16mo 1.00
In the Clouds. 16mo 1.25
The Story of Keedon Bluffs. 16mo 1.00

Thomas Frederick Crane.

Italian Popular Tales. Translated from the Italian. With Introduction and a Bibliography. 8vo . . . 2.50

F. Marion Crawford.

To Leeward. 16mo 1.25
A Roman Singer. 16mo 1.25
An American Politician. 16mo 1.25
Paul Patoff. Crown 8vo 1.50

Maria S. Cummins.

The Lamplighter. 12mo 1.50
El Fureidîs. 12mo 1.50
Mabel Vaughan. 12mo 1.50

Parke Danforth.

Not in the Prospectus. 16mo 1.25

Daniel De Foe.

Robinson Crusoe. Illustrated. 16mo 1.00

Margaret Deland.

John Ward, Preacher. 1 vol. 12mo 1.50

P. Deming.

Adirondack Stories. "Little Classic" style. 18mo . .75
Tompkins and Other Folks. "Little Classic" style. 18mo 1.00

Thomas De Quincey.

Romances and Extravaganzas. 12mo 1.50
Narrative and Miscellaneous Papers. 12mo . . . 1.50

Charles Dickens.

Complete Works. *Illustrated Library Edition.* With Introductions by E. P. Whipple. Containing Illustrations by Cruikshank, Phiz, Seymour, Leech, Maclise, and others, on steel, to which are added designs of Darley and Gilbert, in all over 550. In twenty-nine volumes, 12mo.

The Pickwick Papers, 2 vols.
Nicholas Nickleby, 2 vols.
Oliver Twist.
Old Curiosity Shop, and Reprinted Pieces, 2 vols.
Barnaby Rudge, and Hard Times, 2 vols.
Martin Chuzzlewit, 2 vols.
Our Mutual Friend, 2 vols.
Uncommercial Traveller.
A Child's History of England, and Other Pieces.
Christmas Books.
Dombey and Son, 2 vols.
Pictures from Italy, and American Notes.
Bleak House, 2 vols.
Little Dorrit, 2 vols.
David Copperfield, 2 vols.
A Tale of Two Cities.
Great Expectations.
Edwin Drood, Master Humphrey's Clock, and Other Pieces.
Sketches by Boz.

Each volume $1.50
The set. With Dickens Dictionary. 30 vols. . 45.00
Christmas Carol. Illustrated. 8vo, full gilt 2.50
The Same. 32mo 75
Christmas Books. Illustrated. 12mo 2.00

Charlotte Dunning.

A Step Aside. 16mo 1.25

Edgar Fawcett.

A Hopeless Case. "Little Classic" style. 18mo . 1.25
A Gentleman of Leisure. "Little Classic" style. 18mo 1.00
An Ambitious Woman. 12mo 1.50

Fénelon.

Adventures of Telemachus. 12mo 2.25

Mrs. James A. Field.

High-Lights. 16mo 1.25

Harford Flemming.

A Carpet Knight. 16mo 1.25

Baron de la Motte Fouqué.

Undine, Sintram and his Companions, etc. 32mo . . .75
Undine and other Tales. Illustrated. 16mo . . . 1.00

Johann Wolfgang von Goethe.

Wilhelm Meister. Translated by Thomas Carlyle. Portrait of Goethe. In two volumes. 12mo . . . $3.00

The Tale and Favorite Poems. 32mo 75

Oliver Goldsmith.

Vicar of Wakefield. *Handy-Volume Edition.* 32mo, gilt top 1.00

The Same. "Riverside Classics." Illustrated. 16mo   1.00

Jeanie T. Gould (Mrs. Lincoln).

Marjorie's Quest. Illustrated. 12mo 1.50

Thomas Chandler Haliburton.

The Clockmaker; or, The Sayings and Doings of Samuel Slick of Slickville. Illustrated. 16mo . 1.00

A. S. Hardy.

But Yet a Woman. 16mo 1.25

The Wind of Destiny. 16mo 1.25

Miriam Coles Harris.

Rutledge.   A Perfect Adonis.
The Sutherlands.   Missy.
Frank Warrington.   Happy-Go-Lucky.
St. Philips.   Phœbe.
Richard Vandermarck.

Each volume, 16mo 1.25

Louie's Last Term at St. Mary's. 16mo 1.00

Bret Harte.

The Luck of Roaring Camp, and Other Sketches. 16mo   1.50

The Luck of Roaring Camp, and Other Stories. Riverside Aldine Series. 16mo 1.00

Tales of the Argonauts, and Other Stories. 16mo . 1.50

Thankful Blossom. "Little Classic" style. 18mo . 1.25

Two Men of Sandy Bar. A Play. 18mo 1.00

The Story of a Mine. 18mo 1.00

Drift from Two Shores. 18mo 1.25

Twins of Table Mountain, etc. 18mo 1.25

Flip, and Found at Blazing Star. 18mo 1.00

In the Carquinez Woods. 18mo 1.00

On the Frontier. "Little Classic" style. 18mo . . 1.00

Works. Rearranged, with an Introduction and a Portrait. In six volumes, crown 8vo.

Poetical Works, and the drama, "Two Men of Sandy Bar," with an Introduction and Portrait.

The Luck of Roaring Camp, and Other Stories.

Stories and Condensed Novels.
Frontier Stories.

  Each volume $2.00
  The set 12.00

By Shore and Sedge. "Little Classic" style.
 18mo 1.00
Maruja. A Novel. "Little Classic" style. 18mo . 1.00
Snow-Bound at Eagle's. "Little Classic" style.
 18mo 1.00
The Queen of the Pirate Isle. A Story for Children.
 Illustrated by Kate Greenaway. Small 4to . . . 1.50
A Millionaire of Rough-and-Ready, and Devil's Ford.
 18mo 1.00
The Crusade of the Excelsior. Illustrated. 16mo . 1.25
A Phyllis of the Sierras, and A Drift from Redwood
 Camp. 18mo 1.00
The Argonauts of North Liberty. 18mo 1.00

Wilhelm Hauff.

 Arabian Days Entertainments. Illustrated. 12mo . 1.50

Nathaniel Hawthorne.

Works. *New Riverside Edition.* With an original
 etching in each volume, and a new Portrait. With
 bibliographical notes by George P. Lathrop. Com-
 plete in twelve volumes, crown 8vo.
Twice-Told Tales.
Mosses from an Old Manse.
The House of the Seven Gables, and The Snow-Image.
The Wonder-Book, Tanglewood Tales, and Grand-
 father's Chair.
The Scarlet Letter, and The Blithedale Romance.
The Marble Faun.
Our Old Home, and English Note-Books. 2 vols.
American Note-Books.
French and Italian Note-Books.
The Dolliver Romance, Fanshawe, Septimius Felton,
 and, in an Appendix, the Ancestral Footstep.
Tales, Sketches, and Other Papers. With Biograph-
 ical Sketch by G. P. Lathrop, and Indexes.

  Each volume 2.00
  The set 24.00

New "*Little Classic*" *Edition.* Each volume contains
 Vignette Illustration. In twenty-five volumes, 18mo.

  Each volume 1.00
  The set 25.00

New *Wayside Edition.* With Portrait, twenty-three
 etchings, and Notes by George P. Lathrop. In
 twenty-four volumes, 12mo 36.00
New *Fireside Edition.* In six volumes, 12mo . . . 10.00

A Wonder-Book for Girls and Boys. *Holiday Edition*. With Illustrations by F. S. Church. 4to . $2.50
The Same. 16mo, boards 40
Tanglewood Tales. With Illustrations by Geo. Wharton Edwards. 4to, full gilt 2.50
The Same. 16mo, boards 40
Twice-Told Tales. *School Edition*. 18mo 1.00
The Scarlet Letter. *Popular Edition*. 12mo . . . 1.00
True Stories from History and Biography. 12mo . 1.25
The Wonder-Book. 12mo. 1.25
Tanglewood Tales. 12mo 1.25
The Snow-Image. Illustrated in colors. Small 4to . .75
Grandfather's Chair. *Popular Edition*. 16mo, paper covers .15
Tales of the White Hills, and Legends of New England. 32mo 75
Legends of Province House, and A Virtuoso's Collection. 32mo 75
True Stories from New England History. 16mo, boards .45
Little Daffydowndilly, etc. 16mo, paper 15

Franklin H. Head.

Shakespeare's Insomnia, and the Causes Thereof. 16mo, parchment-paper 75

Mrs. S. J. Higginson.

A Princess of Java. 12mo 1.50

Oliver Wendell Holmes.

Elsie Venner. A Romance of Destiny. Crown 8vo . 2.00
The Guardian Angel. Crown 8vo 2.00
The Story of Iris. 32mo 75
My Hunt after the Captain. 32mo 40
A Mortal Antipathy. Crown 8vo 1.50

Augustus Hoppin.

Recollections of Auton House. Illustrated. Small 4to 1.25
A Fashionable Sufferer. Illustrated. 12mo . . . 1.50
Two Compton Boys. Illustrated. Small 4to . . . 1.50

Blanche Willis Howard.

One Summer. A Novel. New *Popular Edition*. Illustrated by Hoppin. 12mo 1.25

William Dean Howells.

Their Wedding Journey. Illustrated. 12mo . . . 1.50
The Same. "Little Classic" style. 18mo 1.00
A Chance Acquaintance. Illustrated. 12mo . . . 1.50

The Same. "Little Classic" style. 18mo $1.25
A Foregone Conclusion. 12mo 1.50
The Lady of the Aroostook. 12mo 1.50
The Undiscovered Country. 12mo 1.50
Suburban Sketches. 12mo 1.50
A Day's Pleasure, etc. 32mo 75

Thomas Hughes.

Tom Brown's School-Days at Rugby. *Illustrated*
    Edition. 16mo 1.00
Tom Brown at Oxford. 16mo 1.25

Henry James, Jr.

A Passionate Pilgrim, and Other Tales. 12mo . . 2.00
Roderick Hudson. 12mo 2.00
The American. 12mo 2.00
Watch and Ward. "Little Classic" style. 18mo . 1.25
The Europeans. 12mo 1.50
Confidence. 12mo 1.50
The Portrait of a Lady. 12mo 2.00

Anna Jameson.

Studies and Stories. New Edition. 16mo, gilt top . 1.25
Diary of an Ennuyée. New Edition. 16mo, gilt top . 1.25

Douglas Jerrold.

Mrs. Caudle's Curtain Lectures. Illustrated. 16mo . 1.00

Sarah Orne Jewett.

Deephaven. 18mo 1.25
Old Friends and New. 18mo 1.25
Country By-Ways. 18mo 1.25
The Mate of the Daylight. 18mo 1.25
A Country Doctor. 16mo 1.25
A Marsh Island. 16mo 1.25
A White Heron, and Other Stories. 18mo 1.25
The King of Folly Island.

Rossiter Johnson.

"Little Classics." Each in one volume. 18mo.

I. Exile.	X. Childhood.
II. Intellect.	XI. Heroism.
III. Tragedy.	XII. Fortune.
IV. Life.	XIII. Narrative Poems.
V. Laughter.	XIV. Lyrical Poems.
VI. Love.	XV. Minor Poems.
VII. Romance.	XVI. Nature.
VIII. Mystery.	XVII. Humanity.
IX. Comedy.	XVIII. Authors.

Each volume $1.00
The set 18.00

Joseph Kirkland.

Zury: the Meanest Man in Spring County. 12mo . 1.50

Charles and Mary Lamb.

Tales from Shakespeare. 18mo 1.00
The Same. Illustrated. 16mo 1.00
The Same. *Handy-Volume Edition.* 32mo 1.00

Harriet and Sophia Lee.

Canterbury Tales. In three volumes. The set, 16mo 3.75

Henry Wadsworth Longfellow.

Hyperion. A Romance. 16mo 1.50
Popular Edition. 16mo 40
Popular Edition. Paper covers, 16mo 15
Outre-Mer. 16mo 1.50
Popular Edition. 16mo 40
Popular Edition. Paper covers, 16mo 15
Kavanagh. 16mo 1.50
Hyperion, Outre-Mer and Kavanagh. 2 vols. crown
8vo 3.00

Flora Haines Loughead.

The Man who was Guilty. 16mo 1.25

S. Weir Mitchell.

In War Time. 16mo 1.25
Roland Blake. 16mo 1.25

Mrs. M. O. W. Oliphant and T. B. Aldrich.

The Second Son. Crown 8vo 1.50

Elizabeth Stuart Phelps.

The Gates Ajar. 16mo 1.50
Beyond the Gates. 16mo 1.25
The Gates Between. 16mo 1.25
Men, Women, and Ghosts. 16mo 1.50
Hedged In. 16mo 1.50
The Silent Partner. 16mo 1.50
The Story of Avis. 16mo 1.50
Sealed Orders, and Other Stories. 16mo. 1.50
Friends : A Duet. 16mo 1.25
Doctor Zay. 16mo 1.25
An Old Maid's Paradise, and Burglars in Paradise.
16mo 1.25
Madonna of the Tubs. Illustrated. 12mo 1.50
Jack the Fisherman. Illustrated. Square 12mo . . .50

Marian C. L. Reeves and Emily Read.

Pilot Fortune. 16mo $1.25

Riverside Pocket Series.

1. Deephaven.   By Sarah Orne Jewett.
2. Exile. ("Little Classics.")
3. Adirondack Stories.   By P. Deming.
4. A Gentleman of Leisure.   By Edgar Fawcett.
5. Snow-Image, and other Twice-Told Tales.   By N. Hawthorne.
6. Watch and Ward.   By Henry James.
7. In the Wilderness.   By C. D. Warner.
8. Study of Hawthorne.   By G. P. Lathrop.
9. Detmold.   By W. H. Bishop.
10. Story of a Mine.   By Bret Harte.

Each volume, 16mo, cloth. 50

Josiah Royce.

The Feud of Oakfield Creek. 16mo 1.25

Joseph Xavier Boniface Saintine.

Picciola. Illustrated. 16mo 1.00

Jacques Henri Bernardin de Saint-Pierre.

Paul and Virginia. Illustrated. 16mo 1.00
The Same, together with Undine, and Sintram. 32mo   .75

Sir Walter Scott.

The Waverley Novels. *Illustrated Library Edition.* Illustrated with 100 engravings by Darley, Dielman, Fredericks, Low, Share, Sheppard. With glossary and a full index of characters. In 25 volumes, 12mo.

Waverley.	The Antiquary.
Guy Mannering.	Rob Roy.
Old Mortality.	St. Ronan's Well.
Black Dwarf, and Legend of Montrose.	Redgauntlet.
Heart of Mid-Lothian.	The Betrothed, and The Highland Widow.
Bride of Lammermoor.	The Talisman, and Other Tales.
Ivanhoe.	
The Monastery.	Woodstock.
The Abbot.	The Fair Maid of Perth.
Kenilworth.	Anne of Geierstein.
The Pirate.	Count Robert of Paris.
The Fortunes of Nigel.	The Surgeon's Daughter, and Castle Dangerous.
Peveril of the Peak.	
Quentin Durward.	

Each volume 1.00
The set 25.00

Tales of a Grandfather. *Illustrated Library Edition.* With six steel plates.   In three volumes, 12mo . . $4.50

Horace E. Scudder.

The Dwellers in Five-Sisters' Court. 16mo 1.25
Stories and Romances. 16mo 1.25
The Children's Book.   Edited by Mr. Scudder.   Small 4to 2.5c

Mark Sibley Severance.

Hammersmith : His Harvard Days. 12mo 1.50

J. E. Smith.

Oakridge : An Old-Time Story of Maine. 12mo . . 2.00

Mary A. Sprague.

An Earnest Trifler. 16mo 1.25

William W. Story.

Fiammetta. 16mo 1.25

Harriet Beecher Stowe.

Agnes of Sorrento. 12mo 1.50
The Pearl of Orr's Island. 12mo 1.50
Uncle Tom's Cabin. *Illustrated Edition.* 12mo . . 2.00
The Minister's Wooing. 12mo 1.50
The Mayflower, and Other Sketches. 12mo . . . 1.50
Dred.   New Edition, from new plates. 12mo . . . 1.50
Oldtown Folks. 12mo 1.50
Sam Lawson's Fireside Stories. 12mo 1.50
My Wife and I. Illustrated. 12mo 1.50
We and Our Neighbors. Illustrated. 12mo . . . 1.50
Poganuc People. Illustrated. 12mo 1.50
The above eleven volumes, in box 16.00
Uncle Tom's Cabin. *Holiday Edition.* With Introduction, and Bibliography by George Bullen, of the British Museum.   Over 100 Illustrations. 12mo . 3.00
The Same. *Popular Edition.* 12mo 1.00

Octave Thanet.

Knitters in the Sun. 16mo. . . . . . . · . 1.25

Gen. Lew Wallace.

The Fair God ; or, The Last of the 'Tzins. 12mo . 1.50

Henry Watterson.

Oddities in Southern Life. Illustrated. 16mo . . . 1.50

Richard Grant White.

The Fate of Mansfield Humphreys, with the Episode of Mr. Washington Adams in England. 16mo . 1.25

Adeline D. T. Whitney.

Faith Gartney's Girlhood. Illustrated. 12mo . . . $1.50
Hitherto: A Story of Yesterdays. 12mo 1.50
Patience Strong's Outings. 12mo 1.50
The Gayworthys. 12mo 1.50
Leslie Goldthwaite. Illustrated. 12mo 1.50
We Girls: A Home Story. Illustrated. 12mo . . 1.50
Real Folks. Illustrated. 12mo 1.50
The Other Girls. Illustrated. 12mo 1.50
Sights and Insights. 2 vols. 12mo 3.00
Odd, or Even? 12mo 1.50
Boys at Chequasset. Illustrated. 12mo 1.50
Bonnyborough. 12mo 1.50
Homespun Yarns. Short Stories. 12mo 1.50

Justin Winsor.

Was Shakespeare Shapleigh? A Correspondence in
Two Entanglements. Edited by Justin Winsor.
Parchment-paper, 16mo 75

Lillie Chace Wyman.

Poverty Grass. 16mo 1.25